FURY'S CHOICE

Visit us at www.boldstrokesbooks.com

By the Author

Fury's Bridge

Fury's Choice

FURY'S CHOICE

by
Brey Willows

2017

FURY'S CHOICE

ISBN 13: 978-1-62639-869-6

This Trade Paperback Original Is Published By
Bold Strokes Books, Inc.
P.O. Box 249
Valley Falls, NY 12185

First Edition: September 2017

CREDITS
Editor: Cindy Cresap
Production Design: Susan Ramundo
Cover Design By Sheri (graphicartist2020@hotmail.com)

Acknowledgments

Thanks to my editor, Cindy, who makes the process painless and always makes me laugh more than she makes me cry. Thanks to Radclyffe and Sandy, who gave me the chance to do what I love on an entirely different scale with a concept that's a little on the fringe. Thanks to all the Bold Strokes staff who do so much behind the scenes to get the books to readers.

Unquestionably, thanks goes to my wonderful partner, Nic; my biggest cheerleader and fan, who keeps me writing even when I get stroppy about it.

Dedication

For Nic, who saves me each and every day.
Thanks for not giving up on me, babe.

PROLOGUE

Kera Espinosa woke slowly, sweating, chilled, breathing fire through parched lips. "Please. Water."

The head of the rebel group smiled down at her with his broken, blackened teeth. "I told you. As soon as we've got the rest of your information, we'll take care of you. Our scientists are working through your formulas, but you've done a superior job of making them senseless. All you have to do is give us what we need, and you'll be free to go with all the water you like."

"Don't do this. It wasn't meant to kill people."

His laugh was like sandpaper on a chalkboard. "Stupid woman. You know as well as I do you can't control nature. You wanted knowledge not meant for people, and you got it." He squatted down next to her to look her in the eye. "Just like the man who created the nuclear bomb. What did he think the information would be used for? Geniuses seem to be the stupidest idealists. Fortunately for us, you're an attractive one, which makes trying to get you to talk far more interesting."

He was right. She'd known what could be done with it, with any number of the deadly airborne illnesses she'd investigated, but the incredible power it gave her, the feeling of being God, had been a temptation she couldn't fight.

She would have spit on him if her mouth didn't feel stuffed with dry cotton. He gave her cheek a hard pat and left, his bad guy whistle echoing off the cell's cement walls.

She coughed and winced at the pain of a broken rib. A scream from another cell crashed through the silence, until it was abruptly cut off.

As she slipped back into blissful unconsciousness, she briefly wondered if anyone would answer her prayers.

They say you always reach for God when you're at your lowest. She knew another few days of this, and her body would give out entirely. *If you're listening, whoever you are…please.*

Chapter One

T hank you, Lord Shiva, for that enlightening information. And with that, we'll leave our audience to, as always, consider what's been said, think critically about it, and make their own decisions. Good night."

Tisera Graves laughed as Selene signed off on her weekly TV talk show. When they'd begun the process of the gods coming out months ago, after several more months of administrative wrangling, she hadn't been sure what would happen. None of them were. But once the ball started rolling, there was no stopping it. God after god appeared to their followers, primarily in their places of worship. And then Selene started the show, where she not only interviewed the deity of the week but asked them some tough questions. Foremost, she asked the audience to think, to really consider what the gods' answers were, what they were offering, and the way of life they embodied. She asked them not to follow blindly, but with forethought.

Tis wasn't sure how she felt about all of it. When she and her sisters were in their heyday, the gods had been public figures. They'd appeared to their people all the time in various forms. There hadn't been any question they were real, and people took prayer and sacrifice seriously. But then the gods had moved away from the public view as the world expanded, and new gods made their way into new lands. Humans continued to worship, but soon they started to take it on faith that their gods existed. Proof was no longer necessary.

The phone startled her from her reverie, and she glanced at the display. She smiled as she answered. "Hey, superstar. How's my celebrity sister?"

Alec laughed. "Glad I kept my day job. Dealing with murderers and psychopaths is easier than dealing with gods and their egos. I'm heading to a job on the East Coast. Want to come?"

"Sure. Tough one?"

"I think it might be. One of those cult leader things. With the gods out in force, the extremists are coming out of the woodwork. I think we've got a Kool-Aid situation."

Tis sighed inwardly. This was the kind of thing she was worried about. There was no telling how humanity would react. Apparently, following people who made promises, but only if their followers offed themselves, was one of those reactions. "Sure, when do you want to leave?"

"About an hour? We'll take the Hummer, unless you want to drive?"

Tis's top-of-the-line Range Rover Evoque had a glass roof, and the inside was like sitting in an upscale hotel suite. "Since it's a long one, let's take mine. We'll see the night sky that way." She'd gotten the car for that reason. She didn't like the openness of a convertible, especially as it messed with her hair and wings, but she hated feeling boxed in. Gone were the days they'd fly everywhere, and she missed them, but larger territory meant longer trips, and it wasn't practical to go everywhere on their own.

"Cool. See you soon."

Tis hung up and wandered into her bedroom. Every wall in the house was floor to ceiling glass. The back of the house looked out onto the Pacific Ocean, with a steep cliff path leading past an opulent gazebo-cum-guesthouse and down to a private beach. Trees surrounded the house, providing a deep sense of privacy, even though the outside world had no idea the house was even there. It reminded Tis of the old days, of nature and peace, away from the constant noise and distraction of the modern world. It was her sanctuary, and she protected it fiercely. Only her sisters had ever been inside, and even then, only when she invited them.

She heard Alec's Hummer a short time later and grabbed her things. She was outside before Alec had climbed out. "Hey."

"Hey yourself. Feeling okay?"

Tis winced slightly. If anyone would notice something wasn't right, it would be Alec. Their other sister, Meg, wouldn't notice unless someone pointed it out. "Yeah, fine. Just had a long job in Africa. I've only been home a few days."

"Damn, Tis. You should have said. I can do this job on my own, no problem."

Tis shook her head. "No, it'll be nice to spend some time with you. Really, I'm okay."

Alec looked at her searchingly before she smiled. "Let's get on the road then."

They got into the Range Rover and set off. Soon, scenery was whizzing past at the typical supernatural rate they often traveled. Alec put her seat back and stared at the sky as they drove in silence for a while.

Tis asked, "So, how is life in the limelight? How's Selene handling things?"

"So far, it's going okay. A lot of questions are coming up in the organization, and plenty of people are coming back to the office more than a little frazzled. It's been a long time since the gods had to work instead of lounge around, but their egos are growing with the flock of believers. It all feels a little unstable, and Selene's in the middle of it. But the gods seem to respect her, and she's doing better than she thought she would on stage." She shrugged. "We'll have to see how it goes, I guess." She looked at Tis. "How are you holding up? Really. No bullshit."

No bullshit. Then what is there to say? More than anything, Tis wanted to tell Alec the truth. But it wasn't the right time. She didn't know if there would be a right time, but now definitely wasn't it. She wasn't ready. "Honestly, I'm okay. Better than the last time we talked, I guess. You know how it gets to you. Sometimes I wish we were angels, or leprechauns, or tooth fairies. The beings who get to see the good stuff, hand out miracles or gold, or pull pranks on people. Not the ones always dishing out the nightmares."

Alec nodded and closed her eyes. "I sure as hell get that. It's funny, I didn't really notice it until I met Selene. Now, being around someone so...human, I get to see the nicer side of life a lot more than I used to." She opened her eyes and grinned. "Maybe you just need a girlfriend. Maybe one of the happy goddesses. What about Ame-no?"

"The goddess of orgasms? Too much sex is distracting, as well as boring. Have you ever had to sit on a chair after her? She always leaves a wet patch. No thanks."

Alec laughed. "Okay. So Aphrodite is out too."

"Without question. I couldn't deal with all the orgies, and that whole lingerie line she has going makes me vomit in my mouth a little every time she brings it up."

"Let me tell you, there's nothing wrong with lingerie." Alec grinned. "Is there anyone you *would* consider?"

Tis thought about it. She pictured their various colleagues and discarded them quickly. "Not a one. I've been with the ones who were options, and they're old news. And besides, everyone is busy getting back to their followers. I'm not looking for anyone right now." She sighed and swallowed back the feeling of isolation she really felt. "I would need to be with someone who could take me like this. All the time, not just when I'm working. Or having sex." She threw Alec a small smile to show she was teasing. She shifted to adjust her wings, liking the way their pearlescent white glowed against the black interior of the SUV.

"I get that. I'm not bothered by staying in my more human form, but I know you've never been totally comfortable in it." She reached over and squeezed Tis's hand. "Just remember you're not alone, okay? You've got me and Meg. And of course the rest of Afterlife."

Tis squeezed her hand in return. "I know. You and Meg are my rocks. You always have been."

"Good. I think we're nearly there. Take the next exit."

Alec guided them to the farm in the middle of a massive cornfield. There were no neighbors, but a dozen cars were parked behind the house. Only one light was on inside.

Tis parked a distance away so they could get a feel for the scene before they got too close. It was always good to know if there were victims beyond the immediate area, so they could be counted among the perpetrator's crimes. They got out, and Tis stretched her wings. She sniffed the air, and mixed in with the fresh earthy smell was the scent of the recently deceased, underscored by the harsh tang of fear. She looked at Alec and saw her wings were out, her eyes had gone completely black, and her fangs glinted in the moonlight. Tis raised her arms and let her true form come completely to the surface.

Her white hair was replaced by a multitude of thin, long white snakes with eyes the same color red as her own. She welcomed their presence like old friends and felt her fangs extend. Together, she and Alec flew toward the house, following the smell of human destruction.

❖

An hour later, Tis and Alec leaned against the Range Rover and stared up at the night sky. The full moon looked back at them, and Tis wondered, as she often did, how so much ethereal beauty could be matched with so much violence and death.

"That was messy." Alec sounded tired.

"I think it will get messier. With the gods coming out, humans will have a hard time coping, especially those not strong enough. It's like some bizarre, paradoxical natural selection."

Forty of the people inside were already dead, having ingested the "elixir" their leader promised would take them straight to the home of the gods, where they'd be welcomed as gods themselves. Of course, at the last minute, he'd chickened out and not had any himself. They'd found him in a corner, wide-eyed and mumbling about new worlds and other planets. When he'd looked up and seen them, he'd begun to laugh. That laugh had quickly turned to screams as Tis punished him for the murders by creating a terrible, painful illness in him that would lead to a short, horrible death, and Alec punished his lack of morality by giving him nightmares he'd endure for the rest of his brief life. Such was the punishment of the furies.

"Hey there."

Tis looked over to see Dani walking toward them, dressed in her ceremonial garb of black cloak and massive scythe.

"You look fancy," Alec said, giving her a hug.

"Yeah, well, wouldn't do for Death to show up looking like a slob, would it?" She threw her hood back and breathed in the night air. "Besides, we're being watched so damn closely these days, I have to have my A game on all the time. I've warned my team to do the same."

Tis winced. "I hate that we're being monitored that way. Like we're under some kind of performance review."

Dani nodded. "I know what you mean. Thankfully, some of us don't really need approval. In fact, maybe it would be better if they saw me as just a normal person, doing a different kind of job. Maybe they wouldn't be so afraid…"

She stopped talking, clearly lost in thought. Tis cleared her throat slightly. "Guess we'll leave you to it."

Dani looked startled and then laughed softly. "I'm always distracted lately. Yeah, I'd better get to work." She pulled her massive hood back up and gave them a little wave. "See you at Meg's party Friday?"

Alec shook her head. "Not me. Selene's got a press release thing going, and I want to be there to support her."

Tis couldn't imagine the pressure Selene was under. She didn't envy her at all. "I think I'll head to Venice, actually. Meet up with a friend and relax away from it all."

Dani started toward the house. "Okay, well, don't be strangers." She disappeared into the house, and the air around the area cooled dramatically.

"I wonder why that happens?" Alec wrapped her wings around her to ward off the cold.

"Weird, isn't it? There's no logical reason for it. It's as though the souls give off heat, and when she takes them, there's a void." She shrugged. "Or something."

"I feel like we're asking questions we've never had to ask."

"That's because it's a new era. We just have to learn to live in it, right?" Tis flexed her wings. "I think I'll catch that flight to Venice today. Get away for a few days. That okay with you?"

Alec nodded thoughtfully. "Sure. Meg and I can handle it for a few days, and I'll get another department to jump in if things get too crazy." She punched Tis's shoulder. "Just come back, okay?"

Tis turned and hugged her tightly, suddenly overwhelmed by their love for one another. "Always."

Chapter Two

Tis took a deep drink of merlot and sighed happily. Water lapped lazily beneath her feet as the tides of *aqua alta*, the Venetian term for high water, brought the lagoon surging into the city, right to the doors of the restaurants and shops. Still, people moved through it easily, walking on the bridges of trestle tables set up in the squares, or splashing through the water in rain boots. Cafés like this one, alongside the Grand Canal, kept their outdoor seating open, the tables on slightly raised platforms so the water wasn't deep, and gave patrons blankets to wrap up in. Venice was too beautiful a city to stay indoors, even in the winter during high tide.

She looked up when her closest friend splashed through the water to their table, looking for all the world like a child playing in a puddle. She jumped up to give her a hug.

"Aulis. You look amazing, as always."

Aulis, one of the Praxidice, or oath keepers, held Tis at arm's length and studied her. "And you, my lovely terrifying friend, look tired."

They sat down, and Aulis ordered a Bellini. The waiter nearly tripped over himself in his hurry to please her. Men and women often fell over themselves when Aulis was around. Her diminutive frame, together with her thick, long brown hair and stunning purple-blue eyes made an exotic, enticing package. Though she wasn't Tis's type and never had been, it was easy to see why so many others fell willingly into her bed.

Tis waited to speak until Aulis had taken a drink of her Bellini. It was a tradition for them—no one spoke of anything serious without first taking in a bit of alcohol.

"Beautiful. Now. Tell me why those lovely gray eyes of yours look more like hurricane skies than wispy summer clouds."

Tis smiled wryly. "You make them sound elegant rather than drab."

Aulis tilted her head slightly. "You're the only one who has ever thought them drab, my love. Others see the beauty you don't. Spill it."

Tis stared at the dark, lapping waters of the Canal, and tried to put her thoughts in some kind of order. "Before the exodus, I didn't know why we do what we do. I mean, we serve justice, but the humans just seem to find new, awful ways to hurt one another. For every one we punish, five more take their place. Do you know, in 2015 alone, nearly two hundred thousand people were killed in various wars? And those are just the ones reported. In America, nearly fifteen thousand were killed in gun related violence. How are we supposed to keep up with those numbers?" She finally looked at Aulis, who appeared to be listening intently. "And why do we want to? Why not let them kill one another off, if that's what they're so intent on?"

Aulis took a sip of her drink, looking at Tis thoughtfully over the top of her glass. "And now that the exodus is happening?"

Tis sighed. "I don't know if it changes anything. Some of the really bad stuff has gone down, I think while the humans figure out what it means to their ways of life. But I'm worried it will get worse when they figure out that the gods have human-type limitations. And then? What does that say about us?"

"Heavy questions, my friend. In fact, those sound like questions of a pre-fader." She looked at Tis searchingly, waving off the waiter headed their way. "Are they?"

Tis stayed silent for a long time. She didn't want to acknowledge the truth of it. "I can't let my sisters down," she finally said.

"If you live for someone else, you'll never be happy. Believe me, I know."

Tis was reminded of Aulis's last love affair, which had resulted in the inferior goddess she'd taken to her bed becoming a burnt shadow on a wall after she'd insulted one too many of the immortal kind.

"I know. But if I'm not a fury, what am I?"

"You. Tisera Graves. Bookworm, lover of bland food and rich wine. Cave and mountain dweller. Intelligent, sincere, kind—"

"Okay, okay. I didn't come for an ego boost, though it doesn't hurt." Tis laughed, feeling a bit better. "I don't know who I'd be if I didn't have my job and my sisters. It's all I've ever known."

"Do you really think your sisters would turn their backs on you? I've known them almost as long as I've known you, and I seriously doubt it."

Tis thought about it. "Alec would be disappointed, but she'd be okay with it, as long as I was happy. Meg...I don't know. She's not like Alec and me. She's more..."

"Temperamental? Volatile? Moody? Unpredictable?"

Tis laughed and held up her hand to stop her. "Yes. All those things. I think she might take it personally if I quit." It was the first time she'd ever mentioned that possibility out loud, and it made her feel slightly dizzy.

"Well, you have to do what's right for you. At the end of the day, you can't do anything but." Her eyes widened, and she leaned forward. "You didn't take an oath to do this job, did you? For eternity?"

Tis thought back to when she and her sisters had been born. They'd frolicked as children, testing their wings and their mother's fortitude. Fortunately for them, Gaia had immeasurable patience and more love than anyone could ever know. She'd taught them what their roles would be when they were of an age. "No. No oaths. Our mother instructed us, but we never swore to it. We just...are."

Aulis sat back with a sigh of relief. "Thank goodness. Then there's no reason for you to stay in a job you no longer want to do."

"But you know what happens if I walk out. A pre-fader can't just go back to Afterlife. There has to be a damn good reason to let someone back in once they've left the fold. What if I make the wrong choice?" A police boat went by, sirens blaring. The officers on board waved as they went past. *That's Venice. Always overtly friendly.* She loved that about this special city. Nowhere else in the world was like it. She felt her tension begin to ease.

"Lady, you can't tell me they wouldn't let a fury back into the fold? Please." She took Tis's hand and said seriously, "I'm not going to say there isn't a place for you at their table. The world will always need you and your sisters, as well as the others who do your line of work. But that's the thing." She let go of Tis's hand and sat back with her drink. "The world will always need you, and there are lots of you doing the work. If you need to leave…" She shrugged. "We're all replaceable."

Tis thought about it as they silently sipped their drinks. Could that be true? Could someone replace her? The thought of someone taking her position with her sisters made her distinctly uncomfortable. And yet, the thought of being free, of not having to face the worst of humanity each and every day, ignited an excitement she hadn't felt since her first serious girlfriend, several centuries ago.

She looked up when Aulis stood up abruptly. "Enough of this serious talk. Let's go to every café in the city and see who has the best cake and wine."

Tis laughed and stood. "We've done that. Several times."

"Indeed we have, beautiful. But we haven't done it yet this decade, and time changes even places like Venice."

They headed down one of the narrow side alleys Venice was famous for. For the moment, Tis could let go of her worries, her doubts, even her inhibitions. She could pretend, for just a little while, that life was meant to be enjoyed. As Aulis took her hand and started to run through the flooded square, Tis thought that maybe, just maybe, there was truth to that idea.

Tis groaned and grasped her head in both hands. The pounding hangover made her want to fade. Her stomach rebelled at the scent of bacon and eggs. She staggered into the bathroom and splashed water on her face. Her eyes were bloodshot, and her hair was a tangled mess. She did her best to finger comb it, but it would take a shower and brush to tame it properly. She shuffled into Aulis's kitchen, her wings dragging, and squinted against the sunlight coming through the lovely old windows. "How on earth are you not dying of alcohol poisoning?"

"I live here. I have a wonderful tolerance. You, my friend, have lived too long among the fruits and nuts of California. There was a time you could drink like Bacchus and fuck like Aphrodite. Now you eat granola and fall asleep cradling a book instead of a breast. Coffee?"

Tis nodded and gratefully accepted the mug. She sipped the potent brew and slowly felt like she could live again. "Thanks for the character update. When did I become so boring?" Her phone buzzed on the table, and she glanced at it.

"It didn't happen on my watch. And your phone's been doing that for hours," Aulis said.

Tis sighed and read the numerous text messages. Several were from Zed, and a few were from Alec. The overall idea was that she was needed back home, urgently. She closed her eyes and felt the familiar sinking sensation of work calling. She opened her eyes when Aulis put a gentle hand on her shoulder.

"It seems like your decision needs to come sooner rather than later. Listen to your heart, not your head."

Tis hugged her tightly. She trusted few people and had fewer friends. Aulis's friendship meant more to her than Aulis could imagine. "That's never been my forte, but I'll think about it. I promise." She let her go and headed for a shower. "But now, duty calls."

When she arrived back in LA, she was surprised to see Meg in the airport waiting for her. She threw her arms around her and hugged her with typical exuberance.

"I'm so glad you're here. Did you have any idea you were going to be the next savior? I mean, not of the world, or anything, I don't think, but of our sanity?"

Tis laughed, as always buoyed by Meg's boundless energy. "I have no idea what you're talking about, but you've never been sane. What's going on?"

Meg tossed her flaming hair over her shoulder as they slid into her Z4 convertible. "I'll let the big man explain. You know how much I hate details." She pulled into LA traffic and glanced at Tis. "But if the hubbub is anything to go by, you're in for a ride."

Tis sighed, the sinking feeling from earlier deepening. *What I wouldn't give to be a librarian, or an accountant. Or...anything else.*

Chapter Three

G et down!" Kera flung herself over the woman and child as the building exploded around them. A large piece of concrete hit her back and knocked the wind from her. She held her breath to keep from inhaling the acrid smoke and dust. As soon as she could, she wiped the soot from her eyes and looked around. They'd managed to get most of the women and children out, but there had been a few stragglers, like the ones beneath her. She sat back on her heels, letting them up. Coughing, she pointed at the massive military style truck, and the mother quickly grabbed her child and began climbing over the rubble toward the vehicle. Kera watched them go, then began her own scramble over the debris, looking for any other survivors.

A soft sob caught her attention.

A small child, malnourished and already careworn, rested its head on a woman's chest. Kera knew right away the woman was gone. She looked up when she heard the telltale thrum of a truck coming their way. She grabbed the child, who didn't have the energy to fight but kept crying, and made her way to the waiting truck and the crew yelling for her to hurry. She quickly passed the child up to her chief's waiting hands before climbing in behind them and reaching up to yank down the armored shutters.

Before she lowered them, she saw her.

It was the pale woman, the one she'd seen before at another bombing site. With enormous white wings and snakes for hair, she was probably terrifying to anyone else. To Kera, she was awesome in the truest sense of the word. Almost as though she knew she was being watched, the being slowly turned and looked at her with eyes the color of fresh blood. The truck rumbled away, and Kera could swear she saw surprise in the being's expression. The bombers pulled into the site and started crawling all over it. The pale woman turned toward one of them and held up her hand. Red smoke that almost looked like oil paint rose from her palm, and the man in front of her began to scream.

Thank fuck I'm one of the good guys. Kera slammed the door shut and slumped against the side of the truck. The child she'd pulled from its mother crawled into her lap silently and lay there still and light as a feather. She stroked its head, unsure whether it was male or female. She asked its name in what she hoped was its native language, and the soft reply confirmed female.

"That was too close. We need to close shop here, boss." Her chief, Ajan, also held a child in his lap, while the mother rested against him, tears streaking down her dirt covered face.

"I know. I just hate giving in to these bastards. But we can't lose any more people. We'll close down and get everyone home. Once they've razed it to the ground and have moved on like the locusts they are, we'll try to come back and rebuild."

He nodded and passed the child back to its mother. "We got twenty out of the main building and all ten out of the secondary building. Yang and Deek are already en route to the rendezvous point with the other group, and the plane is ready. As long as we can avoid any ground-to-air missiles, we'll be in France by morning."

Kera sighed, exhaustion and frustration finally sweeping away any adrenaline she had left. "Take off after dark, unless we need to get up before that."

"That's only an hour away. Shouldn't be a problem."

The rest of the ride to the plane was made in silence, except for the soft crying of the women and children. As she studied them, remembering their names and places of origin, she felt the weight of her work more than usual. An unbidden image of the pale woman came to mind. *It's time for a vacation.* When she started to see the *orishas* her mother had told her about as a child, it was time to take a break and get away from the daily horrors she dealt with.

Once they'd loaded the women and children onto the passenger plane, along with some of her staff, she and the rest of her senior staff boarded her own private jet. It would get to France faster, which meant she could have things moving before the other plane touched down. They buckled in, and it was only minutes after full dark that the two planes took off.

Ajan fell asleep almost instantly in the plush leather seat opposite her, and all the other staff were either asleep or subdued. Once in the air, Kera headed for a quick shower, needing to wash off the dust and death of the educational outpost in Nigeria that was now nothing but a pile of blasted stone. She let the water sluice over her, and slowly she felt almost normal again. *It's all part of the job. That's what I tell everyone, and it's as true for me as it is for them.* She knew without asking they didn't see the pale woman. She'd learned as a child to keep silent about seeing the beings no one else could.

She headed back to her seat and closed her eyes, determined to dream about the mysterious being rather than the destruction they'd barely lived through.

❖

The six-hour flight to France had gone quickly, and once on the ground, Kera took control and made the necessary arrangements for the next steps. The refugees would be taken to a safe house, where they'd receive medical care and food. Then, with the help of interpreters, they'd be asked where they wanted to go next. If they wanted to stay in Europe, the paperwork would begin. If they wanted to go to family somewhere else, that would be arranged too. It was entirely up to the women, and because they'd hardly known a time with that kind of choice, it often took a little while for them to decide. There was no rush.

Kera met Ajan for breakfast in the hotel the next morning, feeling refreshed and ready to get moving. He didn't look quite as good.

"You look like you got hit by a bomb," Kera said with a smile after taking an appreciative sip of her coffee.

"Funny. You look like you just left a Beverly Hills salon."

"Yeah, well, I'm lucky that way. It's hard to be this good-looking, you know. It takes enormous effort and self-control not to let it go to my head."

He rolled his eyes, and she was glad to see his trademark smile beneath the lines of exhaustion.

"I'm sure it does. I can't tell you how much I'm looking forward to getting home, to my own bed."

Home. It feels like a place in a dream. She pushed away the loneliness that thought always brought with it. "Me too, buddy, me too. I can't wait to have a conversation with my favorite scotch again. You?"

"Ice cream. The good stuff. I'm going to spend the night in an ice cream locker and eat myself into a cookie dough coma."

She laughed and relaxed. It was well known that Ajan had the most intense sweet tooth on the planet. It was one of the best ways to bribe him. "Everyone get settled in okay last night?"

"Fine. Lots of tears and plenty of fear. That bombing really shook things up. But I think everyone will figure out where they want to go before long."

"Medical?"

"Starting with the kids, then moving on to the mothers. Mostly dehydrated and malnourished, though they're checking for cholera and TB."

Kera picked up her phone and rang the main office. "Hey, Shell. We've just made a drop-off at the French location from our base in Nigeria. Be ready for influx, will you? And have status reports available on Kenya, Madaya, and Ethiopia. I'll also want to check in with the medical unit, so let them know I'll need reports and concerns by Friday. And get the president of Full Drum on the phone for me tomorrow morning."

She hung up, and Ajan shook his head. "I don't know how you keep all this stuff in your head." He leaned forward and took her hand in his. "Make sure it isn't *staying* in your head, hear? This stuff..." He swallowed hard. "Once it gets hold, you have to scrape it out, like a cancer. Don't let it get hold, girl. I can see it sometimes. It's like watching ghosts in your eyes."

You don't know the half of it. She squeezed his hand and returned his serious gaze. "I know, old friend. I do. I don't think you can get through what we do without carrying some of it with you. But that's okay. I'd rather carry them than forget them. Because then the world would forget them too, and to have lived and died, with no one to mourn you, is a tragedy." She let go of his hand and grinned, needing to lighten the moment. "Besides. We're taking a vacation. You and I, and a few of the others from this mission. We all need a break to, as you say, scrape the stuff away."

He nearly jumped from his seat he was so excited. "You mean it? Real time off?"

"Real time off. Go see your family, go see the Great Wall of China, whatever. But take the entire month off. The world will still need saving when we get back. And I could do to spend some time on the money side of things instead of the saving people side of things."

The hotel steward came over to tell them it was time to go, and that their bags were already in the car. Ajan was on the phone as they walked out, making reservations for a flight to Haiti. He held the phone away from his mouth and put a hand on her arm to stop her. "Come with me? You know your aunties would love to see you."

A fresh wave of pain hit her as she thought of her mother's sisters. "Thanks, but I'm not ready. You go ahead."

He nodded sympathetically and went back to his call.

As they headed to the jet, Kera considered what she might want to do with her time off. Suddenly, the idea of taking a vacation seemed ludicrous. There was so much to do—more research to focus on, heads of state to visit. *I can do some of it from the house in France. At least I'll feel like I'm away.* They were on the tarmac, heading for the plane steps, when she noticed a commotion at a nearby plane. Reporters jostled for a place near the front and cameras were all pointed at an impossibly tall man with a thick, black beard and almost shiny swarthy skin, wearing a turban. Instinctively, Kera knew it was Mohammed, the prophet of the Muslims. He nodded solemnly at those waiting for him but ignored the cacophony of questions thrown at him by the reporters.

Since the gods had shown up, life had become more complicated. Praying to someone who may or may not be listening was one thing. Asking that person over a cup of coffee about things like cancer and genocide was something totally different. She knew for a fact the women who'd been in her facility had prayed just as hard as those who prayed in temples. But many of them were still buried beneath the rubble, their prayers silent on their bloodless lips. What had belief gotten them?

Kera tried to stay out of it all. No matter what, people needed help, and that's what she was going to give. *Even if the gods don't.*

Chapter Four

W hy me?" Tis crossed her arms and glared at Zed.
"You know why. You're among the oldest here, you
have experience with legal matters, you've spent the most time with
the varied religious personnel, and you're the most rational of your
sisters." He grinned at Alec. "No offense."

Alec shrugged. "None taken. It's all true."

Tis felt like she'd been ambushed, and there was nothing she
hated more than being backed into a corner. She needed time to
consider every angle, but they were pushing for an answer now. The
room was filled with the heads of every major religion, as well as a
few of the larger minor ones. They all waited expectantly, to see if
she'd be the one to draft the new constitution and business plan for
Afterlife, Inc. Now that the gods had moved into the public sphere,
entirely new issues had been raised, and the department heads felt
boundaries had better be drafted sooner rather than later. It made
sense, of course. But drafting a new rulebook with gods whose egos
had gotten serious boosts from the corporate changes was going to
be a nightmare of vanity and narcissism.

She sighed. "Okay. But I'm not squabbling. You decide on the big
things, hell, decide on as many of the little things as you can as well,
before I start. I'm not sitting in on the preliminary discussions. I don't
have the patience, and I'd end up feeding all of you to my snakes."

Alec coughed behind her hand, and Tis knew she was trying
not to laugh. Maybe threatening a room full of deities wasn't a great
idea, but she didn't care.

"Once you've decided on whatever you can agree on, I'll come in and start drafting the new constitution, and I'll ask questions to clarify the rules. I'll also try to think of any situations which might need addressing, so when I do come back, they can be dealt with accordingly."

"That sounds wise and as though we've chosen the right person."

Buddha's smile was gentle, and as always, looked slightly mischievous. Tis smiled back at him, glad he was there. He'd been a friend and mentor for longer than she could remember. Although not technically a god, so many people prayed to him as an enlightened being they wanted to emulate, just as the other's followers did, he had developed god status.

"Thanks, Bud. I'll do what I can."

Zed stood and surveyed the table. "In that case, why don't we let Tis go, and we'll begin bullet-pointing our guidelines."

Tis gratefully headed for the door. As it closed behind her, she heard Zed say, "Now, let's begin with territory and how we publicly discuss our own religions in comparison with others."

Alec and Meg followed Tis, and they both burst out laughing the moment the door was closed.

"What? What have I missed?" Tis stared at them, bewildered.

"You just told a room full of egomaniacal gods how to act, what to do, and that you'd feed them to your hair if they didn't behave. I love you so much." Meg wrapped her arm around Tis's waist.

Tis leaned into her embrace. "I'm thinking ahead. Can you imagine what's going to happen in there? It will be a miracle if the building is still standing by tomorrow."

Alec shook out her wings as though shivering. "I don't envy you, Tis. I mean, every religion has its own take on war, the afterlife, death, submission...how do they say theirs is the right version without stepping on someone else's toes?"

The elevator let them out into the reception area, and they each stopped to pet one of Cerberus's enormous heads. She rarely stayed in human guise these days, preferring her normal three-headed canine form now that the building had become visible to the world at large. A cluster of humans constantly waited outside to catch a glimpse of their god. A strange phenomenon of "spiritual autograph hunter" had sprung up, along with bizarre trading cards. As press cameras flashed whenever a god left through the front door, humans pressed forward for inhuman signatures. Tis couldn't help but find something about it distasteful, though she wasn't sure why.

"I have an idea." Meg took both their hands in hers and headed for the back door, which led into the safety of the compound. "Let's fly."

❖

Tis closed her eyes as she soared over the black-jade Pacific Ocean, the sun warming her entire being. She reopened her eyes when she heard laughter. Ahead of her, Meg's red wings looked like they were on fire as she twisted, spun, and dove through the air like a bird freed from a cage. She glanced behind her at Alec, who looked as relaxed and free as Tis felt. Her onyx wings looked like a living shadow, and her black eyes were alight with the freedom that only came with flying unhindered.

Tis couldn't remember the last time they'd flown together just for fun, without having to head to a job site or business meeting. She concentrated on the way the wind lifted her hair and caressed her feathers, the way the warm ocean air felt against her skin. The tension she'd been carrying, the worry and frustration, dropped away into the ocean's white caps. Meg's shout made her focus, and she looked down to where Meg was pointing. Below them, a pod of humpback whales surfaced, and Tis laughed as they blew water high enough to hit all three of them.

Alec called from behind, "Let's head to the Rim of the World."

Meg banked hard and dove toward the water. She dipped one wing in the water and created a wave of spray. Tis dipped her other wing, sent up a line of spray to the other side, and giggled like a girl when Alec followed suit behind her. They hadn't played in the water together since…no, Tis couldn't think of when.

She followed Meg inland, and they flew high above the smog layer and heat rising from the dry desert landscape into the cool air of the mid-level atmosphere. The constant human noise abated, and Tis drank in the silence like a tonic to her frayed soul. Desert turned to mountains, and she felt another part of herself return. She missed the forests and caves of their old life.

Meg finally slowed and landed on a heavily treed cliff, closely followed by Tis and Alec. She walked straight over to a massive oak and hugged it like an old friend.

Tis smiled, glad to know she wasn't the only one missing the peace nature used to bring them. She sat on the edge of the cliff, and Alec sat beside her. Soon, Meg let go of her tree friend and sat on Tis's other side. For a long while, they sat in silence, staring out over the thick blanket of clouds below them. They'd always loved this part of Southern California and had come here often when they'd first moved to Afterlife. This part of the San Gabriel Mountains was always above the cloud layer, and often empty. There were even a few caves in the cliff face below where they sat, and every once in a while Tis would sleep in one, just so she could feel like her old self again.

Eventually, Alec said, "I forget how noisy the world is now, until I hear the trees speaking again."

"Mmm," Tis murmured, not ready to break the silence.

"You know I like a lot of the changes, but I'll always love this." Meg wrapped her wings around herself, still staring out at the clouds.

They listened to the wind in the trees, the sounds of small animals rustling in the underbrush, and when Meg silently pointed, they watched a mountain lion stalk a rabbit in the valley below.

This is what life should be. Not squabbling gods or corporation contracts. Good and bad, moral and not moral. Nature, not concrete.

Almost as though she could hear Tis's thoughts, Alec said quietly, "Want to talk about it?"

"I don't know. I'm not sure what it is myself."

Meg bumped Tis's shoulder with her own. "Start with the emotion. Then go from there."

Tis thought about it. Naming emotions had never been something she enjoyed. She preferred logic, justice, facts. Emotions were so nebulous, so unpredictable, and often irrational. "Okay.

Frustration. I'm frustrated that it never changes. We do what we do, and then there's another case, and another. I don't know if humans have gotten worse, or if we're simply more aware of them because we work a larger area. And granted, they've gotten a little better since the gods have appeared among them. But how long will it last?"

Her sisters listened without interrupting, and Tis could see them taking her seriously. She continued. "Tired. But not just had-a-long-day tired. I'm tired in my soul, in my being. We never get any real time off, and seeing the worst in people, and never having any fun...it's exhausting. I want to go to bed, but when I do, I lie awake wondering when I'll be called out on the next case, or I'm thinking about previous cases. And now, the company wants me to do this extra thing, and I feel like...like I don't have a life outside work anymore."

"Have you ever?" Meg asked, sounding genuinely curious.

"We did. We had relationships, we had friends, we went to cafés and bars and traveled just to travel, and not to work." They stayed silent, and then it hit her. *They* still had all those things. They had relationships, and friends, and all the other stuff. She was the only one who didn't. She felt the tears come, and she didn't try to hide them. "Lonely. I don't know how it happened, or when. I don't know when I became this shell. Aulis reminded me—"

"Oh my god, how is she? Does she still drink like a whale? Is she still with that beautiful Norwegian with the huge—"

"Meg! Hush." Alec frowned at her.

"Sorry. Go on, Tis." Meg looked slightly contrite, but not entirely.

"Anyway, Aulis reminded me I used to be someone else. Someone fun, and daring, and sexual. What happened?"

Birdsong filled the air, and a slight breeze ruffled Tis's feathers. She let her sisters think, knowing they'd give her question real consideration.

Alec said, "I don't really remember it happening. I don't think there was a moment when things changed. I think you were gradually taken over by the new way of life. It's so different. And you know, I don't think humanity has gotten any worse. I mean, when you think about Oedipus, Orestes, and even Clytemnestra, you know how awful people were, way back then. The Crusades, Vietnam, World War II. I think we just had fewer of them to look after. Now, with this global workload, I agree it's overwhelming sometimes."

"Maybe you need a break?" Meg's brow was furrowed, and she leaned forward, as though into a thought. "I don't mean a vacation. I mean a break. As in, we take over your workload, and maybe even grab someone from another department, and you take the time to figure out what you want. For as long as it takes."

"Go find myself?" Tis gave them a wry grin.

"Well, yeah. Why not? Being immortal doesn't mean we don't get ennui. In fact, maybe we're even more prone to it. Or maybe you're having a midlife crisis."

Alec snorted. "I think you have to have a life end to have a midlife." She avoided the pebble Meg threw at her. "But you know, I think she's right. With people behaving now that they think their particular afterlives are real, it's a good time to do it. Go have some fun. Travel. Go to libraries in other countries and have sex with women between the stacks. Go see friends you haven't seen in ages. Fly."

Can I? Really? Then she realized. "What about Zed and the company stuff?"

Meg laughed. "How soon do you think they'll figure out the answers you need? They're going to come up with new ones every day they're out among their fans. I'd say you've got time."

At the same time, both sisters put an arm around Tis, and she felt safe, and more importantly, she felt hope. Maybe with some time away, she really could turn things around. She didn't want to be this person anymore.

But who do I want to be?

CHAPTER FIVE

Kera woke to sunlight warming her naked skin. The thin curtains blew in a soft morning breeze and parrots called to one another over the lapping water beyond her deck. The beautiful woman next to her stirred and gave her a sleepy smile.

"Time?"

Kera kissed her forehead before getting out of bed. "Who cares?"

Anabelle stretched, and Kera appreciated, as she always did, her sculpted, toned, and tanned figure. Whenever Kera made it to her place in Port Grimaud, France, she and Anabelle spent some quality time together. Anna was a journalist, and they'd met when she was covering one of Kera's projects. Ever since, they'd been close friends, and the benefits were truly an aside to an exceptional friendship.

"Coffee, then?"

"Always." Kera loved being naked, and as she moved about the kitchen making coffee and chopping fresh fruit for their breakfast, she paid attention to the feel of the cool slate tile beneath her feet, the way the warm air caressed her skin, and the glorious smell of fresh coffee. For a long time, when she'd been younger and far more foolish, life had been about pleasure, whether in the form of women or daily living, it didn't matter. It still was, to a large degree, and she didn't apologize for it. When Anabelle's hands slid over her stomach and moved up to cup her breasts, she was glad she spent so much time in the gym.

"I have to get going," Anabelle murmured in her ear. "Work just called."

Kera turned around in her embrace and cradled her face in her hands. "Busy lately?"

Anabelle sighed. "Since the gods have reappeared, there's never a moment when something isn't happening somewhere. Crime rates are down, but you can feel the tension in some places… like believers are just waiting to explode. When people could say God works in mysterious ways as an excuse, they were content. Now that they're getting answers, or not getting them, as the case may be, they're not sure where they stand."

Kera rested her forehead against Anabelle's. "Be careful, okay? Zealots are zealots, and knowing their gods are real isn't going to make them less so. They'll just find new levels of crazy."

Anabelle placed a kiss on Kera's nose and grinned before she walked back toward the bedroom. "I'm always careful. And if I didn't know better, I'd think you cared."

Kera laughed. "You know I care. If I didn't care, we'd do this at your place."

Anabelle ducked back around the corner to look at her. "I know you do. And it's not just because I'm the best lay you've ever had."

After Anabelle left, Kera took her coffee out to the deck. The little village south of St. Tropez was a hidden gem. Built on canals by someone who wanted to re-create Venice, every house had a boat dock and a view of the water, often both in front and behind the house. Her sixty-four-foot yacht, the *Madaline-Rose*, bobbed gently, covered until it warmed up a bit more. She couldn't wait to take it out again. Being on the water was freeing, not only because she felt at one with the waves, but because it was so hard to get hold of her. Thanks to no Wi-Fi or phone reception, she was forced to live in the moment, and there'd never been a time she wasn't grateful for that. It was something her mother had tried to teach her, which was why she'd named the boat after her. But she hated the cold, and being stuck inside, even on the water, wasn't what it was about. There was nothing like having sex on the deck in the sun—

Her phone rang, calling her back to the moment. She grabbed it. The head of a company couldn't take a real vacation, not the way other people could. She accepted that and was just glad she had the kind of staff she could leave in charge so she could get away physically once in a while.

"Hey, boss. Sorry to bother you. There's a situation."

"There's always a situation, Ajan. Which one are you talking about? And why are you working? You're supposed to be in Haiti under some woman."

He laughed. "Who says I wasn't? I just got a call from HQ. You know I only care about the people-based situations. It's the child, the one you took off the deceased mother. We can't find any relatives, and the people we got out don't want her. Apparently, there's some superstition involved because she was taken from her mother's body."

"What, if they'd been hit by the bomb separately it would have been okay?"

"Yeah, pretty much."

She sighed. "Okay, get hold of the adoption agencies we use. See if we can get her on the books."

"I will. In the meantime, do we keep her in the medical center?"

She thought about it. The child had been terribly malnourished, a late arrival to the project who hadn't had time to make use of the facilities in place for health care. Without family, the child had no one to visit her in the care center, but she wasn't strong enough to go live among children yet either.

"Put her in the children's ward once she's strong enough. Let's integrate her slowly, and see that she gets into some English classes right away, so she doesn't feel so helpless. We'll go from there."

"I'll pass it on. Enjoying your break?"

"You know it. See you soon."

She hung up and thought about the child as she stared at the water without seeing it. Before the gods had come out, she couldn't imagine wanting to bring a child into the world. There was constant war and chaos. Even Westernized countries had their share of homelessness, addiction issues, poverty, and violence. She'd never understood the biological calling people felt to pass on their genes or create a being. Ego always seemed to be at the heart of it—the desire to make sure the nature of who a person was continued on through time. Once, that might have been necessary to propagate the species. Now, in a world with a population overrunning the planet's resources, it seemed so…frivolous and narcissistic. Not that she had anything specific against being frivolous or narcissistic—she was known for being both, labels she considered part and parcel of being who she was. But when there were orphaned children in desperate need of someone to care, having one of your own seemed a lot like going to a dog breeder for a special breed, rather than saving one from a pound.

Was I wrong to save the child? Did the mother have time to pray before she died? Is that why I found the girl? Before, those answers would've been simple. She'd logically searched for survivors, found one, and helped. Simple cause and effect. But now, with the gods answering prayers, she wondered about free will and fate more than she ever had before. It irritated her. Who were they to dictate what she did and why? What made it okay for them to use her as a tool for other means? Or were they involved in her life at all, when she didn't pray to any of them? Did that mean she had free will or only to the point she didn't involve herself with believers?

She rubbed the back of her neck to stave off the impending tension headache. If she wanted answers badly enough, she could go to one of the meetings the gods were having with their followers and simply ask. But she didn't want to. She didn't want to acknowledge their power, or lack thereof, and she knew if she did talk to them, she'd be less than respectful. Insulting a god by telling them they were ineffectual, childish, naïve, and vengeful probably wasn't going to help her plans. Staying away from them, and under their radar, seemed like a better idea.

Stop thinking. Be in the moment. Once again, she focused on the way the sun felt, the smell of the air, the sounds of the small tourist motorboats and the flaps of sails in the breeze. She closed her eyes and slowly drifted back to sleep, cradled in her deck chair, brief images of the woman with the white hair rising to the surface before she fell into a deep, dreamless sleep.

❖

When Kera woke, the sun was sinking below the horizon, and she shivered in the cool evening air. *Jesus. I must have been more tired than I realized.* She hadn't slept so well, and for so many hours, in longer than she could remember. Energized, she wanted to be around people, but not anyone she knew. She quickly showered and dressed and headed down the coast a few miles to St. Maxime. With luck, she could find a sexy woman with long hair and large breasts to spend the night with. Flirtation and sex were a game, one she was almost magically good at. *Venus has nothing on me.* She grinned at the thought of giving the goddess of love some tips. *Like don't fall in love.*

She valeted her petrol blue Maserati at the far end of the paseo and strolled along, enjoying the sounds of music and laughter coming from the varied restaurants. Couples walked hand in hand, children raced one another onto the sand, and the sun cast a final gasp of dusky orange light before it sank beneath the horizon. She loved this part of France. Far enough from the impossibly rich people of St. Tropez and Cannes, but close enough to be cosmopolitan, she'd bought her house there after she'd started the company, knowing she'd need a genuine getaway at some point. Her mansion in Malibu was great, and served as an office as well, but this area felt more like home.

There was only one restaurant with a deck that led onto the beach. The others were across the street, and right now, she wanted to be near the water. She went in and smiled at the waitress, a woman whose bed she'd enjoyed once or twice, until she'd come back to find her married and pregnant. She kissed her cheek and waved her out to the deck before she turned and started making Kera a classic mojito with Wray and Nephew rum, Kera's favorite drink.

When she stepped onto the deck, she froze. *What...is it possible?* The woman with the white hair sat alone at a table in the corner, reading a book with a tall glass of what looked like iced tea in front of her. Unlike the times Kera had seen her in war zones, she didn't have wings or writhing snakes on her head, and she could easily pass for normal, if incredibly beautiful and unusual looking. Kera's waitress friend nudged her and nodded toward the table with her eyebrows up.

"Go ahead. I doubt she bites."

Little do you know. Kera figured she did a lot worse than bite. *What the hell.* She went over and quietly cleared her throat. "Of all the gin joints, in all the world..."

The woman looked up, startled, and stared at Kera for a moment before she gave her a small smile. "She had to walk into mine." She motioned at the chair across from her. "Please."

Kera sat down and extended her hand. "Kera Espinosa." The woman shook her hand, and Kera noticed how dry and cool her skin was.

"Tisera Graves. Friends call me Tis. Nice to meet you, finally."

Kera nodded, glad there wasn't going to be any pretense about them not having seen one another before. "It's strange, though. To see you here, in the quiet, without bombs going off or people screaming. I almost feel like I should make a scene, just so we know what parts we're playing."

Tis nodded, looking deeply contemplative. "It seems more than strange, to be honest. The world is a big place, and yet here we are, at a tiny port town in France." She took a sip of her iced tea, her gaze never leaving Kera's. "Rather, it seems almost...fated. And I always know what part I'm playing. I'm sure you do as well."

Kera tried to shrug off the slight chill she felt at the words and smiled. "Whatever the reason, I'm incredibly glad for it. I've wanted to meet you for a long time."

She sat back and thanked the waitress, who left her drink and a small plate of hors d' oeuvres on the table with a quick wink.

"Truth be told, Kera, I've wondered how you managed to see me at all. If I'm not mistaken, the first time you saw me, in Baghdad, was years before the gods came out and the veil thinned. Usually if people see me, it's because we're having a...discussion. Granted, one person in a century might see me who isn't on my client list, but it's beyond rare."

Kera sipped the cool, minty mojito, savoring the high-end rum, and considered the implied question. "My mother was a vodun priestess, as was her mother. From the time I was born, she introduced me to the orishas, and I started seeing whoever she was praying to, for whatever thing she was praying about. I always assumed I could see you because you were one of them."

"A goddess of the voodoo religion? No, I'm afraid I'm nothing so interesting."

Kera waited for more information, but it wasn't forthcoming. Tis appeared to be lost in her thoughts. "If it's not insulting, may I ask what you are, then? I can assure you, a woman like you is far from *not* interesting, in my rather vast experience with women."

Tis focused on her, looking almost surprised to find her there. "I'm sorry. I've been incredibly overwhelmed lately, and I kind of just drift off sometimes." She folded a napkin corner, then folded it back again before she looked up. "I'm a fury. One of the three ancient furies of Greece. My sisters and I deliver justice to those who perpetrate crimes against one another. And good to know you're not spending nights pining about being alone."

Kera nodded and hoped she didn't look as daunted as she felt by the information. There weren't a lot of people who got to sit across from an immortal thousands of years old. *Well, there didn't used to be.* "That's why we've crossed paths. I'm in places helping the people who are being hurt by the people you're there to deal with."

Tis inclined her head. "That makes sense. Tell me what you do."

Talking about her business was one thing Kera knew how to do. And it made talking to a stunning supernatural being a bit easier. "I run a company called Global Relief and Development Experts, or GRADE. We go to war torn, poverty-stricken places and try to help. In some places that means working out how to get them clean water and mosquito netting. In others, like the one in Nigeria where I saw you, we run full-scale rescue and relief programs, taking in women and children who are displaced and in danger. We get them medical care, education, and help them get on their feet so they don't have to depend on other people. If we have to, we evacuate them to other countries."

Tis stared at her as she talked. It was slightly unnerving, the way she focused so intently and didn't break eye contact. Kera rarely felt like someone was truly listening, but there was no question of that with Tis.

"That sounds noble. But it must take an astounding amount of money and time."

Kera wondered if there was an implied rebuke or question of integrity in the statement. "It does. Fortunately, I made a lot of money working in the biomedical field before I started GRADE, which I invested extremely well, mostly in tech and medical companies that surpassed expectations. And in order to make GRADE work, I've developed partnerships with massive corporations as well as some smaller ones." She sipped her drink, wondering how much to explain. Did it matter if this mysterious being, this fury, questioned her ethics? *Damn right it does.* She'd examine why later. "It's not totally altruistic, if you're wondering. I've always believed that in order to do good in the world, you have to be doing well yourself first. If you're struggling to put food on the table, you won't be able to focus on helping others as much as you want to. If you're doing okay, though, then you can really work on making a difference in the world. I, and my staff, make good money. We still live in hovels when we're working, often in war zones, ducking bombs and trying to help, even when dealing with the worst of humanity. But when we're home, when we're able to take some time off, we can enjoy it. And I do…enjoy it, I mean."

"And with the money you've earned, you have the ability to develop these programs in other countries."

She was glad Tis seemed to understand. Something about having a harbinger of justice based doom give you the thumbs-up had to be a good thing. "Exactly. I can't do good without doing well. When I do well through my various business ventures, I try to make the world better. I do what I have to in order to get things done."

Tis finished her iced tea about the same time Kera finished her mojito. She looked uncertain before she said, "I need to go, I'm afraid. Perhaps we could do this again one day."

Kera was disappointed. *Guess I said something wrong after all.* "Sure. That would be great."

Tis seemed to sense her feelings, and her hand covered Kera's. "I mean it. I'd like to see you again."

You run into minefields to save kids. You've slept with queens. You can ask a woman out. "Okay…tomorrow? Would you like to come to dinner at my place at, say, eight o'clock? I live in Port Grimaud."

Tis frowned slightly and was silent for a long moment. Kera swallowed, wondering why it really, really mattered that she said yes.

"I'd like that. Thank you."

She raised her translucent light gray eyes to meet Kera's, and Kera felt her stomach flip. She'd been with plenty of beautiful women, but never someone, something, as stunning as Tis. "Excellent. Fifty-six Ile des Pins."

Tis stood and moved away from the table. She gave Kera a tentative smile and inclined her head slightly. "See you tomorrow, Kera Espinosa."

Kera watched as Tis walked to the edge of the water. Her slim, lithe body glowed against the dark night. She knew the moment Tis moved into what Kera thought of as spirit territory, where they weren't visible to all and sundry. It had always reminded her of the heat waves that came off the pavement on a hot day. Tis looked as though she was surrounded by them. She looked over her shoulder at Kera and unfurled her magnificent white wings. With a final smile, she leapt into the air and soared off over the water. She was gone in an instant, leaving Kera holding her breath and in awe of her surreal, powerful beauty.

She sat back in her seat and motioned for another mojito. As her pulse slowed to a normal rate, she had a thought. *What the hell does a fury eat? At least I know she drinks iced tea.* She pictured Tis's stunning eyes and sweet, though sad looking, smile. *I've got a date. With a fury. Mom would be so proud.*

CHAPTER SIX

"Why did I say yes?" Tis sat on the veranda of her rented apartment, sipping an iced coffee and debating the necessity of existence over the phone with Aulis.

"Because if you didn't, you'd molder away with your books, waiting for some cat lady's cats to come eat you. Because you don't even have your own cats. And then they wouldn't eat you, because you're so bony and muscly. Not even cats would eat you, and you've got wings. So you may as well go on a date and see if you can find something interesting to do with your life."

Aulis always had a way with words. "Thanks for that little pep talk. I should date because cats wouldn't eat me. I'm not sure your logic is sound."

"Tisera, listen to me. You need this. You said yes because deep down, you miss being with someone." Her tone gentled. "Give yourself a chance."

"She's human, Aul. What's the point?"

"The point, ancient one, is to live. It doesn't have to be forever, but it can be incredible while it lasts."

Tis remembered that Aulis had once taken a human lover, and if she remembered correctly, they'd been together most of his life. Aulis had disappeared for a decade after his death, and when she'd returned, she'd been a deeper, more sensitive creature. *Could it change me? Not likely.* But Aulis was right. She wanted meaning in her life. Maybe developing more relationships outside Afterlife was a good start. Even if it didn't get romantic, it would be nice to have a non-work friend other than Aulis.

"Okay, you're right. I'll go. But that doesn't mean anything will come of it. It'll probably just crash and burn."

"No, it might not. And I'm glad you're going into this so open-minded."

"Sarcasm is unnecessary. I'd better go get ready."

Aulis laughed again, and it made Tis smile, as it always did. "Call me with the dirty details when you finally get out of bed. Let me tell you, that woman has achieved demigod status when it comes to sex. I'd absolutely go there if I could."

Tis hung up and went through her limited wardrobe. Since this was a last-minute trip, she only had a small bag with her. She pulled out the flowing silk sundress with the light red flower print. *That will do. I don't want to look desperate or overdressed.* The thought of going out with someone with the kind of reputation Kera had was daunting. What if it did go somewhere, and she forgot how to do it? *You can't forget how to have sex, moron.* She took out a light wrap to go over the dress, and within a few minutes, she was ready. She didn't wear makeup. Unlike Meg, she didn't think it added anything, and it wasn't as if they had blemishes or wrinkles. All three of them had porcelain skin and always would. When she saw commercials advertising anti-aging potions, she was glad she didn't need to worry about it, and was bemused by the human fight against it. It wasn't as if it could be helped, and the alternative to not aging was death, which seemed a rather drastic measure.

She hadn't bothered with a car, and given that Kera knew what she was, she decided to fly. It had felt amazing to stretch her wings just because she wanted to and not because she was on her way to a job. She leapt from the balcony and dropped into the warm air current, glad the clothing she wore always stayed intact, though she never understood how that worked. It had been that way all their lives, and their mother had said to simply accept that some things were without reason.

She flew over the beautiful glistening waters of the French Riviera to Port Grimaud. When she spotted Kera's address, she saw her in the kitchen, chopping knife in hand. Spontaneously, Tis decided to surprise her. She landed with a soft thump on Kera's deck, her wings fully extended, blocking out the sunlight in front of the open French doors.

Kera looked up, apparently not fazed, and smiled widely. "That's quite an entrance. Do you do it at parties?"

Tis laughed. "At the kind of parties I go to, there are far more impressive beings than me."

"I seriously doubt that," Kera said. "I don't think that could be true anywhere, not just at parties."

Tis had no idea what to say. Compliments from attractive women hadn't come her way in a very, very long time.

"Please, come in. I'm just finishing the salad. Wine?"

"Yes, thank you. Your home is lovely." Tis stayed in her more human form, keeping her eyes round and her fangs sheathed. But she folded back her wings and let them drag along the cool tiled floor. She hated hiding them, and being able to keep them out was novel.

Kera looked around her place, as though seeing it through Tis's eyes. "It is, isn't it? I hardly ever get to spend time here, and then when I do, I forget to really look at it. Feel free to wander around."

Tis took her glass of wine and did just that. The house was massive, with high ceilings and curved archways leading from room to room. Cool terra-cotta flooring offset light terra-cotta feature walls, and beyond the spacious kitchen and small informal dining area was a large formal dining room. The living room was long and open, with sofas that looked like she could sink into them like clouds. The house was modern, not packed with furniture, and had very little about Kera personally. The paintings on the walls were black-and-white female nudes, but there were no photos anywhere of family. Tis liked to know people, really know them, and so far, there wasn't much about Kera except her appreciation of the female form and the fact that she had considerable wealth.

"I thought we'd eat on the deck, if that's okay?" Kera called from the kitchen.

"That sounds great." She looked at Kera's bookshelves. She'd always thought it was possible to tell a lot about someone by the books they read. Almost all the books were nonfiction, about things like architecture, water filtration, social conscience organizations, and psychology. There were biographies on various women throughout history and quite a few books on anthropological studies. There were also a number of language guides and dictionaries. *So, she's not an escapist.* Tis wasn't sure if that was a good thing or not. She didn't need to be around someone like herself, who was always consumed with work and the tribulations of the world. She needed…light.

She wandered back to the kitchen and found Kera setting out the dishes on the deck table. The outdoor patio was also huge, with a massive covered lanai area, again with cloud-like sofas, and a few feet away, a long, thin lap pool that ended shortly before the dock, where a small boat bobbed in the water. She watched as Kera set everything out, carefully arranging the plates and silverware. She moved with fluid economy, not wasting time or energy. Tis liked the way her muscles bunched under her baby blue T-shirt and the perfect fit of her jeans. She looked strong. And sexy. Very, very sexy. When she looked up and saw Tis watching her, she grinned, and Tis swallowed against a rush of desire.

"My father taught me that presentation matters. We should enjoy our food on every sensory level, not just as sustenance. So, when I'm not in a war zone of some kind, I try to take my time." She motioned to an empty chair. "Shall we?"

"Thank you." Tis sat and watched as Kera dished their food. "Are your parents still alive?" Kera flinched slightly, and Tis berated herself. Humans didn't like talking about death. She often forgot how sensitive they were about losing loved ones. Since Tis had never lost anyone, she couldn't really empathize. "I'm sorry, that was insensitive."

"No, it's okay, really. My father is still alive, and we're very close. He's currently in Haiti with my mother's family. She passed away eleven months ago. Cancer."

Tis wasn't sure what to say and floundered for a moment. *Think like a human, idiot.* "I'm sorry. It sounds like you were close."

They ate silently for a moment before Kera smiled. "We were extremely close. She was incredibly religious and wanted me to follow in her footsteps as a priestess, the way I followed her into science. But I saw the suffering and misery around me, and I couldn't fathom why God would allow that kind of thing. The weird thing is, I knew he existed, or at least, elements of faith did, because I often saw the orishas." She laughed. "And you. I saw you."

"But you still didn't believe?" Tis began to eat but kept her attention on Kera.

Kera shook her head. "It wasn't so much that I didn't believe as I didn't care. They weren't helping people, as far as I was concerned, so they didn't have anything to do with my life." She motioned at the food. "How do you like it?"

Tis finally noticed the flavors in her mouth. She'd been so focused on Kera, she wasn't paying attention. "It's all delicious. Perfect, in fact. And beautiful."

Kera blushed. "I'm glad you like it. My father is a chef, and I learned my appreciation of food from him. You know, cooking for you is way more pressure than cooking for a regular date."

"Why is that?" Tis took another bite, enjoying the idea of it being a date.

"I've seen you in action. What if you didn't like the food? I could end up on the other side of those fangs." Kera laughed.

Taken aback at how lightly Kera took what she'd seen, Tis looked blankly at her for a moment before she started to laugh too. "Unless you poisoned me, or a family, or an animal, I don't think you'd need to worry. Fortunately, I'm not so volatile. My sister Meg, on the other hand, might torture you for hurting food. That's always possible."

Kera ate and sipped her wine. "Then I simply won't cook for her. I'll reserve that for you."

Tis finished her meal and closed her eyes. "That's probably a good idea." Her eyes popped open when she realized how that sounded. "Not, I mean, that you should only cook for me. Or that I expect you to, ever again—"

Kera held up her hands. "Are you always this concerned about what you say?"

Tis thought about it. "I don't know. I suppose I've become that way."

Kera refilled their glasses and then motioned toward the deck chairs. Once they were seated, she said, "So what changed?"

"Is this normal? Is this really small talk? Aren't we supposed to be talking about favorite colors and pets we had as children?"

Kera looked amused. "Do you like small talk? Personally, I loathe it with all my being. And I wouldn't think someone with your experience would find that interesting."

Thank the gods. "No. I despise it. But do you want to know the dark things so soon? In fact, maybe you could tell me more about yourself. For instance, why do you help people? Why go through all the trouble when you could have been a rich, successful businesswoman without a care in the world?" Kera's laugh made Tis smile, but not the way Aulis's made her smile. Kera's went right through her, like a warm caress along her nerves.

"I think business people have some troubles, too. The hours are insane, and when you move the kind of money and resources I do, it's high stakes, high intensity, and incredibly emotional work. Frankly, I made a few bad decisions, and I decided some things had to change. I took some time off, sailed all over the world, saw the Seven Wonders, and enjoyed the hell out of life."

Tis liked watching Kera talk. She looked so relaxed, so peaceful, stretched out on the lounger, talking with her hands as she spoke. She certainly didn't look like the person rescuing women and children from rubble Tis had seen in other parts of the world, though she definitely looked like the playgirl billionaire she'd Googled. "And then?"

Kera sighed quietly. "You know that story about Buddha? How he was a prince, and once he saw true poverty, he couldn't go back to being a prince?"

"Of course. We've talked about that moment often through the years."

Kera gave her a brief incredulous glance and then started laughing. "Of course. How silly of me." She shook her head and continued. "Well, I was on a cruise in South America. We stopped at some quick tourist port, and we were instantly beset by the locals, selling handmade crafts, children begging for money, women offering to braid people's hair."

"And that bothered you?"

"Not that, so much. That happened in a lot of places. It was their eyes. They were talking to us, but they weren't. It was like they were looking through us, accepting that these rich people, who could afford to take this insanely expensive luxury trip, weren't going to give them the time of day. It was like…they'd accepted they were less than." She shrugged, obviously still haunted by the memory. "I started a conversation with an old woman who was sitting and watching it all. Then a few other women and kids joined us. I ended up going back to the old woman's house. I never got back on the ship. I had a friend pick up my things at the next port, and I stayed with the villagers for three months. I learned how little they had, what they needed, and who they were as humans. I'd been trying to figure out what to do with my life, and they gave me the direction I was looking for."

They drank silently for a while, watching the boats drift by on the water. Tis processed what Kera had told her. She'd been a good scientist doing good work. The news articles had blamed her disappearance on a breakdown after a bad business decision, but it had never been confirmed. She wondered how bad it must have been in order to cause someone like Kera to drop everything and run.

Kera looked at her. "Can they see you?" She tipped her glass at the passing boats.

"No. I've got my wings out, so they can't see me. Now that we're open, people often stare, or worse yet, corner you into a conversation you don't have the time or inclination for. But if it's a problem, I can change, if you need me to?" She didn't offer to let them see her with her wings out. It was hard enough going to and from work and having the press and curiosity seekers everywhere. She didn't need it when she was trying to relax.

Kera laughed loudly. "Please, don't ever change on my account. It just occurred to me it will look like I'm sitting here talking to myself." She looked at Tis, her gaze clearly on her wings. "But to be able to sit next to you, next to your beautiful wings, I'll gladly look crazy to my neighbors."

Tis giggled and put a hand to her mouth, surprised at the sound coming out of her. "Humans are no crazier than gods, I can assure you."

Kera reached out tentatively and stroked the edge of Tis's wing, making her shiver. "I've never seen someone so beautiful. I'm glad you came tonight."

Tis smiled, and the genuine feeling of being happy was so foreign, she wondered if she were drunk. "Me too. Thank you for inviting me."

Kera looked like she was going to ask a question, then settled back instead.

"What is it? Do I have spinach in my teeth?" Tis figured joking was the human way of making things less tense. When Kera smiled, she knew she was right.

"Forgive me if this is too forward. Are you involved romantically?"

It was a forward question, and Tis was glad she asked. "No, I haven't been for a long time." She took Kera's hand in her own and marveled at how delicate, how fragile the human hand was. "I don't have the time. You've seen me at work. You work in the same places. You know how busy this world keeps you."

"So true. I'm not with anyone either, if you were wondering." She grinned and squeezed Tis's hand. "For the same reason, really. I don't have the time. And women aren't great with the whole 'I don't know if I'll be coming back' thing, either. But I have to be realistic."

The thought of Kera dying in some war torn country made Tis's chest hurt in a way she'd never felt. "Yes, I can imagine," she said.

Kera stood and stretched. "Enough of the heavy stuff! Why don't we go listen to music at the bistro on the beach?"

Tis nodded, glad for the distraction. "I'll put my wings away. The press comes up with enough rumors about you. You don't need talking to yourself added to your list of accomplishments." Tis pulled the magic around her that made her visible, and palatable, to humans. Kera studied her, and she was amazed at the insecurity running through her. She hadn't been insecure for four and a half thousand years. The first five hundred of her existence she'd had a few vanity issues, but after that…

"I wish I could say the press make stuff up, but most of it's true, and I'm good with who I am. And I hope you don't mind me saying, I like that people will be able to see me with you. There's nothing like being with the sexiest woman in the place."

Tis felt the heat rush to her face. *Oh gods. Blushing? What on earth is wrong with me?* "No, I don't mind you saying that at all."

They left Kera's and strolled away from the port and down to the beach where they walked along the water. "What brought you to this part of France?"

Tis had wondered the same thing. "You know, I have no idea. There isn't a place on the planet I haven't been, and I have several favorites. But for some reason, I felt pulled to this area. I'm on... vacation. Just for a few weeks."

"I didn't know gods took vacations. That's good to know. Maybe now people will get an out of office message when they pray." Kera looked at her mischievously.

"I'm not a god, so I don't know about that. People don't pray to furies. They pray to whoever they believe in when they see us though, I can tell you that."

Kera laughed. "Oh, I've seen you. I bet they pray to anyone listening, not just the ones they believe in."

"Am I that scary, truly?" Tis asked, genuinely curious. She was who she was, and although she knew she and her sisters were terrifying to those they sought, she hadn't considered how people they weren't speaking with perceived them.

"Honestly? If I were looking up at you, and I knew you were there for me, I'd probably need new underwear, instantly. But from a distance—"

Suddenly, a water sprite leapt from the sea and landed in front of them, water dripping from her seaweed hair, her algae green skin glowing eerily in the moonlight. Her high-pitched voice sounded completely out of place when she said, "Zed says you're needed back at headquarters, right away. Tonight." Her sharp little teeth made her smile look malicious.

"I'm on vacation. He knows that."

"There's been a commotion, and they need the voice of reason." She shrugged and leapt back into the water. As she sank beneath it, she said, "He said to tell you it wasn't a request."

When she was gone, Tis heard Kera let out a windy breath.

"What was that?"

"A water sprite. They're excellent messengers, given how much of the planet is covered in water, but I've never liked them."

Kera swallowed audibly. "I can see why. They're like horror movie dolls. With nasty teeth."

Tis stopped and faced her, glad when Kera took her hands in her own. "I'm sorry. Work calls. But if I can get things settled quickly…"

Kera gently kissed the tops of Tis's hands. "Then come back, and we can pick up where we left off. And if not? Who knows, maybe we'll run into one another while saving humanity." She brushed another kiss along Tis's knuckles. "The world isn't that big, right?"

Tis was surprised at how much she wanted that to be true. "I'm hoping to get back, I really am. But for now…" She stepped back and released the magic, allowing her wings to unfold. She liked the look of appreciation and awe in Kera's expression as she watched. "I'm afraid I have to go."

She leapt into the warm night air, turning to look at Kera standing on the beach below her. Kera raised a hand in farewell, and Tis flapped her wings hard in response.

Zed had better be about to fade, or choking on a donut or something. For the first time in centuries, she couldn't wait to see someone again.

Chapter Seven

Tis pressed her fists to her tired eyes. They'd been at it for hours. Every time a god brought up a new rule, someone else started asking questions. Eventually, they lost sight of the rule altogether, and around it went. All she really wanted was to be sitting on Kera's deck, sipping wine and watching the passing boats.

"This is why I asked you to iron these things out before I got involved. There's no point in me being here."

Zed slammed his fist on the table, and the room was instantly silenced. "We're here to begin the process of setting things in place, and I want to let Tisera leave soon." He looked at each individual just long enough to make them squirm.

That he could do so to a room full of gods meant he was back in full power, and Tis had to admit she liked the reminder of the old days.

"The first thing we've agreed on is this: every single religion states a no violence policy. No killing in the name of any of us."

Most every god nodded their agreement, though Tis noticed one or two who sat stone-faced. "And how are you rolling out this policy to your followers?"

"We're going to our individual meeting places, or sacred sites, and speaking directly with the followers. We're having our words inscribed there and then, and then we're reading them to make certain they've been transcribed properly."

Tis wrote as Zed talked. "I'm marking that as rule one, procedure A. Each god will instruct their followers in a no violence policy and see to its instruction and dissemination. Is that correct?" Again, there were plenty of nods, but she could sense the tension in the room. "Is this decision by majority vote?"

"There are a few dissenting voices who aren't sure about the wording, but for the rest of us it's clear. So yes, it's by majority vote, and those outvoted will adhere to the policy."

Tis wrote it down. "Next?"

"This is bigger, and we haven't worked out the dissemination yet. However, the idea is for us all to reach out to our followers and devise new, updated texts. Wording to be in current language usage, so there's less ambiguity, and the rules of the religion apply to today's world. This will provide a common base for the followers, and any questions with regard to the text can then be put directly to the deity in question."

"I still don't understand how we're going to do that. It will take years. Maybe decades." Confucius looked glum, his normally pensive expression pained.

"Then edit yourself. Pare it down to the important stuff. Sure, teach other things. But only document the big rules, the really important items."

"And leave what we say out loud beyond those rules open to interpretation? Isn't that counterproductive?" Horus glared at Zed, his falcon eyes black and unblinking.

"That's the point of being back among them. You can actually talk to them, get them to understand what you really mean. When they go off on tangents about killing and hating, you can set them straight."

"And if we don't want to?" Shiva sat rigid, his fingers drumming lightly over his necklace of small skulls.

"That's why you're here. As part of Afterlife, you agree to the basic rules. If you go against the rules, if you fail to tell your followers, then you'll be penalized. That's the way we've done it since coming together, and it's even more important now."

Mohammed stood, his dark skin an almost shocking contrast to Zed's paleness. "Zeus speaks true. If we are going to be what the humans need us to be, then we must abide by the constitution set in place. Those who willfully refuse to help make humanity better, as we should, will be fined or, should they continue to refuse, an announcement will be made, and they will be stripped of their godhood. They can fade, or they can live among humans. But they will no longer live as gods."

Stunned silence filled the room. Tis knew there would be consequences, there had to be, but to strip a god of their title…

"Why would you put such penalties in place?"

That came from a god Tis didn't recognize. Now that humans knew the gods existed, many of the ancient religions that had only had a few figureheads suddenly had many more followers, and were developing new ideas of their gods all the time. She'd been talking to someone before the meeting, and their face had blurred for a moment before changing and becoming defined. Some important follower had described the god in detail, and the followers, believing that description, had actually changed the face of the deity altogether. It was distracting and, she thought, a little scary. If humans truly understood the power they held over their gods, she couldn't fathom the consequences.

"Because by placing ourselves among humans once again, we must hold ourselves accountable to the highest degree. We are supposed to make their lives better, help them understand something beyond themselves. As such, we must give them guidance, and be above reproach ourselves. Failing our followers, we fail in the essence of our existence." Zed spoke softly, but his command was clear.

Tis cleared her throat. "I've put that in writing. So, to be clear: no violence, redo your texts for clarity. Anything else?"

The Christian God stood up, his presence heavy in the room. "I propose we hold one another to a level of respect. Now that humans know we all exist, there is no reason to say one of us is better than the other, or correct while another is not. We teach as we believe, as our followers want to believe, and let them choose between us. We don't put one another down or disrespect one another. The world isn't divided into religious sections anymore. Our followers live among one another, and dividing them can lead to conflict."

Again, the room stayed quiet as everyone contemplated it. For a god who'd admitted to being jealous and offed vast groups of people for praying to other gods, it was a grand gesture indeed.

"I like it," Tis said. "It's competition at its most honest. Answer questions truthfully, directly. If you lose some followers because of it, so be it. You'll probably gain them from elsewhere. Maybe by showing respect for one another on a celestial level, you can show them how to behave toward one another." Again, there were nods of agreement, while others seemed reticent. "Can I write it down?"

Zed placed his thunderbolt on the table, and other gods placed their own items of power on the table to show they agreed. Those few who didn't, mostly gods of dissention and destruction, were outvoted. Tis wrote it down.

"Okay. No violence. New texts. Show respect." She pushed the parchment toward Zeus. "I suggest we get everyone to sign this one. It seems like these are the most important rules for the moment. You can handle the other stuff without me in the meantime."

He waved his hand and his thunderbolt signature appeared on the bottom. So it went around the table, until it came back with all the signatures on it, even from those who weren't happy about it. Tis took it and put her own signature below theirs. "This document is binding. Those who don't abide by it will face the indicated consequences." She stood. "Now, if you don't mind, I'll be going back to my vacation."

Ama stepped outside with her. "I can't imagine how difficult this must be, Tis. I'm sorry so much has fallen to you."

Tis shook her head and shoved her hands into her pockets. "It's just strange. There are so many beings at Afterlife who are capable, but they've chosen me?"

"It's because you think that way that you've been chosen." Ama laughed lightly. "Do you truly think anyone else in this building is capable of being as impartial as a fury?"

Tis sighed. It was true. Furies were, by nature, lawgivers, and because they didn't require followers, they could stay above the fray. "Okay. I get it." She gave Ama a hug. "Keep the old man in line."

She smiled, but there was tension in her eyes. "I'm doing my best. Many of the old religions are gaining strength, especially the Greek and Roman pantheons. Hera is coming back for a visit next week. That should be…interesting."

Tis winced. Hera was cold at best and irrationally ruthless at worst. "Well, if you need some time away too, come find me."

Ama turned to go back into the conference room, where one of the newer gods was gesticulating wildly, looking decidedly ungodly. "Oh believe me, I will."

Tis had to decide what to do. Should she head back to France or go talk to her sisters? Just as she was making up her mind to head to France, Dani walked in.

"Hey, Tis. I'm surprised to see you here. I thought you'd be with Meg and Alec."

"Why? Is there a job?"

Dani looked less tired and far more alert than she'd seen her in years. "Yeah, a mass shooting at a university in Tennessee. Some kids saying they were told by Satan to do it. One took his own life; five others are still alive."

Tis looked over her shoulder. Neither Satan nor Hades was in the conference room, and they were two beings who definitely should be. As major figureheads in their religions, they often weren't given god titles, but nevertheless, people prayed to them, which gave them divine status. She realized none of the underworld gods were there, and that they'd intentionally been left out. That wouldn't be good for anyone in the long run. "Would you mind letting Ama know and telling her I suggest getting the underworld gods involved in signing the legal documents too? I'll head over to the shooting."

Dani nodded and squeezed Tis's shoulder. "Will do. One of my team is working that one, but if you feel like I need to be there, just give me a shout."

Tis gave Dani a quick hug and hurried out the back entrance. She wanted to get there, understand what had happened, and who they felt had told them to do what they'd done. If they'd done it on their own, as was most often the case, they'd be punished as usual. But if one of the gods really had instructed their followers to harm others, it became something else entirely. She sent a mental message asking her sisters to wait until she got there.

So much for France. She wondered if she'd ever see Kera again.

❖

"Thanks for waiting."

She gave Alec and Meg quick hugs before closing her eyes and feeling the scene. Death was everywhere, and the five shooters still alive were strangely calm.

"No problem. We could have handled this one, Tis. You didn't have to come." Meg snapped her gum, looking at her curiously.

"It's not that, Meg. I know you could have. Can we go see the shooters? I want to get a sense of them before we act. Then I'll explain."

Alec pointed toward a set of large double doors. "They're in there, against the back wall."

They went in and stood before the five young people. Tis thought they were all in their early twenties, if that, and for the most part looked like normal university students. But their calm silence was bizarre. They looked at the furies without fear, without any emotion, really. Until one smiled slightly.

"You look like minions of our Master. Are you?"

Suddenly, they all looked interested.

Tis asked, "Who do you consider your Master?"

The boy smiled, and if she didn't know better, she would have thought him a demon.

"Our Lord and Master Satan, of course. The one true Master. It must have been—" He began to choke, and his hands went to his throat as though trying to pry something away.

Tis and her sisters hissed, and their snakes came to life. Tis looked around but couldn't see or feel any other deity in the area. She looked at Meg and Alec, who also looked confused. The boy choked and writhed, his eyes bulged. Tis searched his mind, but it was an oozing mass of black strings—chaos and anger. There wasn't anyone in it, nor was there anything tangible for her to take hold of. The boy took a last gasp and was still, an eerie smirk on his lips.

The other four kids stared at him impassively. A girl said, "He knew better than to talk about it. We all know." She settled back against the wall and closed her eyes.

What the hell just happened? She searched the girl's mind but found it utterly blank. No thoughts, no emotions, no…anything. It was the same with the others; they were empty except for strange spaghetti-like strings of black muck. Shaken, she turned to go. One of Dani's team on the death crew came in.

"Weird. I thought I'd gotten them all and was just about to go. Then this one…but it feels really different."

Tis looked at the boy. "Does he? How so?"

The Death girl squinted as though trying to see something. "It's like death came from an attack on the inside—not illness, but someone else causing it. Humans can't do that, can they?"

"Not without weapons of some kind." Alec looked irritated and turned to Tis. "Does this have something to do with why you came?"

Tis nodded and indicated they should go outside. The Death girl knelt to take the boy's soul but stopped short. "Um, guys? You should probably know…his soul is already gone." She looked stunned. "Dani's going to be totally pissed. No one else can do that, right? Damn, is she going to be mad at me?"

Alec raised her hands to get the girl to stop talking. "Dani won't be angry with you. This is new, and we'll have to figure it out. Let her know what happened, though, and tell her we'll come talk to her when we get back."

The girl nodded, hitched her bulging backpack higher, and ran through the back wall.

Tis, Meg, and Alec went outside and sat next to a large fountain.

"What's going on?" Meg asked.

"I got called back to the office today to start writing down some rules. I hadn't noticed at the time, but neither Satan nor Hades were there, nor any of the other underworld gods. These kids say they were told by Satan to kill their fellow students and that boy died while trying to tell us something. What do you think?"

"Would Satan be that ballsy? Or Hades? The others definitely wouldn't. I mean, to tell humans outright to commit murder…"

"This feels more like demon work to me," Meg said. "They tried that stunt with Selene last year, after all."

"Without their leader, they won't be organized enough to do it on their own." Tis sighed, thinking furiously. "Here's the larger issue. Can we, legally and ethically, punish the kids in there if they were told by a god to do what they did? What if the god has a hold of them on a deeper level, if their free will has been taken away?"

It was a question they'd had to deal with five thousand years before, when gods freely mingled with humans, and there weren't laws in place to protect them. Apparently, they'd have to look at the question again.

"I think we should head back to the office. I'll get someone from Purgatory to place them in holding until we can figure out what to do with them, and so they don't go killing anyone else. Let's talk to Zed and see if we can get hold of the underworld gods. We'll go from there." Alec opened her wings and leapt into the air.

Tis and Meg followed Alec, but Tis barely saw the land below them slip away as they flew. If there were gods openly advocating violence, what did it do to the decisions the other gods had made? If they didn't come to an agreement, what would happen to humanity? Was it now possible for the gods to become more than what their believers made them? If they developed autonomy, who was going to stop them?

The weight of the questions made her wonder how she managed to keep flying. And as the sun sank below the horizon, she fleetingly wondered what Kera was doing.

Chapter Eight

Kera smiled and shook people's hands as she made her way through the party. A benefit of having parties at her place meant she could escape to the office, or to one of the upper floors, whenever she was tired of the corporate douchebags.

Tonight's soiree, though, was about being present. GRADE was a sought-after partner by corporations all over the world, and she wanted a few new contracts so she could start some new projects she had in mind. She smiled for a photographer as she shook the president of OilCo's hand.

"Nice to see you doing so well, Ms. Espinosa."

His smarmy grin and flappy jowls made her want to wipe her palm on her date's off-the-rack dress. Her date smiled prettily while holding on to Kera's arm. To be sure, she looked the part; her red gown was cut down the front, all the way to her navel. Generous, probably fake, breasts were barely covered, and her long brown hair shone to perfection. She was stunning, and Kera would have no problem enjoying an hour or two between the sheets with her.

"Nice to see you too, Ed. How are the missus and the kids? And Marcy?"

He laughed again, but his expression was shrewd. "Only you would so indelicately bring up a man's mistress, Ms. Espinosa." He shrugged. "But everyone is fine, thank you for asking. Now, I wanted to talk to you about that parcel of land in Albertine Graben."

Kera inclined her head slightly. "Happy to talk about it, Ed. But you know how popular that particular piece is. There must be a dozen other people here interested in it as well. What kind of terms are you interested in giving?"

His fake smile receded, and she saw the ravenous CEO rise to the surface. "I know your terms. And you know how we work. We haven't had an accident or leak in more than a decade, and I know damn well no one else here can say that. We'll hire thirty percent of our workforce from the local community."

"Thirty percent? I hire more than that as kitchen staff. Enjoy your night, Ed." Kera turned away, ignoring him as he tried to call her back. Each player in the game upped the stakes, and by the end of the night, she'd have not only that deal done, but half a dozen others as well.

They made the rounds, and she soon tired of her date hanging on her arm. "Feel free to roam, darling. I'll catch up with you later." She wasn't worried about the woman's discretion, nor her intelligence. She had clear parameters when it came to her dates. They needed to be smart, well-read, and able to handle themselves in a high-flying crowd. She didn't have time to police what her date might say or do, and having a beautiful woman on her arm played nicely with the powerful old white guys. More than once, her date had overheard conversations that had proven extremely lucrative for Kera. Her dates were women she knew and liked, and even better, they all knew the rules of the game. She offered a good time, excellent wine, and even better sex. But that was all. She didn't have time for more, and the dates she took to events like this one respected that. Briefly, she wondered how Tisera would do in a crowd like this. Kera looked around the room and studied her guests. *How many of them are on Tis's naughty list?* The thought was sobering. *Could I be one of those people?* Although the thought of being on the receiving end of Tis's disciplinary action was chilling, more disturbing was the thought she wouldn't want to disappoint her that way.

"Kera!"

Yanked from her thoughts, she focused on Ajan's bear hug.

"You look like a promotional ad in a lesbian magazine."

She straightened her waistcoat and tux shirt. "Yeah, well, you look like an ad for terrifying celebrity bodyguards."

He laughed, looking decidedly uncomfortable in the expensive suit she'd had made for him. As her chief of staff, she needed him at functions like this occasionally, and he'd never buy something so extravagant for himself. She knew how important image was in the high stakes games they played, and she made sure they looked the part. Granted, she *always* looked the part, but it didn't hurt to surround herself with people who looked like they knew the game too.

He touched her arm and gently guided her down the hall toward her office. "Can we speak privately for a second?"

"I'm not accepting your marriage proposal, no matter how many times you ask."

He put a hand over his mouth. "That always makes me feel a bit sick. I've told you, you're way too muscly and hard. I like my women soft."

"Something we have in common, my friend." She closed the office door behind him and flipped on the music to cover their conversation. "What's up?"

He stared at her seriously for a minute. "I thought you should know, we've got a lead on Degrovesnik."

She gripped the edge of her desk and leaned toward him. "Tell me."

"Boss, are you sure you want to go down this road—"

"Ajan. Tell me."

He sighed. "He reached out to one of our contacts. He wanted weapons, but our contact isn't running them anymore. He left a number in Dermenino, Russia."

"That area of Russia is mostly abandoned now. It makes sense that chickenshit would hide out someplace like that."

Ajan waited quietly while she thought. That was one of the things she liked about him. He didn't mind silence.

"Okay. Get hold of Petra Skinner. Give her whatever info we have, and tell her I want more. Pay her whatever she asks, and tell her to move fast, before Degrovesnik moves on." Petra, a former CIA operative and now GRADE's own private investigator, was efficient, dependable, and just a little bit crazy. In Kera's estimation, a perfect employee.

He nodded, looking resigned. "I'll do it now."

"Good. I'm going to go back out there and figure out the Ugandan deal. Let me know what Petra says." She squeezed his rock solid bicep as she left the room. "I won't do anything stupid."

He rolled his eyes.

"Okay, I won't do anything *I* consider stupid. Better?"

"Go get us some money. Let me know who I need to talk to when I'm done in here."

"Will do. Come find me."

She left the room, adrenaline pumping through her. *At last.* It had been five years, and after the chaos he'd caused, he'd disappeared. *I'm coming for you, asshole. Just like I said I would.*

Kera smiled at her date as she moved back to her side.

"It's Joy, if you were wondering," the woman said quietly.

Kera grinned at her. "I knew that." Joy smiled, and the sharp wit Kera liked was clear in her eyes.

"I'm sure." She moved as though to whisper seductively in Kera's ear, her breasts pressed against Kera's bicep. "The guy from OilCo was discussing your proposal with the guy who smells like sweaty socks from PelicanGull. They were saying your terms are ridiculous, and you should be shown your proper place at the table. The classy woman from Enviro told them not to underestimate you and ditched the conversation." She placed a small, light kiss on Kera's cheek and looked at her adoringly. "You're welcome."

Kera took in the information, the usual rush of the game drawing her in. She pulled Joy close and ran her hand over the perfectly round, if slightly too muscled for her taste, ass. "I hope you'll allow me to thank you properly later."

"I like my coffee with two sweeteners and milk in the morning."

"Noted."

Joy pulled away and said more audibly, "Excuse me while I attempt to find the ladies' room."

"Hurry back." Kera watched her walk away, her confidence screaming femme fatale.

She caught the eye of the woman from Enviro, who seemed agitated by the conversation she was having with a doctor Kera had long found irritating. She made her way over and nearly laughed out loud at the look of relief on the woman's face.

"Emily. Nice to see you again. I'm glad you could make it." She turned to the doctor, who looked as sour and grumpy as he always did. "Glen. You're looking well."

He snorted slightly. "Always the charmer, never a truth-teller."

"You know, I always forget why I invite you to my little get-togethers. Do remind me, and for Emily's sake, explain so she doesn't think I have abysmal taste in friends."

He glared at her. "You invite me because I work harder than most of the people in this room, and I'm the best at my job." He looked at Emily. "I'm a biomedical researcher, and I worked with Kera's mother on diseases in poverty-stricken countries."

Emily nodded as though she now understood. When Kera saw that, she smiled and turned to Glen. "Thank you for the reminder. If you don't mind, please go irritate those two squirrely looking gentlemen over there. The ones who've forgotten who invited them to this playground." She said it loud enough to be overheard, and Glen, who sorely lacked a sense of sarcasm, wandered over to the two flush-faced CEOs.

She turned back to Emily, who looked extremely satisfied. "Now. I believe we have business to discuss."

"Let's cut the crap, Kera. I want that land and the oil rights that come with it. We haven't been around long, but our standards are higher and our environmental impact is one of our greatest concerns. What are your conditions?"

Kera liked a woman who didn't mess around and knew what she wanted. As much as she enjoyed the game, she also loved direct women in power. "You'll rent the land from me on a twenty-year contract. I want sixty percent of the workforce hired locally and not just in grunt positions. I want twenty percent of the profits, and I want yearly accounts showing staffing and environmental impacts."

Emily stared at her for a moment. "You know the life-span of an oil rig isn't nearly that long. Make it a ten-year contract. I'll accept sixty percent of the workforce, and if you'll take ten percent of the profits instead of twenty, I'll put an education program in place, on-site. Impact accounts are no problem."

Kera ran the numbers. Ten percent still meant nearly half a billion dollars a year coming into GRADE, which meant funding a large number of projects. The bulk of it would go into the local Ugandan community, which she'd already assessed when she'd bought the land, choosing an area with the least amount of conflict and the most need. She'd brought in the geophysicists necessary to determine the land was oil rich and had taken the chance. Many companies, even the large oil companies, wouldn't touch war zones in Africa. So Kera sought out areas she knew could be controlled, which were often the most desperate, and made deals with the local governments. In turn, she brought in businesses that provided jobs and then funded the kinds of programs needed in poverty-stricken countries. It wasn't always a clean way of doing things, but ultimately, it meant more people got the help they needed. She could live with it.

"A twelve-year contract, and you fund the reclamation if the wells are empty at the end of it, using the local workforce over the course of no more than three years. I'll have my lawyers send over the contracts next week." She shook Emily's hand.

"You know, I don't know how you do it, and I probably don't want to know all the people you're in bed with, but I like your style." Emily finished her drink and placed it on a table. "And now that I've sold my soul to you, I'll be leaving."

Kera laughed. "I've got a bank of souls, Emily, but I can assure you yours isn't one of them. Give me a shout when you're ready to start moving."

Emily gave a little wave over her shoulder as she left, and Kera scanned the room for her next move. *God, I love this game.*

❖

By the end of the night, Kera had brokered enough deals to keep GRADE going for the next ten years. Her own lifestyle, as well as her staff's, would continue to be more than comfortable as well. Once the deals were signed, she kept in contact with every company she worked with, to make sure they were adhering to the stipulations of the contracts. She often stopped by their bases in the various countries, mostly because she'd be working there, setting up water plants, educational facilities, and medical institutions. She didn't care what their businesses were, as long as they didn't involve weapons or war. There wasn't much point in working with people who would just tear the region down again.

When most of her party guests had gone, she took Joy's hand. "I don't suppose I could interest you in a nightcap?"

"If, by nightcap, you mean the kind of fucking that'll mean no one else will ever be good enough again, and I'll mourn the loss for the rest of my life, then yes, I accept."

God bless direct women. "Well, then..." Kera led the way upstairs.

By the time they reached the bedroom, there was a blur of clothing flying off and scorching kisses. Kera gave her exactly what she'd asked for, fucking her furiously, not bothering with foreplay or protestations of beauty or love. She was sexy, in a hard work kind of way, and plenty responsive. When she went to touch Kera in the early hours of the morning, Kera gently moved her hand away. She gave her a kiss on the forehead. "I'm more of a giver than a taker, love. Get some sleep."

Joy gave her an exhausted smile and rolled over. She was asleep within seconds, and Kera lay there staring at the ceiling. As much as she enjoyed sex, it was a rare woman she allowed access to her body. Too often that meant an emotional connection, and she had neither the time nor the inclination for that. Her parents' relationship had been as close to perfect as she could imagine, but that kind of thing didn't happen for everybody. Just a special, lucky few, and she wasn't going to be one of them, not with the life she led.

She closed her eyes and drifted to sleep, wondering what Tisera was doing and if she ever thought of their shared dinner in France. *I hope I get to see you again, beautiful lady.*

Chapter Nine

Tis sat on her balcony overlooking the Pacific. A light breeze played in the trees, and she closed her eyes to listen. She'd taken a few days off, but decided not to go anywhere. It was pointless to do so, since she'd likely be called back, either to work on the constitution at Afterlife, or to go to a new job with her sisters. Localized, singular murders and violence were way down, but large scale freak-outs were up.

She'd considered going back to France, just to see if Kera was still around, but thought better of it. She liked her and wanted to spend time with her, but her life was far too complicated right now. She didn't want to try for something she couldn't have. *Coward. I'm being a total coward.* Of course she could have a friend. There was no real reason she couldn't. The truth was, she was afraid. Life felt tenuous; the world was at a crossroads, and Tis wasn't sure how it was going to play out. What if she started to care for her and then it all went to hell? She was also human, and there was no good way for that to end. Because for one of them, it *would* end. And then the other would be left to deal with the loss, for eternity.

The phone rang, and she sighed. She was lonely when she was alone, but lonelier when she was surrounded by people. If Aulis weren't so far away, she'd go spend more time with her. Maybe she could get her reassigned? Washington, DC, wasn't so far away, and there were plenty of oath breakers there. The phone rang again, and she finally reached for it.

"Hi, Tisera. It's Cerberus at Afterlife."

As though there's another Cerberus, not at Afterlife. "Hi, Cerb. What's up?"

"I've got a message for you. A woman named Kera Espinosa called and left her phone number and said she'd appreciate it if you could give her a call."

"I didn't think people could just call the office?"

"They can't, technically. I'm not sure how she did it. Anyway, want her number?"

"Sure, thanks." Tis wrote it down and hung up, lost in thought. How had Kera managed to get through to Afterlife? They didn't make the number public, even though the gods were out now. If their followers wanted to leave a message, they did so via prayer, not the phone. *Do I want to see her?* When she'd gotten home, she'd done some more research on Kera, and not everything she found painted her in a good light. She toyed with her phone before dialing.

"Espinosa."

"Do you always answer using your last name? Why?" Kera's warm laugh made her smile.

"It's an old habit, I guess. My only phone is my work phone…"

"Meaning if you do have friends, they get your business side first. I understand." Tis only had one phone, and it too was a work phone.

"I'm really glad you called. I wasn't sure your office would pass on messages. Or if you even worked out of that office, actually."

"They wouldn't, normally. How did you get the number? And yes, I work out of that office. A vast number of us do."

"I have friends in high, and low, places. One of them managed to get me the number, from a friend of theirs who used to work there but is now a hairstylist." Kera hesitated for a moment. "I was thinking, our dinner date kind of got interrupted. Would you like to try again?"

Tis bit her thumbnail, thinking. She wanted a friend. She wasn't sure if she wanted more than that, although sex was certainly welcome. Sex with Kera seemed particularly attractive. "Sure. You're in Malibu, right?"

There was a moment of silence before Kera asked, "Researching me, are we?"

Tis nearly smacked herself in the forehead. "Well, you sounded interesting in France, and I wanted to know more. I wasn't sure if I'd see you again, so—"

"Tisera, I was teasing. I'm flattered, actually. I'm sure you've met some remarkable people, far more worthy of your time. Well, actually, I'm pretty amazing, so I don't blame you. Anyway, yes, I'm in Malibu, at the old Robert Redford place. You know it?"

"You could say that. Did you have a day in mind?"

"That sounds interesting. How about tomorrow night?"

"I'd like that. But you know, if work calls…"

Kera laughed again. "Oh, believe me, I know. I'm making dinner though, so if you could let me know if you get called away, I'd appreciate it."

Tis couldn't imagine *not* calling. "Of course." She hesitated a moment. "I'm really glad you called."

Kera's voice was soft, sexy. "And I'm glad you called me back. See you tomorrow."

Tis hung up and exhaled. She stood up and paced for a moment before doing a little spin in the kitchen. She giggled like a girl and covered her mouth. She jumped at a knock on the door and instantly went from excited to wary. She moved to the door and looked through the peephole. Alec and Meg stood waiting, a huge pizza box in Meg's hands.

"You know we know you're watching us, right?" Alec rolled her eyes.

"This box is hot, and I'm hungry. If you don't open the door, we're going to eat it all without you, right now, on your doorstep."

Tis opened the door, laughing. "Sorry. My mind was somewhere else."

Meg gave her a passing kiss on the cheek as she headed toward the kitchen. "I want to know what it is. But you have to wait until we've got food. I'm starving, and you know how I get when I'm hungry."

Alec gave Tis a hug and walked next to her. "I thought she was going to start chewing on the dashboard when I told her she couldn't have a piece before we got here."

"Are you pregnant?" Tis asked, eyeing Meg, who already had a piece halfway in her mouth.

"As if. I haven't wanted a kid in five thousand years, I'm not about to start now." She talked with her mouth full. "This is amazing. The best pizza ever, in the world."

Tis looked at the box and raised her eyebrows. "Since when did Edesia go into the pizza business?"

"You wouldn't believe how crazy things are getting. She decided that now that she can be out, she wants to be *really* out. She's started up a Goddess Food chain, and a whole bunch of goddesses are putting their names on stuff she's selling. People who are really into food are converting to her as a religion, totally separate from the standard religions."

"Quite a few of the gods, especially the younger ones, are really taking to the marketing idea, thinking of ways to tell new followers about their religions. Obviously, Jesus is way ahead of the curve, since he's been doing it for ages." Alec folded her slice in half and ate it like a sandwich.

Tis slid out a piece and sat on the counter. "I'm glad I'm not involved in all that. It seems so, I don't know, distasteful. Shouldn't gods be above that?"

Meg shrugged and started on her third slice. "That's the thing with them all coming out. It used to be you were supposed to believe in your god, and only yours, or it was sacrilege and your god got to turn you into flora or fauna. Now, there's no denying the others, so they can't hold that over people anymore. It's a religious free market."

Tis picked up the pizza box, jumped down off the counter, and headed to the balcony. "Speaking of which," she said, curling up on the outdoor couch, "any news on the gods of the underworld issue?"

Alec took off her boots and rolled up her jeans to put her feet in the pool. "Satan denies it, says although he was slighted by not being allowed on the main council, he wouldn't use humans that way. He said if and when he does it, it'll be out in the open."

Tis looked at Alec, wide-eyed. "He actually said that?"

"Yeah. Zed warned him about the consequences and said he wasn't welcome at the table because he was a fallen angel, not a god, and there are no other angels at the table either." Alec scooped a struggling ladybug from the water and watched her shake her wings before flying off. "But he did make him sign the contract the others signed, so now he's bound to it. No one has any idea where Hades is, but there's a search on for him. He was sent an invite to sit on the lower council, and he declined it with a hole in the messenger."

"So, that's possible then."

"Let's stop talking about work for like, five minutes. What has you so distracted? Is she hot?" Meg lay on her stomach with her chin in her hands, staring at Tis.

Tis wasn't sure if she was ready to talk about Kera. After all, it wasn't anything specific yet. "Hey!" She wiped pool water from her face.

"Stop analyzing it and just tell us." Alec grinned at her, her hand cupped in the pool, ready for another swipe.

"Okay, okay. Her name is Kera Espinosa. I've seen her at a few of our job sites, and I met her in France recently. We really hit it off." Her sisters stared at her, silent. Alec glanced at Meg, and Meg looked...worried. "What? What's wrong?"

Alec's expression was serious. "What do you know about her, Tis? Have you researched her?"

Tis nodded, a hint of panic bubbling inside her. "Of course. I know she's a bajillionaire. I know she's into big business and she's a philanthropist."

"It's not just that, Tis. The people she does business with? We end up meeting a lot of them. Or we would, if they got their hands dirty more often. But a lot of the time they have people doing their nasty work for them, so they're always on our periphery." Meg glanced at Alec, who nodded. "Honestly, I only watch her because she's hot and in all the gossip mags, because she hasn't actually done anything wrong. But her crowd doesn't seem to play nice."

"But...but she's helping people. When I saw her in Nigeria, she was rescuing women and children. She built a filtration system in a dying village in Egypt." Tis looked between her sisters, wanting them to understand, wanting what they were saying to be wrong.

"That's true, she does a lot of good work. But there's also other stuff she's into, and, well, you should be careful." Meg looked at Alec for backup again, and Alec looked pensive.

"You know, the thing with the world we're living in now, is it's a hell of a lot harder to see the lines in the sand. You've got great judgment, Tis. If you think she's worth your time, then you should see where it goes. Just be careful, and go in with your eyes open, okay?" Alec's expression lightened and she winked. "Besides, she's supposed to be something spectacular in bed. You'll have to find out for us."

Tis threw an olive at Alec and started laughing. Meg launched into a tale about her latest romantic interest, and how it was so different being with someone with extra limbs and a tail. When she started explaining about the tail, Alec and Tis threw things at her to shut her up.

After they'd gone, Tis walked down to the ocean and sat on the beach with her wings wrapped around her. She watched as the sky turned from washed-out blue to cotton candy pink, to citrus orange, and finally, to bruised purple before it sank beneath the waves. Should she give Kera a chance? It didn't have to become something or be anything more than a person to hang out with occasionally. And if it did become a thing, it certainly didn't need to be serious. Neither of them were looking for a lifelong commitment. From the rumors, it seemed Kera was far more interested in fun, and fun was exactly what Tis was looking for right now.

But what if she leaves our periphery and ends up directly in front of us? In front of me? She couldn't answer that, and at the moment, she didn't want to. For the first time in centuries, she wanted to live for now, not for what-if.

Chapter Ten

K era stared at her office whiteboards. She'd had two of the four walls turned into full-size, magnetic boards. She hated having her creative space limited, and this way she could draw out plans and see them in connection with one another, which was important for scheduling. She wanted to draw up the contracts with dates, so there was no way the people she'd glad-handed at her party could back out. But to do that, she needed to see the plans laid out in front of her. She loved color-coding each project and seeing the rainbow of plans come into being. She placed sticky notes on the board, jotting down dates and place names, then crumpling them, throwing them behind her, and changing them. She needed to account for breaks for her staff between projects. They saw too many horrors to go straight from one war zone to the next. Finally satisfied, she wrote down the specifics and emailed them to her assistant. She heard the doorbell and glanced at the clock. Tisera wasn't due for another fifteen minutes.

Her intercom buzzed and her housekeeper said, "Ms. Petra to see you, Kera."

"On my way." She closed up, satisfied with the day's work, and headed upstairs. They'd be helping people for years to come. It wouldn't fix the mistakes she'd made in the past, but she could try to make things right elsewhere.

She shook Petra's hand, struck by her beauty as always. She had thick, jet-black hair and distinctly Middle Eastern features. She spoke softly, but there was never any doubt about her confidence or capability. Kera had once made a play for her and had been clearly rejected. Intrigued, as she'd never had that happen, she'd hired her for the company.

"Nice to see you. Drink?"

Petra nodded and glanced around the house. "Iced tea, if you have any."

"Make that two," Kera said to the waiting staff member. She could never figure out their titles, all of which sounded too *Downton Abbey*, so she just thought of them all as staff. There was always one around when she needed something, but they were never obtrusive. She wasn't home often enough to actually get to know them.

Petra sat down and raised her face to the sun. "How're things?"

Kera sat next to her at the table and stretched her legs out in front of her. "Really good. Excellent, in fact."

"No lack of money or sex, then?"

"Lack isn't in my vocabulary, you know that. Just opportunity for growth."

Petra snorted and opened one eye to look at Kera. "That sounds like businesswoman speak if I've ever heard it."

"But you know I think it's true." She waited until their drinks were in front of them and they were alone again. "You have news?"

Petra sighed and turned toward her. "Kind of. But I know I shouldn't give it to you."

"I pay you to give me information. That Jag out there didn't come from you withholding. Spill."

"He was there, along with about fifteen others, mostly men. Two or three women, I think. From the look of the place, they're not doing well. Whatever benefit they got from that stunt they pulled with you, it's long gone."

Kera liked the thought of him scraping by as she planned what to do with billions of dollars. *Eat that, bastard.* "And?"

"And they're gone. The place has been cleaned out except for the trash they left behind. Only…" Petra looked at her indecisively. "I found a single scrap of paper, a piece torn from something else. It said GRADE."

Kera felt the blood rush from her head and grabbed the table to steady herself. GRADE hadn't been in existence when she'd run across him. "He's watching me."

"It would seem that way. Hard to believe it's coincidental. He wanted your resources before. Now…you'd give him a whole new ballgame." Petra leaned back and stared at her. "You know what that means."

"Fuck that. No. I'm not going back to bodyguards. I hated having them with me for that year when I got back. I'm not doing it again."

"That's stupid, and you're not a stupid woman. If you're on his radar, you need to be careful." She watched Kera over her glass of iced tea. "You know, I've got friends you might like. Bodyguards more along the lines of your…preferences."

Kera grinned. "Hot female bodyguards instead of big, stinky men? That sounds more attractive, yeah. But I still don't like it."

"Compromise with me. Let me get you a few guards, and I'll keep looking for our friend. Once I find him, and we can keep an eye on him, you can get rid of the guards."

Kera thought about it. Memories of a damp, putrid smelling cell, of her own vomit and sweat as she lay dying, reminded her of what she was risking by being stubborn. The screams and moans of others dying around her still invaded her dreams. "Fine. But the moment you know where he is, assuming it's far-the-fuck away from me until I decide otherwise, I get rid of the shadows."

Petra smiled, and Kera thought for a moment how cold that smile was. "Consider it done. I'll have guards with you by tomorrow." The doorbell rang, and Petra stood. "In the meantime, see if you can keep yourself out of trouble."

The sound of the front door closing was followed by the clicking of heels on the marble floor.

Tisera stood in the doorway for a moment, the sunlight kissing her beautiful pale skin, making her look even more ethereal than she was. She stepped out onto the patio, and the spell was broken. Kera could breathe again. She stood up and motioned toward Petra. "Tis, hi. This is—"

"'Uzza! Wow, it's been…centuries upon centuries. What are you doing here?"

Petra looked like a child caught with stolen sweets. "It's Petra now, actually. And Kera and I do business together occasionally. What are you doing here?" She threw a suspicious glance at Kera, who shrugged, at a loss.

"We're having dinner," Tis said.

The simple statement sounded slightly ludicrous, and Petra looked at Kera. "That thing I said about staying out of trouble? Way too late for that, my friend." She gave Tis a kiss on the cheek. "Hopefully this means we'll see more of one another, maybe catch up some time."

Tis's smile was genuine, though she still looked puzzled. "I'd really like that."

Petra left, and Tis turned to Kera. "You keep company with old gods?"

Kera blinked, waiting for the punch line. "What do you mean, old gods?"

Tis sat down next to Kera and smoothed her long, silk print skirt. "Al-'Uuzza was a Nabatean goddess, based at the temple at Petra, in Jordan." She laughed. "I suppose it was as good a name as any to take on."

"So what the hell is she doing working for me?" Kera held up her hand. "Wait. I might need alcohol for this. Would you like a drink?"

"I don't suppose you have Guinness?"

Kera wrinkled her nose. "Gross. It's like old pond water. But I can ask."

"Well, if you're asking, could you see if there's black currant cordial available, too?"

"The stuff they water down in England? Why?"

Tis laughed, and it sent a jolt of current directly to Kera's crotch. She was mesmerizing.

"If you add it to the Guinness, it gives it a lovely berry flavor."

"Even more disgusting. I can't believe I invited you here." Kera motioned a staff member over. "I'll have my usual, please, and can you see if we have Guinness and black currant juice?"

Tis explained what it was, as well as the one-third juice to two-thirds Guinness combination.

Kera took Tis's hand and smiled at her. "As bizarre as this day has just become, I'm really glad you came. Now, you were going to tell me why I've got an ex-goddess in my employ as an investigator."

Tis stared down at their entwined hands. "There are ways the gods work, things they don't tell people. Things I'm not free to say. But I can tell you that Petra, at some point, had to make a choice, and she chose to give up her position as a goddess to live among the humans. I'm certain private investigator isn't the only job she's ever had."

Kera took a minute to process that information. "Do all the gods have that choice? Do you?" Tis looked incredibly sad for a moment, and she regretted asking the question.

"Yes, for the most part, we all have that choice. But sometimes it's less of a choice, and more of a…forced retirement, I guess." She squeezed Kera's hand and made an obvious effort to force the sadness away. "What do you need a private investigator for, anyway?"

Kera winced inwardly. If Tis knew what she planned on doing, if she knew what needed to be done, what would she think? She shuddered slightly. "Business stuff, which is incredibly boring. How have you been?"

Tis looked at her searchingly, and she could feel those spirit-type heat waves coming off her, as though she was trying to see past Kera's words. She waited, curious as to what she'd find.

"You know, if you ever want to talk things through, you can. Before you did anything you'd regret." Tis stood up and moved away from her.

That answers that. "Do you make a habit of getting inside people's heads?" Tis turned to stare at her, her eyes cold and tinged with red. It was eerie and incredibly sexy.

"I wasn't in your head. You've got good walls. But I know what a need for revenge feels like, almost like I can taste it. You should know something." She stepped closer and her fangs extended slightly, her eyes more red than gray. "If you do something that puts you in my way, professionally, I won't have mercy on you because you're beautiful, or sexy, or interesting. You'll be extremely sorry we ever met, and I really don't want that to happen."

Kera desperately wanted to run her tongue along one of Tis's fangs. She was unbearably beautiful, even if she was threatening Kera's life. Plenty of people had threatened her over the years, but no one had ever made it look so inviting. "I hear you, and if anything like that comes up, I'll be sure to talk to you first. Okay?" She watched with fascination as Tis's eyes returned to their usual storm cloud gray, and her fangs receded completely.

"Promise?"

Kera raised Tis's hand to her mouth and kissed her knuckles. "I promise. And if talking doesn't work, I'll remind you how beautiful, sexy, and interesting you find me."

A text message pinged, and they both went to check their phones. Kera held hers up with a frown. "It's from Petra. She says you might want to watch the news."

They went inside and Kera flipped on the fifty-inch flat screen. Their drinks were brought in, and they settled on the couch. She noticed the purple circle in the foam at the top of the Guinness and smiled. "If it isn't right, let me know, and I'll fire the person who made it."

Tis laughed. "It's perfect." She focused on the TV. The camera zoomed in on the Afterlife headquarters, where Cerberus could just be seen inside the front doors, all three of her menacing dog heads baring their teeth at the crowd outside. There appeared to be about sixty people, chanting and holding up signs with slogans like, "No gods, no war" and "Save the humans, kill the gods."

"What fresh hell is this?" Tis murmured.

The camera turned to a reporter, standing with a bearded hipster type who wore a T-shirt emblazoned with Humanity First.

"This is the leader of Humanity First, the group protesting here today. Sir, can you tell us a bit about what's going on?"

"Humanity First believes in the human right to live without the interference of gods. We believe the world is safer, more secure, and more honest without the intervention of religion. Although the gods are saying there's more transparency now than ever before, that doesn't mean they're making the world better. In fact, we argue that their presence here erodes the possibility of humans evolving to become a better species."

The reporter looked baffled. "So, you're protesting their very existence?"

"Yes, to some degree. We want them to stop interfering in human matters. They're obviously limited, or we wouldn't have poverty, illness, and war. Humanity First says it's time for them to actually make a difference, or get the hell out of our way."

He smiled for the camera, looking every inch the sincere zealot. He walked back to his followers, waving a sign that read, "What *does* Jesus do?"

The reporter returned to the camera. "Although there's a relatively small group of Humanity First supporters here today, the movement is said to be growing exponentially, with membership already reaching into the thousands, many of whom were ardent followers of Frey Falconi, who was found brutally murdered in a warehouse last year. Will this be the atheist answer to the new religious movement? Time will tell."

An ad came on for a drug to stop hair loss, with side effects that listed hair loss and death, and Kera and Tis sat quietly, taking it in. Kera turned to Tis. "Do you need to head to the office?"

Tis sighed. "I don't think so. But I should call to see if everyone is okay."

"Feel free to use the den, just off to the left there."

Tis's smile was tight with worry. "I know where it is, thanks. I came to several of Robert's parties here in the late eighties."

Kera laughed, glad for a lighter moment. "Redford partied with furies?"

"Well, I came. My sisters were often doing their own thing. I'll be right back."

Kera wandered back outside to wait for Tis. She preferred to make her business calls in private and assumed Tis would want to as well. The news broadcast made her wonder how Tis felt about it, and she wanted to know more about Humanity First. What the creepy looking guy had said made sense, and it wasn't far off from how Kera had felt most of her life. But now, with a fury sitting in her den and an ex-goddess in her employ, the issue seemed a bit more complex than it had before. *Like so many things.*

Tis came back outside. "Thanks. Everyone is fine, if a little rattled."

"Well, then let's put this behind us and have dinner, shall we? Before something happens and we both have to rush off into the real world, capes floating in the superhero heated air around us."

Kera led them to the covered lanai overlooking Broad Beach. The waves of the Pacific pounded their steady rhythm onto the shore, white foam leaving artistic trails in mocha colored sand. They sat down, and within minutes, staff members brought out plates of colorful Thai food. The lemongrass and ginger smelled heavenly, and she was glad to see Tis looking eager to dig in.

Tis began to eat, and Kera liked the way she seemed to savor each bite. The kitchen staff had outdone themselves.

"I've always loved this house," Tis said when she stopped eating for a moment. "I love the big windows."

"That's one of the things that drew me to it. Although I have to admit, since that talking fish jumped out and talked to you the other day, I've had a whole new way to look at the ocean."

Tis grimaced slightly. "I think that's probably a very common thing right now. People looking at the world differently because of the gods coming out. It must be difficult."

Kera shook her head. "I think it's amazing. I mean, you get so used to a place, to things being a certain way, that you take them for granted. There's no magic left in the world unless you go searching for it. But now…" She waved her fork at Tis. "Now, you get to sit across from magic and see it smile at you."

Tis blushed and took a long drink of her Guinness. "What a romantic way of looking at it."

"Yeah, well, I'm a big ol' softie at heart. Don't tell anyone." Kera gave her what she knew was her sexiest grin and was glad to see it had the same effect on Tis as it did on other women. She blushed again and looked beautifully innocent.

"Your secret is safe with me."

They ate in silence for a little while, comfortable, the singing of the ocean their background music.

Kera sat back and was amazed again at who her dinner companion was.

"What? Do I have food on my face?"

Kera shook her head. "I was wondering what it's like, having sex with a goddess."

Tis seemed to consider the question seriously. "For a human? It doesn't end well, but it's an amazing orgasm."

"An orgasm worth dying for?"

Tis gave her a wicked smile that went straight through her. "It depends on how much you like orgasms. And breathing."

"Damn. Here I was, hoping for a long life. But if given the option…"

Tis raised an eyebrow. "Is there a goddess you're considering? Because sex with Petra would no longer have those consequences, although if I remember correctly, she had a penchant for decorating her basement with her lovers' heads for a while."

Thank fuck she turned me down. The thought of her head mounted on a board next to several others was disconcerting. "No, I was thinking more along the lines of one with wings."

"Ah. There aren't too many of those around. But I could put in a good word for you, if you'd like." She leaned forward and gave Kera a perfect view of her full cleavage. "But if you'd be willing to downgrade slightly, sex with a fury wouldn't have the same consequences either, although I've been told the orgasms are rather spectacular. We're not goddesses. We don't hear prayers. But we do have sex."

"Supreme orgasms without death? Now you're talking."

Tis laughed, her body language relaxed and the worry in her eyes gone. Kera found herself wanting to take all her stress away, just to see her looking so relaxed and beautiful.

"Tell me more about yourself, Kera. The real you, not the playgirl magazine version. Then I'll decide if you're worth the incredible orgasms." She grinned to show she was teasing, though the hint of desire in her eyes suggested there was some truth to the jest.

"Okay…let's see. I was born in Haiti. My mom was a biomolecular scientist and won a Nobel Prize for her research on transmittable diseases. My father is Mexican, and he runs a restaurant in Haiti, a fusion kind of thing. He's an amazing chef, and I learned my love of cooking from him. Sadly, I don't have a lot of time to do it, so I usually have staff on hand to take care of that part of my life."

"You said your mother passed away?"

The memory made Kera ache inside. "Cancer. For all her prayers, for all that she was a lifelong devotee, no one ever answered. I'm going to her year and a day ceremony in a few weeks."

Tis nodded, looking thoughtful. "I'm sorry for your loss, truly. I can't imagine how frustrating it must be. Tell me more?"

"Well, I don't have any kids, which I know you must find surprising." She grinned and motioned for another drink. She pointed at Tis's glass, which was finally empty, and ordered one for her when she assented. "I don't have any pets anymore. I had a dog I loved more than life, one I saved from a desert, and when he passed, I decided I'd never get another. He was my one and only."

"That's beautiful. So very human, and such a lovely sentiment."

Puzzled, Kera asked, "What makes it so human?"

"When you're immortal, you never say never, and you don't believe in 'the only one.' If you had another hundred years, or thousand, you might give yourself the chance to have that kind of love again. Life for an immortal being would be very lonely if they lived the way mortals do, restricting themselves to a memory of something, rather than allowing a different form of it into their lives."

Kera shook her head. "I suppose I wouldn't want to be immortal, then. I like the idea of a love so amazing, so perfect, that nothing else will ever come close." She stood up and held the hem of her T-shirt. "Wanna see something?"

Tis raised an eyebrow and looked her over. "Skipping to death orgasms, are we?"

Kera slowly lifted her shirt, enjoying the look of appreciation in Tis's expression. She didn't often show off the six-pack she worked her ass off for. But right now, she focused on showing Tis the tattoo along her ribs. Tis leaned forward to study it and gently traced the outline of a paw print with her fingertip, making Kera shiver.

"The word dog in Thai."

Kera nodded and sat back down. "I've never loved a person as much as I loved that dog. He really was my one and only."

Tis took a sip of her fresh drink. "I think it's lovely you've had that. I know immortals who haven't found anyone to love that much in their entire existences."

She looked so sad, so terribly lonely when she said it that Kera wanted to take her in her arms and show her… *Show her what? How to have sex without strings attached? She probably has that one figured out by now.* There was an awkward silence neither of them seemed to know how to fill.

Tis set her napkin on the table. "I think it's probably time for me to go. Thank you for a lovely dinner and for your company."

Kera sighed. "I'm sorry, that got kind of heavy. We don't seem to do small talk very well, do we?"

Tentatively, Tis took Kera's hand in her own. "Then maybe we should stop talking."

Chapter Eleven

Kera led Tis down a stony side path to a beautiful, enclosed gazebo. Tis liked the massive windows and noticed the dark coating on them, allowing the person inside to have total privacy without blocking out the view of the ocean beyond it.

Once inside, Kera stood close enough that she could smell the earthy cologne she wore. She could also smell her desire, her need.

"Be you," Kera whispered, her lips a breath from Tis's. "I want you as you are, not as you appear to others."

"Are you sure?" Tis searched her expression for any doubts, but the only thing she saw was lust. Kera's lips touched hers, painfully tenderly, making her want more. She let all the magic fall away and opened her wings, which brushed the walls on either side of them, and blocked out the light behind her. She let her fangs extend and her eyes change, and it felt so good to be in her own skin again.

Kera stepped back, her hands still on Tis's hips, to get a good look at her. "I don't think there's anything, or anyone, more beautiful than you, in heaven or on earth." She moved closer again, and this time, the kiss was far from gentle. She crushed their bodies together and pushed Tis back onto the bed. Tis held her tight, their kisses the kind she'd often dreamt of but never managed to find. She heard material rip as Kera pulled at the front of her dress, exposing her as she hungrily sucked at one of Tis's nipples, pulling on it with her teeth, making Tis arch off the bed with pleasure. Kera's body felt solid, muscled and toned, but with the exquisite softness she loved about being with a woman. Her small, tight breasts pressed against her stomach as she continued to suck and bite Tis's nipples, and Tis ran her nails over Kera's back, beneath the thin tank top she wore. When Kera moaned, her own need flared like a match in the dark.

"Please. Kera, please fuck me. Now."

Kera's hand slid between Tis's legs and cupped her, the heel of her hand pressed firmly against her clit as a finger slid inside her. Tis closed her eyes and gave herself over to Kera's insistent touch. "More, please."

Kera added a second finger, then a third, until Tis felt full of her, opened and taken. She plunged in and out, fucking her deeply, intensely. She looked at Kera, wanting to say something, wanting to express how good it felt, but looking into Kera's eyes, suddenly there were no words. She wrapped her wings around her, glad to see the look of surprised pleasure on her face, before she closed her eyes and simply felt Kera inside her. As she crested her orgasm and came crashing down the other side, she pulled Kera tightly to her, wanting, needing, to feel her close.

They lay silent, arms wrapped around one another.

"Babe?" Kera's voice was muffled.

"Hmm?"

"I can't breathe."

Tis opened her wings and started laughing when Kera took big gulps of air, a light sheen of sweat on her face.

"It's like being cuddled by a down comforter." Kera wiped the sweat from her face, grinning. "Let me get some water."

She moved to the small fridge on the side, and Tis instantly missed the feel of her body. *That's new.* She'd had plenty of lovers over the centuries, some for long periods of time, but she never liked cuddling after sex. She'd always preferred some physical space after. Now, all she wanted was Kera's arms around her again. Maybe she'd just been alone for too long.

Tis folded her wings behind so Kera could slide into bed beside her. She curled up against her side, resting her head on Kera's shoulder. Kera continued to shift, and she looked up at her curiously.

"I can't figure out where to put my arm. Is it okay on your wings? Will it be too heavy?"

Tis snuggled down again. "You'd be surprised how tough they are. Put your arm wherever it's comfortable."

She liked the weight of Kera's arm on the tops of her wings, her fingertips light against the top of her arm. While the feeling of not being alone was wonderful, what made it more so was her acute attraction and interest in Kera herself. "Tell me about this place. I don't remember it from the last time I was here."

"I had it built a few years ago. I love the main house, and I wouldn't change anything about it. But just before I moved here, I'd been used to...smaller spaces."

Tis could hear the pain and anger below the surface of her words and wondered just what those smaller spaces were. The part of Kera that smelled of pain and the need for vengeance flared, making Tis's breath catch slightly. She ignored it and listened.

"There were days when I first started living here, the main house was just too big, and I felt lost in it. It made me feel, I don't know, like I was having a panic attack. I needed something smaller, something cozier. So I had this built as an escape. When I felt calm again, I'd go back to the main house. I guess it was my way of acclimating to life again."

The large gazebo contained the double bed they were in, a small fridge, a single dresser, and a place to hang a few coats. It was homey, and because of the large windows, not at all claustrophobic. "I lived in places this size a lot when I was young. Not as warm, and usually not as comfortable."

"Such as?"

Tis debated opening up this line of conversation. She was normally utterly private and rarely talked about old times with anyone but her sisters or Zed, and sometimes Aulis. But given where they were, and how safe she felt, it might be time. "Caves, mostly. We had some truly exceptional mountain caves in Greece, where my sisters and I grew up. In the wet months, we'd use the caves, and in the warm months, we'd live in the trees. Greece was covered in forests at the time, with rivers and lakes everywhere.

You can't imagine how the topography has changed over five thousand years."

Kera was so quiet Tis wondered if she'd fallen asleep.

"Do you miss it?"

How do I answer that? She couldn't even be completely honest with herself yet. "Sometimes. It was a simpler way of life. Clearer." She shivered as Kera traced the edges of her feathers. "But there are still a lot of natural places to get away to, all over the world. And my house is surrounded by trees and overlooks the ocean. There's even a cave in the hill below my place, and if I'm really out of sorts, I go there." She smiled and traced the lines of muscle in Kera's stomach. "A bit like your place here, really."

Tis moved so she could straddle Kera's stomach. Her black tank hugged her taut body perfectly, and she wanted more of it. She slid her hands under Kera's top and dragged her nails lightly over her breasts, making her nipples pucker. She made a low sound of appreciation before placing her hands over Tis's.

"I don't usually receive."

"Do you usually have sex with women like me?"

"There *are* no women like you."

Tis leaned down and gave her a long, lingering kiss. "Then usually doesn't apply." She pressed her fangs into the top of Kera's tank and pulled, tearing the top to pieces and exposing Kera's beautiful body. Tis moved off the bed and quickly tugged off her jeans and boy-shorts. She stared at her magnificent body for a moment before caressing her sides with her wings, even as she sucked and bit her way along the insides of Kera's legs. When she reached her pussy, she inhaled deeply, taking in the smell of her desire. Kera looked down at her, her eyes half lidded, her hands twisted in the sheets. The sight of her so far gone called to the most primal part of Tis, and she felt her eyes narrow as the urge to fuck and devour came over her.

She pressed her mouth to Kera's clit, careful to slide her fangs along her outer lips. Kera cried out, and she felt her hand tangle in her hair as she pressed herself against Tis's mouth. Tis sucked, circled, and lightly bit Kera's clit until she was writhing, begging.

With an expert flick of her tongue, she made Kera come and held her thighs tightly as she rode out her orgasm against Tis's mouth.

When she settled, Tis let go and moved to lie beside her once more. Panic flared when she saw the tears sliding down Kera's cheeks and onto the pillow. "Oh god, baby, did I hurt you?" She pulled the magic around her, hiding her wings and sheathing her fangs. She searched Kera's body frantically for injuries.

"Tisera, stop." Kera gently cupped Tis's chin in her hand to get her to look at her. "You know how I asked if sex with a goddess was worth death?"

Tis nodded.

"I would gladly die for that kind of orgasm. I've never, ever, come that hard."

Tis relaxed and smiled. "Fortunately, I'm not a goddess, so death isn't necessary. Are you really okay?"

Kera pulled her down to lie beside her again. "No. Okay isn't the right word. Euphoric, maybe. Drugged…high. Overwhelmed, definitely."

Tis glanced up at her and said softly, "Thank you for letting me."

"Thank you for wanting to."

They lay cradled in one another's arms as the sun went down, waking only to explore one another's bodies again and again throughout the night.

Tis lay cradled in Kera's embrace, the feeling of loneliness she'd lived with for so long a stark contrast to the secure, warm feeling she had now. Even if it didn't last, it was worth it, just for this night alone.

❖

Tis woke to light kisses on her eyelids. She smiled sleepily at Kera. "Hey there."

"Hey yourself. I don't suppose you'd be interested in green tea? I'm dying for some, and I want a shower. I was hoping you'd join me."

Tis stretched, laughing when her outstretched wings knocked Kera onto the floor.

"Okay, offer rescinded. I've never been tossed off my own bed." Kera looked up at her from the floor, her gorgeous olive skin glowing against the white tile floor.

"Once you make an offer to a fury it can't be taken back. They're the rules. Break a rule, and we eat your mind. So, yes to the green tea and the shower."

Kera went to open the door, and Tis said, "Um, isn't there something you're forgetting?" She looked Kera's beautiful, naked body up and down.

"Are you shy?" She motioned at her body. "I work far too hard at this to keep it covered in my own house." She gave Tis a lascivious once-over. "But then, I don't know if I'd be happy with everyone seeing you naked...I'm feeling a little possessive this morning." She pulled a sheet from the bed and wrapped Tis in it. "Better?"

"Possessive, huh?" Tis let the sheet pool at her feet. "I like the sound of that. Lead on."

Kera took her hand, and they walked back up the path, the morning sun warming Tis's skin and once again making her think of a time when neither she nor her sisters wore clothes. It hadn't taken long, only a century or two, before they wore the loose robes typical of the Greek pantheon, but she still remembered the amazing freedom that came with being nothing but who you were beneath the sun. Even so, she pulled her magic around her. No reason to freak out Kera's staff beyond the fact they were both parading back to the house buck naked.

When they entered the kitchen Tis sniffed appreciatively. "Coffee. Excellent."

Kera went over to a tray that held a pot of tea, along with coffee and the sides to go along with it. "I really do have amazing staff."

They curled up under a blanket on the couch and sipped their respective drinks. "Do you know them all?"

Kera grimaced slightly. "Only the ones that have been here for a while. Because I'm here so infrequently, the staff changes all the time. When I go away for long projects, say six months or so, only two or three stay here and take care of things. I let them know when I'm coming back for longer, and they hire new people. But I never get to know them." She pressed her toes against Tis's. "Do you know everyone who works for you?"

Tis laughed. "Do you think everyone lives the way you do? I cook and clean for myself, thank you very much. I don't go away for as long as you, and I don't really like having anyone in my personal space. There have been times, mostly during wars, when my sisters and I lived together, and we hired a few people to help out around the house, simply because we were always exhausted. But I was never really comfortable with having servants."

"I wouldn't go so far as to call them that," Kera said, wincing.

"You can call them staff if it makes you feel better. But the job role is the same now as it was in the seventeen hundreds. People paid to take care of the things you don't want to." She ran her hand over Kera's foot. "It's not a judgment, just a fact."

"Suddenly, I feel the need to fire everyone."

"Don't do that. But I have an idea—why don't we cook breakfast together? Show me your stuff."

"Oh, I'll show you my stuff…" Kera set her drink down and started to crawl up Tis's legs.

Tis laughingly put a hand on the top of Kera's head to stop her advancement. "If you want more of that, you need to feed me. Give me some fuel if you want me on my back again."

Kera pressed her face to the blanket. "Spoilsport." She ran upstairs, only to run back down with two thick, soft robes. "Cooking naked sounds sexy enough when you're thinking foreplay, but then people run around screaming about burning pubes and splattered oil."

Tis shrugged into the wonderfully oversized robe and followed Kera into the kitchen. "So, what are we having?"

Kera opened the fridge, and Tis started laughing at how packed full it was. "Good god, woman. Do they think they're feeding an army?"

"They're always prepared. You never know when I might decide to throw a party, or have over a guest in desperate need for sex-fuel." She riffled through the contents of the fridge, piling things into her arms. Setting them all on the counter, she said, "Be prepared. You're going to have the most amazing Mexican breakfast burritos ever."

"Give me some chopping to do then." Tis slid a razor-sharp knife from a rack and brandished it.

"Hey now. You said death didn't have to follow orgasms." Kera gave her a teasing smile and handed her a chopping board.

"Believe me, I wouldn't need a knife if I wanted to kill you off."

Kera looked at her with her eyebrows raised.

"What? I wouldn't. You've seen me work, haven't you?"

Kera broke several eggs, then added milk to fluff them. Paprika, cumin, cilantro, and garlic salt followed. "Not really, no. I'm usually escaping by the time you get there, and I have to move it to stay alive. I have to admit, though, as terrifying as you look when you're working, you're also unbearably beautiful."

Tis felt herself blush and concentrated on chopping the green bell peppers. "Well, trust me when I say I wouldn't need a weapon. I *am* a weapon."

She continued chopping when Kera stopped to answer her phone. She cradled it between her ear and her shoulder as she continued cooking.

"Hey, Ajan." She listened as she expertly chopped fresh cilantro and added it to sizzling sausage. "Yeah, I can do that. Tell them I'll be down this afternoon, and if they need anything specific, get a list and get it over to them."

She hung up and looked at Tis apologetically. "You know, I've never been so bothered by having to cut a date short to go to work."

"Problems?"

"There are always problems, but I have a lot of people to help deal with them. The one today is close to home, though. I set up a soup kitchen in Tent City a few years ago, and it's been going really well. It's staffed on a rotating basis by the people who use it. It gives them some work they can do and provides help to the community they've built there. I don't often have to do anything, but Ajan says there's some tension down there, with fights breaking out, and the kitchen needs some backup. I need to go check it out."

Tis thought about it. She and her sisters had to go to Tent City, Los Angeles's largest homeless community on Skid Row, periodically. The unrest of being homeless combined with mental health issues and addictions often led to violence. Tis hated having to serve justice there. As though things weren't hard enough for the people as it was. Yet, the rules were the rules, and they'd followed them for thousands of years. They weren't going to stop now.

"I don't suppose you'd go with me?" Kera carefully poured the eggs into the sizzling pan. "Maybe after we could go grab dinner in Hollywood or something?"

"I'm not exactly popular in Tent City."

Kera acknowledged the point. "I get that. But if you go with me, in…what do you call it? Your more human-like appearance?"

"I've never given it a name, really. I know my sister Alec calls it her daily appearance."

"Boring, but okay, we'll go with that. If you go in your daywear, and you're there with me to help people instead of punish them, they won't even know it's you, will they?" She placed tortillas over the open flame on the burner, flipping them quickly as they warmed and browned around the edges. She put them on warm plates and sprinkled diced green chilies over them before scooping the egg mixture into the middle.

Tis thought about it. It was strange how many homeless people saw easily through the veil. But then, they didn't have to hide anymore. Would it look like a different place if she approached it differently herself? "Yes. Okay, I'd like that. But if people get weird around us, I'm going to leave. There's no point in me ruining the good work you're trying to do by getting people riled up."

"Fair point. Now, be prepared to taste the most amazing thing you've had in your mouth since…me, a few hours ago."

❖

After breakfast, Tis flew to her home in Laguna to get more appropriate clothes, since the others were in tatters in the gazebo anyway, while Kera made some calls and did some work. She'd been so busy with her projects in other countries, she'd let the one in her hometown slip. It was time to rectify that.

Two hours later, Tis knocked on the front door, and she opened it herself. She couldn't remember the last time she'd felt grateful a woman had bestowed their time on her, but right now, she was ready to drop to her knees in thanks.

"Ready to go?" Tis asked.

"Let's do it. You look great." And she did. Simple jeans that fit her lithe body perfectly were teamed with a basic gray T-shirt that matched her lovely eyes.

Kera, dressed in a similar outfit of T-shirt and jeans, grabbed her keys. "Taking a taxi is best, if you're okay with that? Showing up in my car seems like a bad idea on a whole host of levels. But if you'd be more comfortable…"

Tis shook her head. "I've been in places worse than Skid Row, as have you. But I had a thought about it. If we take my car, I can make it so no one sees it. It's a little trick we have, and it also moves a lot faster than your car, or a taxi, so it won't take us the full hour to get there. And that way we've got a way to go to dinner later."

The benefits of dating a nonhuman. Who knew? "Great. Let's do it." She stepped outside and whistled at Tis's Range Rover. "Nice. I love the glass tops on these. And what a great color."

"We do so much traveling in them, it's good to be comfortable. The color is Aintree Green. I wanted it to feel more…earthy, I suppose." They got in and headed toward LA. "Tell me about your soup kitchen."

Kera thought about it. "I started it about five years ago, not long after I got back from…well, from a bad situation. I wanted to do something local, and that was a quick and easy thing to do. I actually have bigger plans, lots of investing I want to do in the area, but I've been focused on the other major projects, and to be honest, I've let this one slide."

"It happens." Tis rested her hand on Kera's leg. "There are so many places that need help in the world."

"Jesus, isn't that the truth?" She covered Tis's hand with her own, loving the way it felt so cool, different from her own, but sexy just the same. "But really, I need to work it out. Homelessness jumped twelve percent in LA in the last two years alone. The estimated homeless numbers in the city are over twenty thousand now, nearly fifty thousand countywide."

Tis shook her head, looking sad. "That's so horrendous in a country with so much wealth and opportunity. What are your plans?"

"I've been looking into building permanent housing. There are a lot of abandoned buildings, and I'm working out how to turn them into livable spaces. I want to start a back-to-work program, offering job skills and mental health services. The thing is, I tried it on a small scale a few years ago, and it didn't go well. In return for providing the services, I required them to donate some time to the shelter or program they were using, or to one of the kids' programs. You wouldn't believe how many people were pissed off they had to do something in return. It's made me rethink how I approach it and how it'll be decided who gets apartments. Do they get them forever? Do I charge some kind of minimum? One thing I've learned is that people rarely appreciate something they get for free." She sighed, the weight of it heavy on her mind.

"That's a lot of decisions to make. Have you asked for help?"

"That's the other problem. City officials just want the homeless gone, as though it's an issue of cleaning house. But when it comes to the paperwork, they want every damn possibility accounted for, and as you know, you can't always anticipate what's going to happen in situations like this."

"Maybe it's not the City you should be asking for help. Maybe it's the residents themselves, the people using your services. Create a way for them to tell you what they need and how it might work."

Kera was so used to making things happen, to having total control and figuring things out, she hadn't even considered that option. She started mulling over the possibilities.

"We're here." Tis rolled to a stop and parked just beyond where a long row of tents began.

"Damn. You weren't kidding about it going faster. That wasn't even twenty minutes."

"It was twelve, actually." Tis grinned and leaned over for a kiss.

Kera held Tis's face in her hands as she kissed her. "I'm really glad you came."

"Me too. Let's go."

They walked past the rows and rows of tents that lined the sidewalk of the busy street. People milled around, some lying or sitting outside their tent, others in groups on the corners. Beyond the smell of urine and human desperation, there was the sense of resignation. Wary men, women, and children watched them walk by, and not a single one asked for spare change or even spoke to them. These weren't just the homeless, they were the Tent City homeless, some who had been there for years, even decades. They passed the Skid Row city limits mural painted on a wall, "Population: too many," stark white against the green background.

When they neared the soup kitchen, Tis took Kera's hand, and she saw the slight reddening of Tis's eyes. *If she was a cat, her fur would be up.* Kera looked around to try to see what Tis saw, and she felt it instead. The air was warm with tension, and instead of looking wary, the mass of people around them seemed angry, aggressive. They went inside, and the large woman behind the counter looked like she was going to cry with relief.

"You're a damn sight for sore eyes, woman." She came around and gave Kera a massive hug. "It's been a long-ass time."

"I know it has. I'm really sorry, Spice. This is my friend Tisera. What's going on?"

Spice gave Tis a nod before turning back to Kera. "You know how bad things have been the last few years. Lots of promises and no help, even though the politicians are talking a storm."

Kera nodded, feeling guilty. "Are they still raiding and giving out fines?"

"Not so much. But now that there's all this foolishness with God showing up, people are getting rattled."

"Why is that? If I may ask," Tis said, looking worried.

"Damn near every one of those people out there are religious. They've been praying since the moment they made it here, for some kind of help. When you don't know if God is listenin', you keep talking. But when you know he can hear you, and he's not doing a damn thing to help? Well, people start thinkin' there's no reason to keep livin'. No reason to pray anymore, because God's only payin' attention to specific people, and the thousands of people here? That's not them."

"So people are getting angry." Kera pinched the bridge of her nose, thinking. "Understandable. What do you need from me tonight?"

"I need food. Lots of it. Your people delivered some, but it's about half of what I need for the next two weeks. And I need you to come through." She touched Kera's arm. "The gods aren't listening, and that was a lot of people's only hope. Now, it may be you're the only one who can keep this place from imploding."

Tis looked outside and turned back to Spice. "We had a thought on the way here, about how to move forward." She looked at Kera expectantly.

"Right. Here's what we're thinking. I have the means to make big changes here. Places for people to live, training, all that stuff. But I don't know how to go about it. You know how it went last time."

Spice scoffed. "Like a fly trying to have gills and swim in the ocean, baby."

"Exactly. So, what would you think about bringing together a group of people, maybe people who are considered leaders here, and getting them to help me figure out how to help? Five or six, including you."

Spice stared at the wall over Kera's head, clearly thinking. "Yeah. I think that might work. I can spread the word, talk to a few people. When do you want to do it?"

Kera pictured her rainbow wall of projects, mentally scanning the dates. "Two weeks from now. Let's meet here, after closing time. I trust you to choose the right people, so don't worry about asking me." She gave her a hug. "I'll have the rest of the food you need delivered tomorrow, and if you'll create a serious, month-long list of what you want, I'll make sure you get it. In fact, make a list of stuff you need every month, no matter what, and I'll make sure it's a standing order you can add to whenever you need to. Okay?"

Spice nodded, tears in her eyes. "I knew you'd come back around."

Kera felt awful for letting it go this long, guilt fluttering inside her like a trapped moth. "I won't let it slide again, I promise. I'll see you soon."

They left, and Tis stopped to look out over the dirty, graffiti covered streets. "How can we expect humanity to evolve, to behave better toward one another, when they continue to allow their fellow beings to live this way? I've never understood it, not in any country this happens in."

"I agree. But I also think Spice has a damn good point about the gods. It's a time bomb waiting to go off."

Tis sighed. "I know. I can feel it, everywhere I go. People are behaving, because now they know an afterlife really is a possibility. But the longer their needs go unmet, especially in places like this, the more they're going to become disillusioned and angry. My sisters and I just talked about it the other day." She took Kera's hand, and they started back toward the car. "I'm not sure how it's going to work out."

"You see why I don't subscribe to religion? That group, Humanity First. I think they've got a point, Tisera. What use are the gods when people are still living like this?" Irrational though it was, she felt as though Tis came from the very group disappointing people all over the world. "Why should they be allowed to interfere, to demand devotion, when all it comes down to is narcissism and greed? What right do they have to judge us if they can't help us?"

When Tis looked at her, she saw a bone-chilling sadness in her eyes.

"I don't have the answers, I'm sorry. I don't know what the next steps are, or what to tell people."

"Well, maybe people should be allowed to live and work without hoping some deity is going to save them. Maybe the immortals should go back to where they came from, and leave the rest of us alone." Surrounded by vast numbers of lost humans and feeling utterly overwhelmed, Kera tried to keep her anger and frustration from coming out. But she wasn't one for hiding her emotions, and the toxic combination of guilt and helplessness threatened to make her say something she'd regret. "I think I need to be alone for a while. I'm sorry." She hailed a passing cab and got in. "I'll call you."

As the cab drove away, she saw Tis in the side view mirror, standing in front of her invisible car, looking for all the world like one of the lost. Kera closed her eyes and her stomach dropped. *What have I done?*

Chapter Twelve

*T*his *morning, the first Peace Convention was held at the Israeli West Bank Barrier. Tens of thousands of people from both sides of the heavily war torn area came together when the Christian God, the Prophet Mohammed, and the God of the Jews showed up* together. *When the area was full, they took turns telling their followers it was time to stop committing violence in the name of religion. They acknowledged that although there are differences between them, the one thing they all stand against is violence against one another. In an astounding move, as a unit they actually demolished the entire wall, which now stands as a four-hundred-and-fifty-mile pile of cement and barbed wire rubble. They have instructed their followers to discontinue their violence and learn to live as a human community, accepting that individuals may believe differently, but what land they reside on has nothing to do with whom they pray to. In another astonishing move, they've decreed, again as a triumvirate, that anyone committing suicide bombings or the like, for any reason, will be forfeiting their souls and will be sent to each religion's version of Hell.*

Government officials have yet to respond to this unprecedented and highly unorthodox intrusion into what was, to some, a secular division.

Will peace prevail? Or will human politics simply create chaos under another guise? Stay tuned here for all our breaking news. "

Tis flipped the TV off despite the broadcaster's instructions. She'd shut herself in at home for two days, mulling over Kera's words along with her own feelings. Kera had a right to say what she did, and her feelings weren't all that far off from what Tis had been feeling for some time. The division between humans and gods was too enormous, and humans were too far gone to help. She hadn't thought about the failings of the gods, not in the way Kera said. But now, the newscast put an entirely new spin on things. With the gods speaking directly to their followers and making extremely clear where they stood, wars all over the world had virtually ceased. As humans listened to their deities, as bombs stopped dropping on their homes, the world was changing drastically. So, while Kera was right, and there was still too much poverty and too much suffering, there were also immense changes for the good happening. *Maybe it will just take time. Can the world really be better?* She thought back to the early days, when there were fewer major belief systems. The gods had behaved terribly, created by the humans in the image of the humans, with every fatal flaw and noble virtue exemplified to the nth degree. But over the centuries, they'd developed some autonomy, come into their own, to some extent. By working together and using the contract slowly coming along, they could do things like they'd done in Israel and Palestine.

Troubled by thoughts of what-if, things far beyond her control, she could only wait and see. In the meantime, she and her sisters found that while the gods were run off their feet busy, the furies had time on their hands. There was still the occasional serial killer or wife beater to deal with, of course. Religion didn't stop the assholes or the mentally deranged, so they still had jobs to go to. They always would. There'd been crazy people, and angry people, and desperate people, since the beginning of time, and believing in a god or an afterlife didn't change that. But it could mean a world that looked a hell of a lot different than it had over the last several centuries.

The phone rang, and she ignored it, as usual. Kera had left several messages, but she wasn't ready to talk to her yet. If they'd had a normal conversation about the limitations of the gods, on a more philosophical level, she could have handled it. But Kera's anger wasn't just for those suffering. She'd wanted to be left alone by immortals—all of them. She seemed to forget Tis was one of them, and by saying they had no right to judge, she was saying Tis herself shouldn't exist. It echoed too closely how Tis felt about herself, and she'd spiraled into a pit of confusion and sadness.

She listened to Kera's latest message.

"Okay, I know you live in Laguna. But I don't know where. I've driven around, looking for a house that looks big enough to house your wings, but the people who live there don't seem to like me knocking on their doors. And then I realized your house might be like your car, some invisible superhero thing, and I could probably drive around here for years and not find you. So, I'm going to park down at the harbor at Dana Point, and I'm going to lie spread-eagle on top of my car, possibly naked, until you come save me from the seagulls and the police, whichever comes first."

Tis couldn't help but smile, and the heavy feeling on her chest lightened a little bit. She grabbed her keys and headed out.

She found Kera exactly the way she'd said she would. Fortunately, she wasn't naked, though her shorts and tank top exposed plenty of skin. Shading her eyes, she grinned at Tis from the top of her car. "I knew you wouldn't let me be seagull fodder."

"I'm not here to save you. I just wanted to see you naked and handcuffed."

"Baby, you can see that anytime you like. Just say the word." She slid down off her car and moved to stand in front of Tis. "Thank you for coming." Her voice was soft, her eyes serious.

"You're welcome. Lunch at Wind and Sea?"

"Yes! Anywhere. Lunch at McDonald's is fine, if you're with me. But please don't make me eat there."

Tis took Kera's hand, laughing. She felt like she could breathe again. "I live on La Senda, on the cliffs. The one with the lighthouse." She shrugged slightly. "For future reference."

They walked to the restaurant, hand in hand, the sun warm and the area quiet. They got a table outside, and Kera took Tis's hands. "I'm sorry. More than I can say. I was upset about the state of things there, and I really, really hate not being in control. It pisses me off, and this whole religion thing has gotten under my skin. I took all of that out on you." She kissed the tops of Tis's hands. "Will you forgive me?"

"If I held grudges against people who were emotional, I'd have no friends, and I'd have killed my sister Meg long ago. I appreciate your passion." She looked out at the water, considering her words. "I won't say it didn't hurt. You have a problem with the gods, with immortals in general, and I'm one of them." She looked at Kera. "I *am* one of them. And I've got conflicts and issues I can't begin to explain in that region. But I won't apologize for what I am, either. I hope you understand that."

Kera nodded thoughtfully. "I would never ask you to apologize for who you are. You're amazing, and exceptional, and beautiful, and the best sex I've ever had, and it didn't even kill me."

"Fortunately, I'm more level-headed than that. Usually. I only thought of destroying you for a second, if that." Tis grinned to show she was teasing. "But seriously, if you can't handle who I am, what I am, then we can move on. No hard feelings."

Kera gave the waitress a distracted smile when she left their drinks, and Tis didn't miss the inviting, slightly too long glance the waitress gave her in return. She wondered if the girl's mind would withstand a snake or two...

"The thing is, I don't want that. I really enjoy spending time with you, when we have it." She wiped at the condensation on her glass with her thumbs, clearly thinking. When she finally spoke again, her voice was soft. "Do you know much about Haiti? Or Mexico?"

"I've done a little bit of work in both, although both countries have their own departments that handle my kind of work, so it's been rare."

"Then you know what it's like. You know that Haiti is one of the poorest nations in the Western Hemisphere, with an average income of four hundred dollars a year, and a life expectancy for both men and women of somewhere in the fifties. And Mexico...well, it's not a haven of fun either. My mom managed to scrape an education and go on to college in Florida, something unheard of there. My dad got into a culinary school in Mexico, the first in his family to finish high school. They both clawed their way out of poverty, and they met when my mom was on a research trip to Mexico. He was their camp chef during their expedition to learn more about medicines from rainforests. They fell for one another right away, and he proposed to her before the end of the expedition, six weeks later."

"That's remarkable. You obviously get your drive from your parents."

"They taught me that there isn't a single thing that can't be done, if you're willing to make it happen. My mom got me interested in science and medicine when I was a kid, and my dad taught me about people. He loves learning about people, and after they'd made enough money to be comfortable, and to keep me in school, he invested in his home town in Mexico and built a library and a youth center for the kids."

"So, you get your business acumen from both parents and your social conscience from your father?"

Kera picked at her salad, moving pieces around but not eating. "They're both amazing people. Were amazing. My dad still is." She looked at Tis, her expression haunted. "But you see why I get so angry at the gods. I didn't think they existed, so that was no big deal. Now that I know they do, I'm angry. I mean, I'm *really* angry. All those people in Haiti who died during the tropical storms, who die in boats trying to get to America…I just don't understand."

Tis hated feeling so helpless. She couldn't explain about the gods, about the way things worked, without revealing their limitations and putting the organization at risk. It wasn't her place to do that, even with a single human. "I can't imagine how frustrating it must be. I'm so sorry. I suppose all I can say is I'm not a god, and I can't speak for them or what they do or don't do. I hope, with time, they can start to fix the many things that are wrong. But if you want to be with me, around me, even if it's just as friends, you can't take your anger out on me. It's not fair, and although I appreciate you have a right to your feelings, you're choosing to be around me. However all this plays out, you have to play fair."

Kera pushed her plate away. "Yeah. I get that, and I'm sorry. I've never been known as a patient person, and my parents taught me to let go and express myself. That's not always a good thing." She closed her eyes and stretched, shaking her hands as though shaking away the feelings. When she opened her eyes again, she looked more like her usual playful self. "Tell me, who gives birth to fury triplets?"

Tis laughed, glad the tension of the moment seemed broken. There'd be plenty of time to talk about the heavy stuff later. *Hopefully.* "The earth herself. Gaia mated with a Titan, Ouranus, and we were born of their union. Creatures of the sky and the earth, meant to watch over those who lived between. When we were children, my sisters and I loved to fly and play in the waves, hiding from our mother in caves and trees. Obviously, she always knew exactly where we were. When we got to adulthood, we simply stopped ageing. What you see is what I've been for nearly five thousand years."

"You've aged all right, I suppose." Kera grinned. "What about your father?"

Tis shook her head. "Have you read anything about the Titans? They weren't really paternal people. One of them, Zeus's father, used to eat all his children to make sure none of them overthrew him."

"And why would he think they would?"

"Ah. That would be because of the Fates. The Wyrd women, who weave every person's fate, even those of the gods, sometimes. They often hand out little fortune cookie oracles just to mess with people. They tell them a piece of a puzzle, a tiny aspect of their lives, and then sit back and watch the chaos."

"That sounds rather bitchy."

Tis laughed, thinking about the many names Selene called them. "That's one way of thinking of them."

The waitress came and took their plates. When the girl had left after lingering, once again, a little too long next to Kera, she reached over and took Tis's hand once more.

"I want to ask you something. And it's absolutely, one hundred percent okay if you say no. I mean, I'll be heartbroken and devastated, and my ego will never recover, but it will be fine."

Tis's pulse sped up at the serious look in Kera's eyes, even though her mouth was smiling. "Go on."

"Will you come to Haiti with me in two weeks? It's my mother's year and a day ceremony, and it would be really amazing if you'd come. You could meet my dad, and my million aunties will be there too. What do you say?"

Tis considered. Work was slow, certainly slow enough that Alec and Meg could take care of it, and she was supposed to be out "finding herself" anyway. Spending more time with Kera sounded perfect, even if it meant being surrounded by people. Did she want to risk getting closer to Kera, though, knowing how she felt about the gods? *It's better than sitting at home moping about being lonely.* "Okay. Yes, I'd like to come. Thank you for asking."

Kera punched the air. "Yes! There's a week of celebration beforehand, lots of food and family stuff, lots of ceremonial things." She tilted her head. "Do you need a plane ticket? Do I get to ride on your back or something? And if I do, can I have reins?" Her grin was wicked.

"That's obviously not the way I prefer to be ridden." Tis bit one of Kera's fingertips. "Yes, I'll need a plane ticket. I can fly that far if I have to, but I'd rather not if there's an alternative." She hated to ask, but she needed to, given the gravity of why they were attending. "Do you need me to stay in my daytime form?" She was in it now and was beginning to understand why Alec didn't mind using it so often now that she was with Selene.

Kera thought about it for a moment. "Maybe initially, that would be a good idea. You know how superstitious the Vodun culture is. If they meet you first, and I explain who you are, they're more likely to accept you in your natural state. I don't know how things are going there, with the gods visiting and whatever uproar that's causing, so it's probably better to ease you in."

They left the restaurant hand in hand, and Tis felt better than she had in days. There were issues and potential pitfalls of varying kinds. But she was looking forward to the weeks ahead, and that was something special in itself. Kera headed back to work, and Tis headed to Afterlife to see if Meg or Alec were around. If Aulis wasn't available, her sisters certainly had enough experience in relationships between them to help a girl out.

CHAPTER THIRTEEN

"Y ou're joking, right? Or are you really this moronic? You'd rather have them living in tents on the streets than in housing?" Kera threw her pencil across the room, completely fed up.

"The mayor feels that by building the homeless permanent housing, we'd be creating a slum area and would be giving complicit acceptance to the homeless situation."

"Has the mayor ever been to Skid Row? You're telling me he really thinks the city's image is better with twenty thousand homeless actually on the street than in buildings?" She squeezed her stress ball so hard the side split and goo started spilling out. She needed to figure out how to spin the situation so the mayor saw the benefit to himself. "Tell him this. Tell him that image comes from visibility. Right now, those twenty thousand homeless people are completely visible, out in the open. If he gives me the leases on those buildings, the homeless move inside, out of view, and it looks like he's done a massive cleanup of the city. He'll look like a big hero, and people will stop talking about his massive truck compensating for other things. Tell him that. I'll call tomorrow for his answer." She hung up and rested her forehead on the desk. She'd spent the entire week trying to work through the mountain of paperwork to get the LA project underway. Some of it had been easier than she'd thought it would be, like the youth center. The current social welfare offices "weren't available," so she decided to start her own job center, and procuring the building for that had been simple too. She had staff working on getting renovation teams in to set it up, along with those for the youth center.

But when it came to housing, it was like firing a water canon into a tornado. Even though she was willing to buy the buildings outright, because they knew she wanted them as long-term housing and shelter, they were refusing to sell them to her. All the buildings large enough for her plans were owned by the city, mostly reclaimed through forfeiture.

Ajan knocked on her open door. "Hey, boss. How's things?"

She got up to give him a hug. "Same shit, different government. No one wants the poor in their cities, but no one wants to do anything about them, either. I suppose we can just be grateful we're not contending with bombs on top of it all."

"Well, if anyone can do it, you can. I wanted to talk to you about something else."

He was rarely totally serious and almost never reticent to say what was on his mind. That he looked both now set off alarm bells. "What's wrong?"

"Nah, not wrong, really."

"Wait. Do I need a drink for this?"

He shrugged, not looking her in the eye. "Yeah, maybe we both do."

She punched his shoulder on her way past him up the stairs. "Beer first."

Once she'd popped two open for them, and they were sitting on the deck watching the sun go down, she said, "Okay. Go."

"You remember that little girl, from Nigeria? The one you took from her mother's body?"

"Of course I do. How is she acclimating to the orphanage?"

"Not great." He took a sip of beer and looked away from her again. "The thing is, when I went over there to check on her and give the instructions you gave me, I sat with her a while. And I've been going back whenever I can, you know, just to check on her. She's a sweet kid, just a bit messed up from it all."

"Okay. And?"

"I want to adopt her." He blurted it out and looked relieved the moment the words were out of his mouth. "She doesn't have a soul in the world, and because of what you pay me, I could give her a really great life. I always wanted kids—"

"Ajan, stop. It's okay with me if you want to do it. Hell, you don't need to clear it with me at all." He looked so excited, she hated to say what she needed to. "But you know what our lives are. How long we can be gone. Are you okay with adopting her and then going away for three, six, eight months at a time? You know the areas we go aren't safe for children."

He looked like he might cry. "I know all that. I'm going to hire people to help me out and to take care of her when I'm not here. She might not have me around all the time, but she'll have a way better life than in an orphanage or in foster care. And when I am around, I'll treat her like she's my own." He finally looked at her squarely. "You know, I'm not getting younger, either. I'm not going to be working forever."

The thought stunned her. She'd never considered what the business would look like without Ajan. She looked at him and really saw him for the first time in ages. There was more gray in his hair than not-gray, and fine lines weathered his face like the veins of a leaf. She tried to smile past the fear of losing her bulwark against the world. "So you're going to be Daddy Warbucks, huh?"

"A Haitian one. That's a story no one would believe."

"Just give me plenty of heads-up before you go, okay? I'll want you to train my next *you*."

He looked at her sheepishly. "Well now, I've been thinking about that. There aren't many people out there I know for a fact would take a bullet for you the way I would. Someone whose loyalty you could really depend on. But there is one person…"

Kera wracked her brain, trying to figure out who he could possibly mean, but she came up empty. She gave him a baffled look.

"Petra Skinner."

She scoffed. "Petra? You barely know her. Hell, I barely know her, although I know a ton more about her than I used to. Did you know she—"

"Is one of those immortal folks? Yeah, I know. I have for a while."

"How did you know?"

He sighed, leaned back in his chair, and put his hands behind his head. "You know, in all the years we've been doing this crazy business, you never asked me why I came with you."

She shrugged. "I assumed it was because I offered you more money than you'd ever seen and a chance to get away from our little shanty town. Not to mention my remarkable charm."

"You can call it charm if you want to. And the money? That didn't hurt." He grinned at her, but his expression was serious. "But you and your parents didn't live there anymore. You'd been gone for a while, just coming back to see family. What you don't know is, on one of those trips your mama asked me to look after you. She said she'd been watching you grow up, and she didn't know why, but you had trouble letting people in. You had lots of friends, plenty of people around you, but you never let them get close. God knows, your mom and dad weren't that way, so she wasn't sure why. But she said she knew you were destined for something big, so she was hoping it meant you would find that special someone when your destiny came for you."

Kera could almost hear her mom talking to Ajan. "Why didn't she tell me any of this?"

"She knew how you felt about religion and destiny. She knew you were far too stubborn to hear what you needed to hear." He wiped a bit of moisture from his eyes. "But she said she knew she wasn't going to be around long enough to see you through. So she asked me to, because she knew I loved you like my own, and I didn't have any reason to stay there."

She'd known she was going to die. That wasn't hugely surprising. Her mother had always seemed to have a sixth sense about things, which Kera put down to her work as a priestess. She tried to push the overwhelming sadness away. "So, what does this have to do with Petra?"

He dropped his hands from behind his head and stood up. "How many of the people who work for you do you really know?

Other than me. I've gone out with them, had drinks, met some of their families. Petra and I have spent plenty of time together over the years, and let me tell you, that's one damn good woman. I'd trust her to be your...*me*." He smiled and the tension eased. "Think about it, okay?"

"Yeah, okay. I will. I don't suppose you know if she's got any more news on Degrovesnik?"

He sighed. "Not that I know of. And that's another thing. I don't think I want to be around when you go down that road, girlie. It damn near broke me when...well, what happened before. I don't want to see what happens next. That time is gone, and you should leave it alone. I told your mama I'd watch after you, and I've done my best. But if you're determined to see this fool thing through, I'll be there when it's over. But I can't watch you do it."

She slammed her hands on the desk. "How can you say that? Knowing what you know? Knowing what he did?"

He didn't back down in the face of her anger like most people did. Instead, he faced her squarely. "Because I do know, and I don't want you becoming like him!"

She flinched like he'd hit her. "I'd never...Is that what you think?"

He turned away and opened the door. "I don't know what to think when it comes to him and you. And I hope when it comes down, I'm wrong."

He left, quietly closing the door behind him, and she slumped back into her chair. Ajan told her the truth, always, whether she wanted to hear it or not. It was part of what made him so valuable, both as a friend and as her most trusted employee. Playing over pieces of their conversation, she quickly felt like the walls were closing in. She grabbed her keys and left.

She considered calling Tis, but decided she needed to be alone for a while. *But that's what I always decide when it gets tough, isn't it? I wish you'd tried talking sense into me when you could, Mom.*

❖

Tis landed in the courtyard of Afterlife, figuring it would be better if she didn't go through the office. She hadn't been called to deal with anything in several days, and she knew it must be coming any moment. With massive decisions like the one taken in Palestine-Israel, there were bound to be more questions and issues that needed clarification and consensus.

Just as she was nearly to Meg's house, Hermes landed in front of her, his lovely winged sandals setting him down gently. She smiled at him but sighed inwardly. *So close.*

"Hey, Tis! So great to see you, really, really great. Sorry to bother you, truly, but Zed saw you come in, and he'd *really* love a word with you, if you have just a second for him?"

She'd always found Hermes's way of tiptoeing around a message awkward. He never wanted to cause offense, and he took the idiom "don't shoot the messenger" to heart. But for all that he hated confrontation, he was a sweet god.

"Sure, no problem. Tell him I'll be right there."

"Of course, absolutely, happy to. I'll go right now. Shall I tell him a time you'll be there? You know how he is about specifics!"

"Give me ten minutes." If Meg was home, she wanted a quick word before she got sucked into the office politics.

"That's perfect, really great, thanks so much, I'll let him know!" His little winged sandals flapped, and he headed off to the office, propelled by his heels.

She knocked on Meg's door, but there was no answer. She turned back toward the office and briefly wondered if she could get away with flying out, saying she forgot...*He'd just find me anyway.* She trudged to the office, wishing she could be out at a job, or better yet, somewhere with Kera. When she got to Zed's office, she stopped in surprise outside. The room was full, but not like usual.

She went in, trying to prepare herself.

Zed stood and gave her a hug, a rarity in itself. When he whispered in her ear, "tread gently," she understood.

Hades, Zed's brother and once her long time employer, kissed her cheek. As always, he was cold, distant. His eyes were black, but there were light specks moving in them all the time; the souls constantly moving in his realm, always under his watch. "You're looking well, avenger. You haven't been to dinner in too long."

She kissed his cheek in return. "The constant noise gives me a headache, and too many of the people I've dealt with bug me while we're eating. Maybe you should come to my place some time?"

He looked slightly surprised. "I'd like that, winged one. Let me know when."

Azrael, mostly known as Satan, leaned across the table and shook her hand. "Tisera. Wonderful to see you again. It's been centuries." He leaned back, his perfect white teeth, golden hair, and tight black T-shirt over his well-defined body making him look distinctly god-like.

"Nice to see you too, Az. You're looking great."

"Thanks. I'm feeling great. Nothing like bringing things out into the open to light up the underworld."

Yama, with his blue skin and bushy beard, sat next to Osiris, with his green skin and slim, pointed beard. They made Tis think of different depths of the ocean in sunlight. Both smiled and welcomed her. She'd had some contact with both over the years, but not enough to get to know them well.

Iblis, Azrael's Islamic counterpart, gave her a distant nod. She and her sisters had plenty of work in Islamic countries where life, particularly for women, was deeply undervalued. Needless to say, they weren't well liked.

Suddenly, she was crushed in a hug that lifted her from the floor. "Beautiful terror! I'd forgotten how your beauty makes the stars and moon seem like nothing more than reindeer shit."

She would have laughed if she could breathe. When she was finally back on her feet, she grinned at Freya, goddess of the Norse underworld. "And you're looking spectacularly well, too, old friend."

Freya puffed up with pride, her blond braids long and healthy, her warrior's metal corset shiny. Her usual companion, a gargantuan tiger of some kind, lay snoring against the wall. Tis and Freya had enjoyed a few decades of companionship, before deciding it was time for them to move on.

"I was close to fading, you know. Barely a shadow moving among the fields of ice. But when the gods came out, there was a revival of interest in the ancient religion, and suddenly the halls of Valhalla and the fields of Folkvangr are ringing with life again!" Her voice boomed off the glass walls.

Zed cleared his throat. "If you don't mind, I'd like to get on with this." Everyone sat down, and he looked at Tis. "As you know, there's been some question as to the nature of the underworld and how those leaders will play in the changes."

Tis nodded and looked at Satan. "Like the issue with the young people recently."

He sighed and shook his head. "I swear, that wasn't me. I don't know who they're praying to, or who they think is talking to them, but it's not me." He pointed at Hades. "You sure it wasn't you, old-timer?"

Hades grimaced. "They used your name, not mine. If it were me, I assure you, they'd know who it was."

Zed tapped the table. "It's entirely possible a human is behind it, brainwashing believers into thinking it's one of you. It wouldn't be the first time." He turned back to Tis. "That's part of why we're here. We need a constitution, a plan of some sort, similar to the one we've devised for the high…other, council." A few of the beings at the table stiffened slightly at Zed's slip. It wasn't good to remind gods they didn't have a place at the decision-making table. "There need to be rules in place to correspond with the other rules, so we can all do our jobs without chaos."

"What is life without chaos?" Osiris motioned with his large wooden staff. "If you take away chaos, if you take away death, what do you have left? Lotus eaters, rotting away on a beach, existing for nothing."

Zed's face turned red, and Tis wondered how many times they'd had this conversation. She thought about the conversations she had with Buddha and Lao-Tse about balance and thought Osiris might have a point.

"Okay. So, I need to show you the rules already set in place, and we need to develop a coda to run alongside it."

Iblis frowned and sat stiffly upright. "I won't be dictated to by a woman. Especially not one who constantly enters my territory and delivers justice she has no right to demand."

Irritated, Tis stood and let her full form show, her snakes coming alive and her fangs extending. She leapt on the table and stalked on all fours to face him. She moved into his personal space and saw the fear in his eyes. "I am far more than a woman, and I suggest you don't pull your sexist gendered shit with me. I do my job anywhere I need to, when I need to, no matter who is ruling. If you refuse to get your people in line, that's not my problem. Insult me again, and god or not, I will take your mind and melt it into the kind of horrors you haven't even thought of yet."

He gave her a sharp nod and looked away, his throat working as though trying to keep from screaming.

She turned away from him and went back to her daily form as she walked back down the table to her chair.

Satan started laughing, and he was quickly joined by the others. Iblis didn't look amused.

"Holy hells, Tis. I'd forgotten how fucking amazing you are." Azrael wiped tears of laughter away. "And you know, I think you'd do it, too."

"You know I would. Now, let's get down to business, shall we?"

Zed slid the file in front of her, and he looked decidedly less stressed than when she'd walked in. "I'm so damn glad I chose you for this position."

"That makes one of us." She opened the file and turned toward the others. "Now. The other gods have declared a no violence edict. There's to be no suicide bombings, no murder in the name of religion, no human-on-human violence at all. Period. Obviously, declaring that isn't going to make it happen, it just might make it happen less."

"I've had an eighty percent decrease in new souls in the past six months." Azrael looked around the table. "You?"

The others nodded, all looking disgruntled.

"I'm sure that's true. Obviously, my sisters and I are seeing less work, as are the Praxidice. People aren't quick to break oaths right now, either. However, we know how humans work. Granted, there's never been this kind of religious transparency, and we can't be totally certain how it will turn out. But I'm willing to bet they'll find other reasons to fight, other reasons to war. It's in their nature."

Yama leaned forward. "The question is, are we allowed to instigate these other reasons?"

Tis looked at Zed, who shrugged. She closed her eyes and thought for a moment. "Let's figure this out. As far as I'm aware, you've always been the instigators of difficulty, correct?" They all nodded, looking slightly brighter. "The other gods have dictated no violence in their names and have told people to love one another."

Freya scoffed. "As our sky colored friend there says, Lotus eaters."

"But if we talk about balance, the kind needed to keep the planet in check and to keep population under control to some degree, then it can't always be that way." She looked at them, taking in their individual personalities. "My suggestion is this: be transparent. Be just as visible as the other gods. But you have to have some boundaries too. You can't instruct people to murder. But if they do, then they should know they're coming your way." She looked at Azrael. "For a long time, you were God's right hand, and you opposed him on a lot of things. You thought humans should think for themselves, that they should question directives that didn't make sense. Well, maybe that's where you come in now. By getting people to question their gods, you may end up getting followers of your own. In fact, I think that's key." She nodded, knowing she was on the right track. "You want followers. Your followers don't necessarily need to cause problems or chaos, not if you're out there talking to them. Decide what each of you can offer them—that's what the other gods are doing. What can you give followers that the others can't? Why should they come to you and start building your altars? If all you're offering is a brimstone and fire afterlife, with nothing but pain and anguish for eternity, you're not going to have a lot of people flocking to you."

"You're saying we rebrand ourselves." Osiris looked at her speculatively.

"Yeah, I suppose I am. I mean, Freya already kind of has it going."

Freya looked surprised, then thought about it. "Because it's not all about death and rotting. It's about glory and honor."

"Exactly." Tis looked at Zed, who was clearly thinking about what she was suggesting. "Now is your chance to be *more*, to clean up your places of business and not only expand, but make it different. Sure, you're still going to need your punishment aspects, that's how you balance out your religions and keep people in line— fear of coming to you. But that same fear means you won't get the followers you want. So, design a new system. And not one based on false promises, either." She pointed at Azrael and Iblis. "If you want it, make it real. Do the work. I've heard Jesus is running a few marketing workshops in the evenings, for those interested. Maybe you should consider attending."

The room was silent for a few minutes as what she said sank in. Yama pulled over a pad of paper. "Shall we get started on a basic set of guidelines we all agree on, and then go away and consider our individual marketing strategies?" He looked at Tis and smiled. "Thank you, most terrifying advisor. I believe you have given us a fresh start in a rather confusing time."

Freya pounded on the table, briefly waking her tiger, who looked up and then went back to snoring. "You've always been the most incredible woman ever born—land, air, or sea. Let's have sex again soon!"

Tis laughed. "Perhaps. But I think your concern should be more focused than that right now."

Zed stood up and motioned Tis to go with him. "When they've got a good list going and it comes time to make it official, I'll give you a call."

They walked out into the hall, closing the door on the already busy conversation behind them. "Zed, what are you going to do about this person masquerading as Satan?"

"I've got the research team on it. They're checking all social media sites, email, and phones for all the kids involved. We'll see if any base communication was made, although none has shown up yet. If not, we'll find another way to check. I don't like that the soul was taken before one of the death crew could get to it." He held Tis's shoulder in one of his massive hands. "Thank you for doing this. I can't tell you how much we need your level head. I never would've thought about the rebranding thing. Hopefully, they'll be so busy remaking their domains they won't have a lot of time to create problems elsewhere for a while."

"I won't say it's my pleasure, but I have to admit, I'm kind of enjoying it. In a twisted, masochistic way."

"Good. Everything else okay?"

"I think so, although I'm a little worried about the tension and the way the humans are going to handle this in the long run."

He waved dismissively. "They're humans, Tisera. You know as well as I do—show them some power, make them understand how lucky they are to pray to us, and they'll fall in line."

He sounded just like he had when Greece felt like the only place in the world, and there was no one to oppose them. But that world was long gone, and she wondered if he really understood the one he was playing in now.

"Okay, well, I guess we'll see how it goes." She gave him a weak smile, and he nodded before heading back into the room to listen.

Tis stood there for a moment, at a loss as to what to do next. Her sisters weren't around, she hadn't gotten a call about a job, and she was done with her duties at the office. She pulled out her phone. Should she call Kera? She wasn't sure, even though they'd made up, if she was ready to see Kera after an afternoon of discussing the ways the gods of the underworld would woo their human followers.

She hit number three on her speed dial. "Aulis? Are you free? I feel like drinking wine and eating ice cream."

Chapter Fourteen

K era sat across from Petra, really looking at her, trying to see the heat wave she saw with the other nonhuman kind. But it wasn't there.

"Do you want to tell me why you're looking at me like I'm something in a zoo?"

Kera frowned. "Why didn't you tell me you were one of them?"

"Why would I? I'm not one of them now, and it doesn't have any effect on my job performance."

"No. I could see how the whole immortal thing wouldn't affect your job. What the hell?" Kera flipped her pencil across the room, to join others sent there throughout the day. She'd been out of sorts since her conversation with Ajan, and the city was still being ridiculous about not giving her the building permits she needed. She hadn't heard from Tis, and with all the stress she was under, she decided Tis should be the one to call her. After all, she'd made the first move by apologizing, so now it was up to Tis to make the next move. They were supposed to be leaving for Haiti the following week, and Kera was beginning to regret inviting her. *Like I don't have enough going on. This is exactly why I don't see women more than once or twice.*

Petra coughed discreetly.

"Sorry, what?"

"I said I'm not immortal. That's not the way it always works."

Suddenly, she had Kera's attention. "What do you mean? You were a goddess, right?"

Petra's smile was slightly sad. "I was. In a beautiful temple, dedicated to myself and my consort. For hundreds of years, in fact. But things changed, the area around the temple was deserted, and eventually, people forgot about us. So I got out while I could."

"Got out? How do you get out of being a goddess? And what does that mean?" Kera's pulse quickened. New information meant new knowledge, and knowledge was always power.

"Tisera hasn't told you?"

Kera thought about their conversations. "She told me there are things she can't tell me. And to be fair, I haven't been very open to the whole gods thing."

Petra stared at the wall, her eyes darting side to side as though she were watching a tennis match. "Then perhaps it isn't my place to tell you either. She must have had her reasons, and trust me when I say angering a fury isn't a good way to keep mind and body together."

"Petra, that's absurd. Maybe she signed a confidentiality agreement or something, I don't know. But I fucking hate being kept in the dark. At least tell me why you got out—if you tell me your story in particular, then she can't be pissed at you for telling me stuff I shouldn't know. I mean, you're allowed to talk about yourself, right?" *I'm getting good at this spin stuff.*

Petra's eyes narrowed. "If you're wrong and someone comes for me, will you be able to save me?"

"Who the hell is going to come for you for telling me? Are all of you this paranoid?"

She sighed and sat back. "My story only. No questions about the bigger stuff. Draw what conclusions you will."

Kera nodded, satisfied. "Done."

Petra closed her eyes and started talking, her voice melodic and raspy. "As I said, I had a beautiful temple, carved from rock by followers who adored me and wanted a place for us that was special, truly unique. I watched over them for centuries, listening to prayers, understanding the ramifications of granting one prayer over another, helping all those I could. When it slowly ended, I began to fade. Literally, to simply cease to be. My consort, devastated by the betrayal and loneliness, faded before I did. I was there alone for some time, mourning him, nearly gone myself. Eventually, I made the choice to stay in the world, but to do so, I had to give up my status of goddess and live among the humans." She opened her eyes and looked at Kera. "When I gave up being a goddess, it meant I wasn't going to fade completely, that I would live. But I'm not immortal. The biggest difference is that, unlike the gods, I can die. I can be killed or have an accident. The gods may be able to kill one another, though they usually just maim each other when they're throwing tantrums, but humans can't kill them, nor can accidents."

Kera had a million questions, though Petra's story had given her more information than she'd ever had. *They fade away if they don't get enough attention. Interesting.* She started to ask, and Petra held up her hand.

"Unless you're changing the subject or asking something about me, then don't."

"What did you do, first thing, when you went out among the humans?"

Petra laughed. "I ate an apple. A green one, so tart it made my eyes water. My followers used to bring them to the temple, but I hadn't had one in forever. I took all the money, jewels, and offerings from the temple with me. Much had been stolen, but there were still vast amounts hidden in vaults and in the caves. I had enough to start a new life, and I used it to see the world and figure out where I wanted to go, and who I wanted to become."

Kera contemplated that. In a much smaller way, she'd done the same after her experience with Degrovesnik. "And here we are."

"And here we are."

"Ajan thinks you can be the next chief of GRADE. I'm disinclined to say a former goddess couldn't handle the job, but at the same time, I don't know if you can. But if Ajan believes in you…" She shrugged, hating the idea of such a massive change.

"If that's your way of trying to hire me, your recruitment skills need work." Petra stood to leave.

"Wait. I'm sorry. He's been with me since the beginning, and I can't imagine replacing him, that's all."

"You won't be replacing him. I don't know him as well as you do, but I don't think he's replaceable. All you're doing is adding a new person to the team. I'm not him, and I never will be."

Kera looked at her speculatively. "Would you want to work for me?"

"No."

"Well, then—"

"But I'm interested in working for GRADE. I find you remote, dismissive, stubborn, and shallow. But what you've created in the company and what you do for the world, suggests you're more than you seem. I'd like to be part of making the world better, and I like the way GRADE does that." Her smile was small, but there. "And if that means occasionally saving your difficult ass, then I can do that too."

Kera stared at her for a moment before beginning to laugh. If there was going to be someone to take Ajan's place, someone to be forthright and tell her what she needed to hear, it looked like Petra was going to be the right choice after all.

"We're heading out on our next project when I get back from Haiti. I'll ask Ajan to get you started so you can learn protocols and get caught up with the details of the project itself." She paused, thinking. "And that means I'll need another investigator, so if you know of any, I'd appreciate it. Do you have any further information on that other issue?"

"Degrovesnik and his crew landed in Cuba two weeks ago. Beyond the airport, I haven't been able to find where they went. You want me to keep on it?"

Kera thought about Ajan and about Tisera. If she kept on this road, there was only one end to it. Would she lose them both if she did what she knew she needed to do? Her skin crawled at the memory of the four-by-four cell... "Yeah. Keep searching. If you haven't found anything more by the time we head out on the project, we'll see what the options are then."

"Fine. How are your bodyguards working out?"

In truth, Kera had barely noticed them. They were burly women, meant for protection, and although attractive, they weren't her type. "They're fine, thanks. They keep their distance so I'm not smothered, and I appreciate that."

"Good. Take them with you to Haiti."

Kera started to protest.

"You think because you leave the country you're safe? You think you'd be fine in a country where people disappear every day without a trace?"

Kera held up her hands in surrender. "Okay, okay. Fine. I'll take them with me. Tisera is going with me, you know. You think those bodyguards are more capable than she is?"

Petra laughed, the first time Kera had ever really heard her do so. "The only creatures as terrifying and capable as Tisera are her sisters. But she might not be with you twenty-four hours a day, so just do it, okay?"

"Yeah, I hear you."

Petra nodded, apparently satisfied. "Good. I'll be in touch if I learn anything." She looked over her shoulder as she stepped out the door. "See you later, boss."

Kera heard her laughing again as she walked down the hall. *A goddess just called me boss. Guess I'm moving up in the world. Speaking of which...*

She grabbed her phone and pressed Tis's number.

"Hey there."

The incredibly sexy smoothness of Tis's voice made her stomach flip like she was seventeen and talking to her first crush. "Hey. I don't suppose you're free for dinner?" There was a slight hesitation, and Kera heard another woman's voice in the background. "Oh. Sorry, I didn't realize you had company. I'll let you go." She was about to hang up, irritated with how distraught she felt, when Tis stopped her.

"I would love dinner, but I've got a friend over. Would you like to join us? We're most of the way through our second, or fifth, bottle of wine. I'll order out rather than cook, so I don't burn the house down."

Relief made Kera dizzy, and the fact it meant so much to her that Tis wasn't actually with someone else was something she needed to think about. "I'd really like that, if I won't be intruding. Can I bring anything?"

She heard a voice call out from the background, "Peanut butter ice cream!"

Kera laughed. "Peanut butter ice cream and wine? That's interesting."

Tis laughed, and Kera hadn't heard her sound so carefree in some time. "Bring anything you like. Sweet is better, though. I'll get pizza."

"Sounds like a plan. See you soon."

Kera hung up and smiled. She liked the feeling of anticipation buzzing through her, and she really liked how excited Tis was that she'd called. She grabbed her car keys and told her burly new bodyguards to bring something to entertain themselves while she played with beautiful women. They barely acknowledged her, and she decided she'd work harder to get a rise out of them. In the meantime, she had women waiting for her.

It may not be forever, but for now, I'll take it.

Tis lay on the ground, her wings fully spread beneath her and her head resting on Kera's lap. Kera, her eyes closed, reclined against the enormous tree on the deck just below Tis's house. Aulis hung upside down in the tree above them, trying to eat her ice cream from the tub before it dripped onto Tis and Kera below her. More often than not, she missed a drop. However, neither Tis nor Kera noticed. The night breeze was warm, the sky a mass of pinpoint eyes staring down at them.

They were all very, very drunk.

"I miss the old days." Aulis hiccupped. "No, I don't. That's not true; it was a stinking mass of sewage and filth covered in plague. I miss little bits of the old days, though. Like when we chased stupid humans through the forest and drove them insane, but they could redeem themselves, so we were doing good stuff." She hiccupped again. "Now, we just drive them insane because we know they're not redeemable." She waved the dripping spoon at Kera. "No offense."

A splatter of peanut butter ice cream hit Kera in the forehead, and she scraped it off with her finger, which she then pressed to Tis's mouth. She made an appreciative sound when Tis sucked it clean. "None taken. I think it's probably true."

Aulis watched as Tis sucked Kera's finger. "That's hot. You're hot. I've always loved Tis, but she's not my type. You know, two deadly people in a bed is a bad combination, generally speaking. But you're hot, and I could definitely sleep with Tis if you were between us."

Tis shook her head and tried to speak around Kera's finger in her mouth before Kera removed it. "I'm not having sex with you again. Ever. The last time we tried a threesome, it was disastrous. Have you forgotten?"

Aulis started laughing so hard she snorted. "Oh gods. I had forgotten. That poor serving wench in the fifteen hundreds."

Tis nodded, her eyes barely open. "You and I came at the same time while we were both inside her..."

Kera waited for the rest, but it didn't seem to be forthcoming. "And?"

Tis opened her eyes and looked up at her. "Ashes to ashes..."

"And boy, did she turn to dust. I didn't know humans could combust that way. Good lesson, though." Aulis nodded sagely. "We didn't make *that* mistake again."

"You exploded a woman by having sex with her?" Though the idea of a threesome had caught her attention when Aulis suggested it, the idea quickly lost its charm.

"Not exploded, exactly. Just..." Aulis waved the ice cream spoon, sending raindrops of peanut butter all over. "Poof."

"Poof," Kera whispered as she drifted to sleep, one hand in Tis's hair, the other resting on her breast. Thoughts of beautiful, immortal women writhing beneath her, around her, all over her, accompanied her throughout the night.

When she woke, the warmth of the sun on her face was quickly accompanied by a blinding, throbbing headache. Her stomach lurched, but when she tried to sit up, she realized she was pinned. She squinted past the pain to see why she couldn't move. *Shit. Shit, shit, shit.* Aulis lay curled against one side of her, Tis lay curled against the other, and both were asleep with their heads on her chest.

And all three of them were newborn naked in Tis's bed.

Kera closed her eyes again, trying desperately to remember what had happened the night before. They'd been outside, against the tree…

"She's panicking," Aulis murmured.

"It's cute, isn't it?" Tis sounded sleepy, but amused.

"I'm not sure. I think I might feel insulted."

Kera vaguely remembered something about someone going *poof* and hurried to stall any such explosive feelings. "I'd just be damn sad not to remember something so extraordinary, that's all."

"Psh." Aulis sat up and stretched. "Nice try. You fell asleep while I was just *talking* about sex. Actually getting you to do anything would've been like trying to get a tree to perform CPR on a snail."

The pounding in Kera's head was slowly making its way to her stomach. She kissed Tis's forehead and said, "Baby, I really think you should let me up. Unless you're into bodily fluid kind of games."

"Ew." Tis rolled over, and Kera bolted for the bathroom.

As she knelt, ridding herself of what seemed like a zillion bottles of wine and God knew what else, she heard them talking in the other room. She pictured them—Aulis's small, olive skinned curvaceous body, and Tis's long, pale, beautiful form. *And I don't remember being in bed with them. Jackass.*

She rinsed out her mouth and splashed cold water on her face. When she came out, she gave Tis a sheepish smile. "Sorry about that."

Tis, wearing a loose fitting black satin robe, shook her head and handed over a cup of coffee. "It's our fault. We know better than to allow a human to try to keep up with us."

Aulis read a message on her phone and sighed. "Sorry, work calls. Something going on back East." She shrugged into her light summer dress and kissed Tis on the cheek before turning to Kera. "Next time, we'll keep you sober enough to give it a try. Who knows, maybe you won't explode on us." She stood on her tiptoes and gave her a lingering kiss before grinning and heading outside. She opened wings that looked falcon-like and leapt into the air.

Kera turned to Tis, totally bemused.

Tis grinned at her. "And that is my best friend, Aulis. I think she likes you."

"Do you two have threesomes with unsuspecting humans often?" Kera hoped her tone sounded lighter than she felt. The idea of Tis with other people made her twitch inside.

"Goodness, no. Not since that unfortunate situation we told you about." Tis sipped her coffee, looking at Kera over the top of the mug. "Jealous?"

Kera looked away, unsure how much she wanted to share. "Maybe a little, yeah."

Tis led the way to the outside terrace, and they sat in the mid-morning sun. "Cute." She put her hand over Kera's. "You understand that being jealous is unreasonable, given the situation, right?"

Kera thought about it. "Okay, yeah. Being jealous of anyone's past is stupid. It's just that there's a lot more of your past than I usually have to deal with, and as extraordinary as I am, I'm willing to admit you may have met some people equally so before me." She traced Tis's fingers with her own. "Do you get jealous?"

Tis winced slightly. "I've never been close enough to someone to bother about who else they were, or are, with." She shrugged. "When you live so long, sex is…functional, sometimes. And fun, and sensual, and cathartic. All the things you want it to be. But I suppose it's also less, well, less serious, I guess. When you live such a short time, sex is part of love, and you hold tightly to it because you know it's finite. When you live forever, you can experience so much more, and it loses its…"

Tis trailed off, and Kera knew it was because she couldn't find a word that wouldn't sting. "Meaning?"

"Yeah, in a way. It means something, and it can be intense. When you have limited time, it becomes a way to hold on to someone. When you live forever, it's simply a way to get close, to enjoy one another, before you move on." She gave Kera a sad smile. "When you're immortal, the word 'forever' means something else entirely."

"So, this thing between us?" Kera hated that she'd asked the question. As if the pounding in her head wasn't enough, she was about to take one to her heart.

"It's interesting. And fun. And I like being with you. Who knows where it will lead?"

Kera pulled her hand away gently and stood. "Except we know it won't lead to forever."

Tis looked at her seriously. "Your forever and mine are very different. But that doesn't mean it can't be wonderful while it's available to us."

Kera felt like someone had kicked the backs of her knees, and she was going to drop. But she nodded and tried to smile. "Sure. I get it." She backed toward the house. "I'm going to head back to work. Thanks for the evening…I think."

Tis smiled slightly, but Kera knew she wasn't fooled. She dressed as quickly as she could without needing to empty her stomach again and called from the French doors, "I'm off. I'll call you about our plans for next week, okay?"

Tis nodded but stayed curled up on the chair, her knees pulled to her chest. "Sure."

Kera got in her car and closed her eyes. She considered the vast differences between them and felt absurd for not having given it real thought before. *What the hell am I doing?*

Chapter Fifteen

The days flew past as Tis got ready to go to Haiti with Kera. Though their texts and short conversations had been cooler and more distant than they'd been before, Kera wasn't walking away, and Tis hoped that meant things would be okay.

"Relationships are so awkward. Why is that?"

Selene reclined on Tis's bed, watching her pack, her bare feet swinging off the edge. "Because there's always an element of uncertainty in communication. Conversations, both physical and verbal, require interpretation from both people involved. As such, interpretation can only be clear once the parties involved have learned one another's communicative idiosyncrasies."

Tis threw a sock at her. "You're saying it takes time to get to know someone?"

"Well, yeah, if you want to put it so basely." Selene threw the sock back, smiling. "And even with time, the very nature of humanity is to attempt to find reason and sense in existence. So situations where those are lacking create discord. Relational chaos, at least to some degree, is inevitable. It's how you decide to deal with that chaos and discord that matters."

Tis loved talking to Selene. Her approach to life made sense, with its logic and reason, even when dealing with emotions. Tis was glad she hadn't lost that part of herself when she'd become part of their world. It reminded her, a little bit, of the conversations she'd had with Plato and Aristotle at the dawn of philosophy. She wished

Selene had been able to enjoy that experience, though they wouldn't have given her much time as a woman. They'd spoken to Tis as a Greek god, not as a female. "How so?"

"Well, you can choose to avoid it, set it aside as an experience better left behind, or you can choose to face it, and further develop the bonds between you and the other person. Deciding to face it rather than turn away from it requires a connection to your emotional self, almost your Id, in order to determine if there's enough interest to continue with the time and emotional investment."

"In other words, we need to really like one another to bother with it if it's hard?"

Selene sighed and shook her head. "Simply put, but yeah, basically."

Tis sat beside her on the bed and noticed how delicate she looked. She'd seen it before, particularly when Selene was in Alec's arms, but sitting beside her made her more aware of her size in comparison to a human's. She'd never thought of Kera as fragile, though. "Selene, can I ask you a serious question?"

"I find that type preferable. By all means."

Tis tried to find a tactful way to ask but couldn't come up with one. "How do you deal with knowing you're going to die and Alec isn't?"

Selene raised her eyebrows. "Ah. Is that what's bothering you?"

Tis nodded.

"Well, I'm not sure I've got the answer for you, I'm afraid. Because of my demigod status, I won't be dying, really. When my time comes, and I assume it will come in some horrible, test-from-the-gods kind of way as usually happens with demigods, apparently, I'll simply give up my mortal status and suddenly be counted among the gods." She shook her head. "That sounds so ludicrous. Anyway, I'm sorry, but I'm not in the same boat." She took Tis's hand in hers. "Surely you've known other gods who've taken mortal lovers?"

"Of course. Aulis was desperately in love with a human, and I believe they were together for his entire life. But when he died…no one heard from her for at least a decade. She's never been the same."

"She shouldn't be."

Tis looked at her questioningly.

"If she really loved him, she wouldn't be the same after losing him. Love changes you. It makes you consider life differently. It makes you better, and sometimes worse. It..." Selene paused, clearly searching for the right words. "It leaves you utterly exposed, like being naked on Mount Everest in January with a helicopter filming you."

"That sounds like fun."

Selene shrugged slightly. "Sometimes it's not. But if you let yourself be that vulnerable, you can find freedom, love, and passion you've never experienced before." Selene traced the black-and-white stripes in a sock as she talked. "I don't know a lot of your history, Tis. But from what Alec and Meg have told me, you're not one to let people in easily. Even if this woman isn't your forever, maybe she's someone who can show you how to let people in." She looked up, her expression cautious, as though trying to gauge if she'd overstepped.

Tis thought about it, and the assessment was true. "The mortality thing scares me. The fact that I'd watch her get old and frail, and eventually die. All while I stay the same. I'm not sure how we cross that bridge. But the thing is, I don't keep people at bay because I don't want to be close to anyone. I guess I've just never found anyone I want. Not the way you and Alec want one another."

Selene blushed. "Well, I don't know how many people find what we have." She stood and kissed Tis on the cheek. "Speaking of, I need to get home. She sent a text to say she and Meg are on their way back from Jerusalem. Apparently, some of the holy sites are being overrun, and the crowding is setting people on edge."

Is this how it starts? Tis was convinced there was going to be a tipping point, where belief, need, and skepticism coalesced into a conflagration of chaos. She just wasn't sure when or how it was going to happen. "Are they getting busy again?"

"Incrementally. Most people are still behaving, given the whole afterlife scenario in every religion. But Humanity First is stirring a lot of people up, and they're gathering an interesting combination of former atheists, as well as believers who are dissatisfied with the answers they're getting from the gods. They say they're pacifists, but when it comes down to it…"

"It's just another type of religion based conflict." Tis threw the last tank top in her suitcase. "It still amazes me that humanity has managed to survive with its inherent propensity for violence."

Selene kissed her cheek and grinned as she opened the door to leave. "Ah, but you're forgetting. Along with that propensity for violence, we've also got an incredible ability to empathize, and a desire for growth. We're apes who created gods. That's pretty amazing, don't you think?" She blew Tis a kiss and left.

As always, conversations with Selene gave Tis plenty to ponder. Seeing things from a human's point of view, even if she were a demigod, always provided new insights. She considered the aspect of vulnerability Selene had mentioned and checked her watch. It was time to pick Kera up at her place, so they could head to the airport. It made more sense to take her Land Rover, so they didn't have to worry about typical 405 traffic.

She grabbed her suitcase and locked the door behind her. *Mount Everest, huh? I've been naked in worse places.*

Kera grabbed her bag and headed out to meet Tis when she pulled up. Her pulse raced and her stomach flipped when Tis smiled at her. *For fuck's sake, it's like being a teenager again.* She'd missed Tis immensely and hated that the sweet beginning they'd forged had turned difficult. But she was also having a damn hard time letting go of the no-meaning relationship thing, even if she wasn't sure she wanted one anyway. Regardless, she couldn't imagine going to Haiti without her and was looking forward to the trip more than she should be, given the reason she had to go.

Tis leaned across when Kera slid into the passenger seat and gave her a lingering kiss. "Hey, stranger."

Kera sank into the feel of Tis's lips on hers, and all the frustration, stress, and worry of her week melted away like ice in the California summer sun. "Hey. I've missed you."

Tis smiled. "Likewise." She nodded at Kera's bodyguards who were loading up their predictably black SUV. "Are they not coming with us?"

Kera wanted to touch Tis, to run her hands all over her, to feel the feathers she couldn't see at the moment. *Focus.* "No, they'll meet us at the airport. I want some alone time with you, and I figured in your magic-mobile I'd be safe enough without them."

"Too true." Tis got on the road, and Kera focused on looking at her. The way the world moved outside the car made her slightly queasy. That, and she couldn't take her eyes off Tis. Although she pictured her every night as she drifted to sleep, often during and after she'd gotten off thinking about their amazing sex, seeing her in person made the mental image pale in comparison. The sunlight on her pale hair, the beauty of her porcelain skin and stunning gray eyes were almost unbearably beautiful. So much so, Kera found her eyes welling up.

As though sensing it, Tis reached over and took her hand. "So, how are you feeling about going home?"

Kera pulled herself together, glad Tis had forced her to concentrate. "I don't know, really. I mean, I miss my mom constantly. It's like a toothache. At first it was so bad I couldn't think of anything but the pain. Now, it's like the tooth has been pulled. It doesn't hurt, but there's a hole." The thought of her mom's laugh made her smile. "I'm looking forward to seeing my family, although I'm not hugely excited about the religious aspects."

"Will you participate anyway?" Tis glanced at her as she maneuvered around traffic.

"I have to really. To honor her memory." She thought for a moment, trying to figure out how she really felt about it. "You know, although I knew the orishas were real, I don't think I ever believed in the religion itself. And now, knowing the gods exist…I'm not sure how I feel about doing the ritual, knowing someone might actually be listening. It feels false, somehow. More so than doing it when I didn't think it was real. Does that make sense?"

Tis nodded, her beautiful brow furrowed. "I understand that. If the gods are there, perhaps you should talk to them. Tell them your concerns directly." She gave Kera a playful grin. "I'll protect you if you stick your foot in it."

"Excellent. My own fury bodyguard."

They got to the airport and checked in. Kera looked at Tis's unusual passport, which had a picture of the symbols of all the major world religions on the front, instead of the standard country name. When they'd walked away, she said, "How do you get new documents? I mean, do yours expire? That seems wasteful as well as ironic."

Tis laughed, a sound that made Kera feel like she was drinking clouds. "It used to be that Afterlife took care of all our documents. They still do, really. But now we can get government issued documents, which is incredibly strange. Who knew Shiva would need a passport, right?"

Kera couldn't think of a response, and after they'd made it through security, they found a café and ordered coffee and croissants. They talked about Kera's work, and she updated Tis on the ongoing issues she was having with the city for the homeless project. They talked a little bit about Kera's upcoming international projects as well, and when Kera's bodyguards arrived, they headed to the gate as a group. As they passed by, people often stopped and stared, and Kera laughed inwardly at the picture they must make. Tis, with her ethereal beauty, Kera with her dark skin and hair, and then two beefy female bodyguards. *Like Charlie's Angels, but with more muscle. And snakes.*

When they boarded, Kera's bodyguards sat behind them in first class, and Kera ordered glasses of champagne for herself and Tis. When they came, she held up her glass in a toast. "To saying good-bye and new beginnings."

Tis smiled and touched her glass to Kera's. "Cheers."

They drank, and Kera relaxed in her seat. When Tis reached over and held her hand, the feeling of rightness with the world surprised her, but she let it in. Soon enough, she'd be back in the arms of her family, and their quiet time would be over for the length of their stay. For now, she would enjoy being with a woman who was starting to mean more to her than she could yet understand.

❖

Kera felt Tis watching her when she woke up. "Am I as absurdly good-looking asleep as I am awake?" she murmured.

"Actually, with your mouth shut, you're even sexier."

Kera forced her eyes open. "Surely my charm and wit are what attract you? If I were silent, how would you benefit from my intoxicating intelligence?"

Tis traced her fingertip over Kera's lips. "I bet I'd find a way to enjoy you anyway."

Goose bumps covered Kera's body, and she bit Tis's fingertip. "You'll have to show me what you mean. I'm afraid I'm utterly lacking in imagination." The lights came on in the cabin, and everyone began to stir. Kera's bodyguards stood and stretched, and Kera decided to do the same. She liked the appreciation in Tis's eyes as she watched her. "Did you get any sleep?"

Tis sighed. "Some. My sisters were in contact, letting me know things are a little…unstable, at work. I may need to make some phone calls when we land."

"Wow, I must have been out cold not to hear you on the phone." Kera moved aside to let her bodyguard past, as always impressed by the woman's size. Too bad she had the personality of a burned out light bulb. She liked that they kept their space, but it would be fun to mess with them occasionally too. Kera returned her attention to Tis.

"I wasn't on the phone. I didn't want to wake anyone."

"So, what? You went and hung out with them on the wings of the plane?"

Tis laughed. "Far too cold up this high. No, my sisters and I can communicate telepathically. Before we learned to block one another it was a nightmare. Especially the first time we all had sex. It was like doing it with a cheerleading squad."

The stewardess came through with hot towels for everyone to wash their hands and face, and Kera wiped down gratefully. Flying always made her feel grimy. Thinking of a young Tis having sex for the first time meant she should have had a cold towel, rather than a warm one. "Seriously, though, I'm sorry I slept all the way through.

It would have been nice to chat some more before we get devoured by my family."

Tis shrugged. "You really are beautiful when you sleep, and I needed the time to talk about work stuff, so it's no big deal. I'm sure we'll have time to ourselves at some point during the week."

"Maybe so. But knowing my family, I'm not holding out hope." She took her toothpaste and mini-toothbrush to the bathroom, waving her bodyguard off when she started to follow her. "Down, girl. I doubt anyone is going to drown me in the bathroom toilet."

The bodyguard sat down, looking unhappy about it. Kera shook her head and went to wait behind two other people with toothbrushes in hand, one in an extremely expensive, and totally wrinkled Armani suit, and another in an ugly pair of brown loafers. Kera turned away from her fellow passenger's fashion debacles and checked out the other people around her. She'd always thought you could tell a lot by watching people on a plane. Whether they were friendly, loud, respectful, or rude, it often showed up clearly after a long flight in cramped quarters, whether you were in first class or economy. The curtain to the economy seats twitched open as a steward came through, and she caught a glimpse of a face she could swear she knew. She felt the blood rush from her head, and her knees went weak. Suddenly, Tis was right beside her, a bodyguard behind her.

"What is it?" Tis said quietly.

"Back there. I thought I saw..." Kera shook her head. It couldn't be. But then, Petra had insisted she take her bodyguards just in case... The curtain twitched open again, and Kera strained to see the passengers beyond it. There was no one there she recognized, just lots of people packed in like cattle. The panic flooding through her receded. "Nothing. It's nothing. My imagination playing tricks on me. I'll be right back." It was her turn, so she ducked into the bathroom and locked the door behind her. She steadied herself in front of the mirror. *I'm just tired. Too much work and not enough sleep. That's all.*

She quickly used the bathroom and brushed her teeth, and felt better by the time she headed back to her seat. If it was him, unlikely as it was, she might get her chance to do what she needed to do. She just had to be ready. A hot breakfast was on the tray in front of her seat, and she dug in with relish. Tis had nearly finished hers and was sipping a strong coffee.

"So, where are we headed after we land?"

Kera answered while still eating. "I've ordered a car to be delivered to the airport. We'll grab that and head south to my parents' house in Petion-ville, about thirty minutes away. I thought we'd stop by Dad's restaurant before we get to the house, just in case we can catch him alone before we're surrounded by everyone else." Kera was looking forward to seeing her father, but wasn't as certain about all the rest of it.

"Perfect. Would it be okay if I made a call or two on the drive there? I don't want to be rude."

Kera laughed and scraped the last of the slightly overcooked eggs from her plate. "Baby, in case you haven't noticed, I don't tend to leave my work behind either. If there's anyone who gets it, it's me."

Tis rewarded her with that beautiful, sincere smile of hers, and she swallowed hard against that same stab of emotion she'd felt before falling asleep the night before. Soon, the announcement for descent was made, and Tis once again held Kera's hand as the plane flew over Haiti. Seeing it appear below them, Kera was struck with a deep sense of nostalgia. When Tis squeezed her hand, as though understanding, she started talking.

"My mom came from Cite Soleil. You know it?"

Tis nodded. "I've had to go there a number of times."

"Then you know what it means that she got out. It's the poorest, most crime-ridden commune in Haiti. Run by gangs, there's no sewage system and only sporadic electricity. Her parents were born there, but when they saw how smart she was, they found ways to get her an education. She walked the hour and a half each way to the college when she started taking classes there, and then got an internship, and made her way to Florida on a scholarship. Her parents were killed when some gang decided to burn down another gang's territory at two in the morning. They set fire to the houses, and my mom's parents never woke up. She was devastated."

Kera looked at Tis to see if she was following and was surprised at the look on her face. "What is it?"

Tis took Kera's hand in hers. "I was there, not long after it happened. Because of the nature of it, and how many people were involved, the Loas asked for help. My sisters and I came to deal with the gang members who had killed so many innocent people."

"YES!" Kera punched the air. "They didn't get away with it?"

Tis shook her head, looking at Kera thoughtfully. "They lived, most of them. But life was far from pleasant." She slipped her hand out of Kera's. "But what I do, the justice I have to serve, is never something I take lightly. Making sure people are held responsible for their actions and stopping those who take other's lives for granted is necessary. But it also comes with terrible responsibility."

"Power, responsibility, seriousness, punctuality, wearing black, solemnity. I get it. It still makes me happy. I'll never be sad when murdering bastards get what they deserve."

Tis frowned and stared at the seat back in front of her, clearly mulling that over. The sound of the landing gear coming down punctuated the tension between them. Kera looked over her seat at her stoic-faced bodyguards. "Isn't this going to be fun?"

Chapter Sixteen

Tis loved the heat of the Caribbean. It was so fantastically intense, so much like the sun had been in ancient Greece. Of course, the earth was warmer overall now, but even so, it was a lovely reminder. They grabbed their bags off the carousel, and Tis rolled her eyes at Kera's attempts to get her bodyguards to lug the baggage out to the car. They were surprisingly good at ignoring her completely, and Tis found Kera's frustration at failing to get a rise out of them more and more amusing. Tis went outside for air, figuring they'd catch up with her. The airport doors swished open, and Tis began to laugh.

"Papa Ghede! What on earth are you doing here?" She returned his massive hug, laughing as he snuggled his face between her breasts. She'd forgotten how short he was.

"Looking for you, of course. Old white beard rang to say you were coming and to make sure you had whatever you needed. Ain't no little Black god ever gonna say no to a White god with lightning in his hands, eh?" His genuine smile belied the sting of his words. His ever present cigarette never left his lips, and his black top hat sat slightly askew, making him look more like a caricature from a movie than one of the older gods.

He turned to Kera who came out telling some bawdy joke to her bodyguards, who didn't look amused. "And I'm here because of your mama, girlie. She was a fine woman, a fine priestess, and she had the finest ass ever slapped on a human. I'm here to help her cross."

Kera stared at him, looking completely bemused. "Did you just talk about my mother's butt? Who are you?" She looked at Tis, who still stood with her arm around him. "And how do you know one another?"

He laughed and flicked his cigarette to the curb as he motioned them into the large SUV. Tis took note of the bulletproof glass and was glad he was looking out for their safety. Gods weren't always cognizant of how fragile human bodies really were. But perhaps the loa, known for "mounting," or inhabiting their followers, were more aware than the gods who only saw them from the outside. She thought about Kera's reaction on the plane when she thought she'd seen someone she'd known. Her fear had called to Tis like a bullhorn, and although Tis had mentally searched the plane for anything dangerous, nothing—and no one—had felt out of place. She was grateful there'd be more of the supernatural sort around if anything went bad.

He got in the driver's side and turned to Kera, who was sitting in the passenger seat. He seemed to grow darker, his clothes blacker, and his eyes became endless pools of night. The scent of summer apples filled the car. "I'm Papa Ghede, child. You've heard your mother talk to me enough, haven't you? I'm the guardian of the gates, and I'm going to make sure your mama gets to the good side she deserves to be on." The darkness faded, he returned to his normal state, and he looked over his shoulder at Tis in the backseat. He gave a loud laugh and slapped the steering wheel. "And as for me and your lady in white, well, that's a tale best told with food and drink."

"So, what? You're god's taxi service?" One of Kera's bodyguards snickered, and she spun around to look at her. "You find *that* funny, but not my jokes? I don't get you at all. I'm going to tell Petra I need shadows with a better sense of humor." She turned back to Papa Ghede. "Sorry, go on. You were explaining why a loa picked us up from the airport instead of the cute redhead chauffeur I asked for."

He inclined his head, another cigarette already perched between his lips. "This is the first time I've been called, actually." He glanced at Tis in the rearview mirror, and she saw the seriousness in his eyes, although he was smiling for everyone else. "You see, it's not often we get visits from the folks at Afterlife these days, so it seemed like a good idea to make sure you were squared away. And that cute girl moved to the States. Now they've got a man who barely fits behind the wheel and smells of old fish every day. Be glad you got me, girlie."

"Hey, no complaints here. A loa picking me up from the airport means I really must have come up in the world. I mean, Dad's going to be so proud." She pretended to wipe away a tear, and Tis leaned forward to flick the back of her neck.

"I believe 'thank you' is the customary response to someone picking you up at the airport."

Kera rubbed the back of her neck and mumbled, "I would have been more thankful if it had been the redhead."

They rode in silence for a few minutes, with Papa Ghede humming cheerfully as he smoked. Tis had been hoping to make her phone calls on the way to the restaurant, but packed in as she was, there was no way. She closed her eyes and thought of her sisters, and was confused when she felt them at a massive gathering of humans, with intense conflict and aggression surrounding them. She certainly wasn't worried about their safety, but she couldn't get a sense of what was going on. She let go of the mental link, not wanting to distract them. She'd call the office when they were stationary again.

Suddenly, Kera said, "Hey, why don't you guys stay at Afterlife HQ? I mean, that's where all the other bigwig magic slingers live, right? Did you kill someone's pet chicken?"

"We're vegetarians now. Didn't anyone tell you?" He laughed. "As if. Can you imagine feeding the loas broccoli? We'd kill you for trying. Zed offered us a place at Afterlife, and we considered it, long and hard. But we don't have followers all over the place like the other gods do. Our home is here, and sometimes we head to Louisiana for a bit of fun, when they call us. There wasn't anything for us in California except some nice tail, and even then, most of them are too skinny for my liking."

Kera shifted around to look at Tis. "Are all gods this crude? Because, really, I would like them a hell of a lot more if they're all like this."

He nodded sagely.

Tis grinned. "Some are, but there's no one quite like Papa Ghede. His interest in sex is unparalleled, as far as I'm aware. Even Aphrodite isn't quite so…"

"Ready to go and willing to get." He laughed.

Tis was glad to see Kera laugh with him. She knew how Kera felt about the gods, immortals, and anything, generally, that didn't die. Fortunately, Papa Ghede seemed to be on her wavelength.

They pulled up outside a small restaurant with a bright green awning and equally bright tables beneath its shade. "Figured you'd want to see your dad first, eh?"

Kera nodded and started to get out, but stopped when he dropped the seat back and pulled his top hat over his eyes. "Not coming? What, my father isn't sexy enough for you?"

"Nope. No ass on that man at all." He peeked at her from under his hat. "Not to mention, he's not a big fan of ours, eh. Never was." He closed his eyes again. "I'll be here when your fine asses want to head to the house. Don't you worry."

Tis took Kera's hand in her own as they headed toward the front door. "You okay?"

Kera took a deep breath and looked at her seriously. "I knew this was going to be strange, that it would feel surreal without my mom here. But we just got picked up by the god my mom used to pray to all the time, as though that's the most natural thing in the world. I've got the most beautiful woman in the world at my side, and she can explode people's heads when she gets pissed off. Surreal isn't really covering it at this point." She looked at the restaurant. "And I haven't seen my dad in ages. What do I say?"

Tis squeezed her hand and placed a soft kiss on her cheek. "Don't overthink it. Start with a hug and go from there." Tis knew she was the last person to give family advice. Aside from her sisters, she didn't have the kind of family Kera was used to. But it still sounded good.

"Didn't you say your father ate his kids, usually?"

Tis shrugged. "We all have our family issues."

"Well, I guess my reunion wouldn't be anywhere near as uncomfortable as yours. Let's get inside."

They entered, and Tis loved the bright décor with typically Mexican murals everywhere. The smell of green chilies and paprika wafted out of the kitchen, and she was instantly salivating.

"Dad?" Kera called. She turned to her bodyguards. "Shoo, little barnacles. I don't need my dad thinking I've joined the mafia. Or a lesbian shot-putter squad."

They winced almost at the same time, though Tis saw one crack a smile. They took seats near the door, looking as inconspicuous in their all black suits as a pair of clowns in a cemetery.

A tall, handsome man with a handlebar mustache came out of the kitchen, wiping his hands on a towel. When he saw Kera, he threw the towel behind him and opened his arms. "Mija."

She stepped into his embrace, and Tis could feel the love they held for one another. She realized how rarely she was around humans who were happy, loved, and desired by one another. *She's showing me so many new things.*

He held Kera at arm's length and studied her. "You look tired. And like you've been living in California, eating granola and grass." He looked over her shoulder at Tis and raised his eyebrows. "But you've obviously done something right." Then he looked at the two women by the door. "Or you've kidnapped her."

Kera turned and motioned Tis forward. "Dad, this is Tisera Graves. She's my…" Kera grinned. "My escort. Tis, this is my dad, Ben."

Tis shook his hand, liking the warm, gentle energy exuding from him. "It's nice to meet you."

"And I, you. Come, girls, sit down and have some of my fresh tamales." He looked at the bodyguards. "Do I feed your dark, probably overheating friends, too?"

Kera slid into a chair. "I'd be interested in seeing them eat, actually. I've come to believe they feed on the essence of black clothing and rocks. Unlike Tis, who eats people and peanut butter ice cream."

He shrugged, as though used to bizarre things coming out of his daughter's mouth. "I don't have any of those things, but I do have tamales and fresh salsa. Be right back."

He hustled back into the kitchen, and Tis liked how incredibly relaxed Kera seemed. "See? Nothing to worry about."

Kera looked contemplative. "He's thinner than he used to be. I don't remember that much gray in his hair, either." She took Tis's hand. "That human limitation thing, huh?"

Tis squeezed her hand gently. "Sadly. But he had your mother and you, and that can make life very much worth living." Even as she said the words, she felt like an utter hypocrite. She, who'd spent decades alone because she'd become disillusioned with her work and yet, buried herself in it at the same time. She had her sisters, and perhaps that was along similar lines. But then, they'd never die, so it wasn't exactly the same. It seemed like a higher value was placed on things and relationships when someone knew they were, one day, going to lose them. It made her wonder if she'd been taking her sisters for granted. And even maybe Zed, who as God relationships went, was kind of like an uncle. Or was she his aunt? Either way, he was family. Perhaps it was time to start treating him like it.

She was startled from her reverie by Ben bringing in large platters of tamales, with sides of refried beans and Mexican rice. It was an enormous amount of food, and it wasn't even eleven in the morning, but Tis dug in eagerly. He then took two more plates to Kera's bodyguards, who graciously accepted the food, and ignored Kera's instructions to put aside their desire for boulders instead.

He sat with Tis and Kera while they ate, and he and Kera caught up on the news of Kera's many "aunties," only two of whom she was actually related to. But her mother had been a popular priestess, as well as a friend to many, and Kera had grown up surrounded by loving women.

"Ben, why did you come back to Haiti?" Tis asked when Kera's mouth was full. "I understand you and your wife lived in Florida for most of your time together?"

He looked at Kera fondly before answering. "We loved Florida. We lived in Louisiana, too, down New Orleans way. Hell, for a while we even lived in New York." He rubbed his arms like he had goose bumps. "Coldest place I've ever been. We hated it, all that concrete and noise. It was like the city just went and gobbled up the night sky." He wiped at the tears in his eyes. "Eventually, we had enough money. We had enough everything, and we wanted a simpler life. I'm from Mexico City, and I didn't have any desire to live in a city again. I loved the weather, the beaches, the slow way of life here, and this place was my wife's heartbeat." He shrugged. "So, with Kera running around the world saving humanity, we figured we'd come back." He took Kera's hand in his own. "She was happy, at the end. You should know that. She was so damn proud of you, and when all those photographs of you and various women would show up in magazines or on TV, she'd just pop another cigar on the altar for Papa Ghede and Erzulie and hope you were having a damn good time."

"You're a follower of Vodun as well?" Tis asked.

"No, *mija*. Not me. I was an atheist, actually. I thought it was all based on superstition and folks who liked incense. Now that they're here…well, I can't say I don't believe in something standing in front of me. But I don't have to like that they're here, and I don't have to agree with them."

"Amen to that." Kera swallowed the last bite of her food.

Tis flinched slightly, trying not to take it personally, though it stung. They'd set aside their differences for the moment, but faced with two people who wished she, and people like her, didn't exist, was not only insulting, it also hurt.

"Well, if you don't mind, I'll go wait with one of those beings now." She stood and shook Ben's hand, allowing her eyes to change ever so slightly. "Thank you for the meal. It was lovely." She turned to Kera. "In fact, maybe it would be best if you spent some more time with your father and got a ride back with him? I'll have Papa Ghede bring me to the house a little later, if that's okay?"

Kera stared at her, clearly oblivious to what had happened. "Sure…okay. You're not going to disappear, are you?" Her tone was light, but Tis could see the worry in her eyes.

"I'll be there, don't worry." She gave her a light kiss on the cheek before heading into the bright midday heat. She climbed in beside Papa Ghede who shoved his hat up slightly to look at her.

"Dancing with the flames, loving a human. Especially that one."

Tis sighed and closed her eyes. "Do you have somewhere the loa go? Somewhere behind the veil?"

He sat up and lit another cigarette before starting the car. "That we do."

They pulled away, and the ache in Tis's heart made her want to turn around, go back in, and listen to more stories. But then, she needed a moment to think about what it meant to be with someone who wanted her, but didn't want her "kind."

CHAPTER SEVENTEEN

Kera's dad cleared their dishes and she followed him back into the kitchen. She puzzled over the conversation and realized where they'd gone wrong. The problem was, as much as she wanted Tis in her life and loved being around her, it didn't change how she felt about the gods and their limitations.

"Well, that was interesting." Her dad placed the dishes on the counter, and she saw his hands shaking slightly.

"Sorry. Maybe she was tired from the flight. Or tired of me, although I can't imagine that being possible." She grinned, and her dad shook his head.

"That's not what I meant." He faced her, a dishcloth pulled tight between his hands. "What is she?"

"Aside from a spectacular woman and a lioness in bed?" Her dad didn't smile. *Well, this is happening sooner than I planned.* "She's a fury. One of three, actually. She and her sisters are in charge of making scumbags pay for doing scumbag things."

His brow furrowed as he thought. "It's been a while since my mythology days. Weren't they supposed to be hideous?"

"Believe me, you wouldn't want to see her pissed off. And in her natural form, yeah, she looks pretty different. But she's stunningly beautiful, in that way that makes you want to drop to your knees and praise whoever gave birth to her."

"So, there's an age gap. Not to mention the everything-else gap." Her father looked genuinely bothered.

"What, specifically, is your objection?"

He leaned against the counter, looking older than she wanted him to be. "The gods are turning the world upside down. Papa Ghede is always out among the women, and the other loas are in bars, clubs, hell, they even come here sometimes. They're not like us, and yet they are. It's like they're the best and worst of us, and nothing in between."

What he said made her think of Petra's story and the issue of fading once people had stopped believing in her. Did that mean they couldn't exist without believers? She needed to give it some serious thought. "Tis isn't like that. Neither are her sisters. They're the ones who try to make the world better by making sure there are consequences to shithead behavior."

He started cleaning, a sure sign he was bothered. "Plenty of the gods say they're good, benevolent. But how many actually are?" He turned and took her shoulders gently in his big hands. "Are you so sure of what, and who, she is? If it came down to her kind or ours, who would she choose, *hija*? When we were praying for your mother, when we begged the loa to tell Bondye to spare her, did they? Of course not. They turned their backs, the way they always do. People here are still living in hovels, in poverty, no matter how much they pray. It isn't right."

He let go of her and returned to his cleaning.

"Dad, they're not going away. They're here, so we have to deal with them in some way. And I really like Tis. She's strong and smart. She cares really deeply about people."

"You agree with me, though, that the gods can go right back to wherever the hell they came from?"

Kera sighed. "I was hoping we could at least have some normal time together before we jumped into the religious stuff."

"And we would have, if you weren't dating…her."

"But I am, and we have enough crap to deal with, without you pissing off the one girlfriend I've had who could make Jell-O out of our brains." She turned him away from his cleaning and hugged him tightly. "I don't know how it's going to work out. Maybe it won't. But she's here, and she's my guest. Play nice, okay?"

He sighed and rested his chin on the top of her head. "Okay, *mija*. I will, because I love you." He moved back and looked down at her. "Did she say Papa Ghede was outside waiting?"

❖

The bumpy road was lined with massive palms that quickly led to a beautiful canopy of lush, tall trees. The air cooled considerably and made Tis's skin tingle. They drove through the small village outside the Saut-d'Eau waterfall, before parking near the one-hundred-foot waterfall itself. "We'll hike up from here. Or you can wrap me in those big ol' wings of yours and fly us on up."

Tis grinned at the cheeky little god. "I could do that. Where are we going?"

He pointed at the top of the waterfall. "There's some caves behind the water toward the top. You have to see it to believe it."

She gladly let the magic fall away and stretched her wings to their full length. She lifted her face to the dappled sunlight and took in the silence and beauty around them. When she looked back at Papa Ghede, he was staring at her open-mouthed.

"Well, damn. I'm glad you folks don't come around here too often. You'd make a god feel downright human. I forgot just how impressive you and your sisters are." He rubbed his hands together. "Now, show me what it's like to fly."

She moved behind him and wrapped her arms around his waist, grinning when he snuggled in closer to her. "Behave." She leapt into the air and laughed when he gave a shout of pure glee. She flew over the trees, allowing his legs to skate along the treetops, before turning and heading toward the waterfall again.

"Just there, next to the rock that looks like a breast."

Water crashed over them as she flew them straight through the fall and into the cave beyond. She set him down, ignoring his excited babble about wishing he had wings, and breathed in the familiar scent of ancient, wet stone. It brought back so many memories, her eyes flooded with tears. A cackling laugh brought her out of her reverie.

"Well, goodness me. It's been a thousand and one years since I've seen you, lady." Loko, the loa equivalent to Tis, came from the back of the cave with a smile. With her shock of white hair and her cane, she looked like a hobbling Q-tip. Tis returned the hug that belied the old lady veneer.

"It very may well have been," Tis said.

Loko shrugged. "No matter, lady. The only reason time matters is because people live and die. For us…well. Come in. We've got a stock of white rum and lots of fresh coconuts."

Tis followed Papa Ghede and Loko toward the back of the cave, where she was surprised to see sunlight. They came to a massive circular area with a huge opening above that acted as a sort of skylight. Water trickled from its edges into a green sea-glass colored pool. Around the pool were lounge chairs and tables covered with drinks. Reclining on one of the chairs was Erzuli, a complex goddess with many roles among the Vodun worshippers.

She raised her glass at Tis. "Welcome back, ancient one. We wondered when Afterlife would send someone to check on us." Erzuli ignored Papa Ghede, as his crass behavior had always been beneath her.

Tis accepted the cold glass from Loko with a nod of thanks and settled by the pool. "Is it okay if I put my feet in this?"

"If you strip down, you can put all of you in it." Papa Ghede laughed around the cigarette in his mouth and wiggled his eyebrows.

"Just my feet is fine. What a remarkable place you've got."

Erzuli nodded, clearly pleased at the compliment. "Isn't it? The whole area is veiled, of course. There are a number of caves and tunnels that lead off this one, and we each have our own area. All of them have openings and pools like this one."

"Magnificent." Tis plunged her feet into the cool water and sighed happily. With her eyes still closed, she said, "I'm not here for Afterlife, by the way. I'm here with a friend, for her mother's year and a day ceremony."

"Mambo Espinosa, over in Petion-ville." Papa Ghede sat next to Tis and murmured appreciatively when he put his feet in the cool water.

Loko sighed. "She was one of the best. A true believer. And boy, did she know how to feed a loa."

Erzuli looked far more interested now. "You've come with her daughter, then?"

"Kera. She asked me to come and meet her family, and go through the ritual with her."

The three of them were quiet, and Tis got the feeling she'd said something wrong. "What is it?"

"You know outsiders aren't welcome at the ceremony, Tisera. I'm surprised she invited you at all, but I'm even more surprised she thinks her family would allow it."

Tis hadn't even considered it, and she should have. She knew the laws of every religion in every culture, but blinded by her desire to be with Kera, she'd forgotten an important aspect of the Vodun belief system.

"Well, it may be that I ask for your hospitality more than I'd intended to."

Erzuli rose, sensual, graceful, and remote all at once. "You know you're always welcome here, snake lady. We have plenty of space. But perhaps you should discuss it with the Espinosa daughter first. If you're involved, hiding here with us isn't going to make things easier."

"You've dealt with her before, I assume?"

Papa Ghede laughed. "Not me, but Erzu came across her more than once. That girl got around before she left, let me tell you. Not a piece of ass was safe if she decided she wanted to play with it. Women threw themselves at her—"

"Enough." Loko's voice was quiet but stern. "You've been spending too much time among them, Papa G. Don't forget yourself, and what you are."

He bowed his head respectfully toward her. "Yes, Mama. Sorry."

She turned to Tis. "The girl had little time for us, like her father. Because her mother was such a supporter, we were often around the family, and the girl often saw us. But she'd act like we were petro loa and avoid us whenever possible."

The petro loa were the bad loa, the ones responsible for chaos and dark magic, and Tis would gladly avoid them as well. "She thinks there's no point to religion, that it only makes people weak and gives them excuses to behave poorly. And that the gods don't actually help people."

Loko waved her hand derisively. "Bah. We help the ones we can. But you know the drill. Their whole system revolves around things being the way they are for a reason. They pray, but it's half-hearted at best, unless it's about health or sex."

"Nothing wrong with praying for sex."

Tis looked at Papa G. "You're not having sex with the human women, are you?"

"When they call me, you bet your fine pretty wings I do. Sometimes as me, sometimes I mount the fellow she's already with, although I have to do that a lot less now that we're allowed to be out with them."

Tis thought about the councils constantly happening at Afterlife and how far removed they were from places like this, where the laws would feel optional rather than obligatory. The next time she was in the office, she needed to consider the ramifications of that.

Papa G began to laugh. "Your girl is calling. She's using prayer to say they're home and asking that I bring you back."

Tis laughed. "Well, at least she knows you're listening." Sad to leave the beautiful sanctuary, she took her feet from the pool and dried them. It felt so much like the places she'd loved when she was young. "No need to bring me back, but thank you. I'll fly."

Loko stood and gave her another long hug. "Come back whenever you want, snake lady. And don't forget we're here when you go back to your big concrete building."

She held Loko tightly, drawing on her strength and sureness.

As she turned to leave the cave, she heard Erzuli say quietly behind her, "You're going to have to make a choice, Fury. The things we see, they stay as shadows in our souls, and we carry the ghosts of the dead with us, even after they cross. The world is being reborn, and that's never painless. When the time comes to choose, do so with your heart as well as your head. Those of us living between life and death don't have the luxury of only using one."

Tis turned to ask questions, but she was already gone, and Tis was alone on the edge of the cave, the waterfall crashing behind her. With a sigh, she turned to fly to Kera's family home.

CHAPTER EIGHTEEN

Kera relaxed into the sound of the drums beating in the background as her aunties gathered for the first night's ceremonies. They came from all over and would have even if her parents' house was too small to accommodate everyone. But it was one of the larger houses in Petion-ville, thanks to her mother's career in science. Her father didn't need to work, since her mother had made enough to set them up for a comfortable retirement, but he'd go stir crazy without something to do, and cooking had always been his second love.

She hugged this auntie and that one. Although she couldn't explain it if asked, she knew the second Tis arrived. She felt like a piece of herself had just come back to her. She looked around and saw her father give Tis a smile as she headed inside to find Kera. Their eyes met across the room, and Kera felt it, as she always did—that tingle that shot right through her, a frisson of electric desire. She smiled and was awed by the beauty of Tis's smile in return.

"Hey."

Kera took Tis's hand in hers. "I was worried you wouldn't come back. That you'd caught a ride back with one of those little sea nymphs or something. Since Papa Ghede got us from the airport, I figured I'd try talking to him telepathically, like you do with your sisters. Did it work?"

Tis kissed her knuckles. "It did, although I'm not sure other gods would take kindly to being a messenger service. And as for running off with the sea nymph, I dislike trying to breathe underwater, and I told you I'd be back. I just needed some time to think. We've got things to work out, but we don't have to do it now." She looked around the increasingly crowded room. "You've got plenty of other things to think about."

"And who is this, girlie?"

They turned to face a behemoth of a woman wearing a red floral print dress with massive matching flowers in her hair. She had a red scarf around her neck and flat red shoes to match. Her smile was broad, but the expression in her eyes was suspicious.

"This is my friend Tisera. Tis, this is my auntie Goslin, my mother's sister."

Goslin shook Tis's hand but looked at Kera. "It's good you have a friend, but you know we don't allow *moun deyò* here. This is for your mama and those who knew her."

"Believe me when I say, I'm pretty certain the loa won't mind Tis being here, even if she is an outsider."

"You can't know what the loa think—"

"Oh, I think we can." Kera kept hold of Tis's hand, liking the way it grounded her. Not that she ever needed grounding, of course. "They're out there telling us all the time these days, aren't they?" She felt Tis stiffen slightly beside her and quickly stopped herself. "Auntie G, she was my mama, and she'd be glad I've found someone I wanted to bring home. It's not up to anyone but me and dad."

Auntie G shrugged and turned to walk away. "It's *your* mama's soul journey. Do what you want."

Kera frowned, and Tis squeezed her hand to get her attention. When she looked at her, Tis was smiling.

"Baby, don't let them get to you. Remember, people believe in different ways because they have different needs. Papa Ghede himself picked us up, and he's coming to make sure your mother crosses over the way she should. None of these people's concerns will make an iota of difference to that. I promise, and believe me, I know. That said, it's true that I'm an outsider. Are you sure you want me here?"

Kera smiled and then laughed loudly. "Nothing like it coming from the horse's mouth. Or fury's mouth, as the case may be." She leaned forward and gave Tis a soft kiss. "Yes. I most certainly want you here. I never liked that auntie anyway."

The head priestess called the ceremony to start. One by one, people placed offerings to the loa on a massive black clothed altar that included a picture of Kera's mother. Cigars, apples, cigarettes, peanuts, and coconuts, as well as little bottles of rum were placed among brilliant white lilies.

The mambo began with the desounen prayers, meant to get the soul to let go of the real world, and the chanting and drumming grew louder as she asked the loa to join them. Tis squeezed Kera's hand and nodded toward the back of the room. Kera looked in the direction she indicated and saw Papa Ghede standing with a beautiful woman, whom she assumed was Erzuli, an entity she'd seen when her mother had called on her during ceremonies. And then, she saw a shimmer, like oil on water in the midday sun, between them. The longer she looked, the louder the chanting and prayers became, the more the figure solidified.

Jolted, she realized it was her mother.

But not her mother. The figure was insubstantial and looked... wet. Puzzled, she looked at Tis. "Why does she look wet? And... why is she here?" She felt shaken in a way she never had before. Her mother used to lead these rituals with passion and fire. Now, she watched impassively, almost like she didn't see what was going on.

"If I'm not mistaken, souls go into the water during the year and a day, correct? So she's come from the water. And souls are often present throughout their leaving ceremonies, in any religion. It's their time to say good-bye as well."

Kera shook herself. "Stupid me. Of course. I guess I'm not thinking."

The chanting grew louder, the dancing more frantic. Kera felt the drumbeat in her stomach, and she couldn't tear her eyes away from her mother, who continued to grow faintly more real looking by the minute. The chanting stopped, and the mambo raised the struggling chicken over her head.

"A gift for Papa Ghede and Erzuli, for the loa who see our loved ones home." She held the chicken over a bowl, and an assistant slit its neck. The blood poured into a bowl, steam rising from it as hot liquid hit cold marble. "Hear us, loa! We pray for our mambo, we ask Loko to get ready to take her home to Bondye."

After about an hour or so, Papa Ghede put his arm around Kera's mother, and he, Erzuli, and Kera's mother walked out. Kera felt a moment of panic swell in her chest. "Where are they going? Why isn't anybody else watching them?"

Tis pulled her close. "Deities don't stick around for long, unless something really interesting is happening, and I have a feeling they're not visible to anyone but us at the moment. Sacred ceremonies can lose a bit of their focus if the god is right there in their midst. Ironic, really. Anyway, the initial prayers have called your mother from the water. Now, everyone can go relax until tomorrow night."

Kera looked at Tis, needing to know. "Can I go see her? Talk to her?"

Tis frowned thoughtfully. "I don't know, but I doubt it. We can ask, if you like?"

"Please." Kera hadn't ever had to beg, at least not in a situation that didn't involve a bed and ropes, but right now, she'd gladly drop to her knees if there was a chance she could say a proper good-bye to her mother. Tis took her hand, and she followed her out, ignoring the glares and frowns of the people around her. They went outside and found Kera's father leaning against an old, bent palm tree, looking up at the sky. He smiled at them when they came out.

"Too much?"

Kera hesitated. From the time she was a child, she'd told him she could see things other people couldn't, and he'd never doubted her, even if he was an atheist. When the gods had come out, he'd actually called and apologized for not being more supportive. But from their conversation earlier, she knew he probably didn't want to hear much about the other world. "Maybe a little."

"You know, I thought I could feel her. Just for a minute, it was like she was this close to me, like I could almost touch her..." He smiled sadly. "Crazy, isn't it?"

Kera's heart hurt for him. She couldn't imagine his pain. She'd lost her mother, but he'd lost his soul mate. "No, Dad. It's not crazy at all. I felt it too. But that's the point, right? To call her back so we can send her on properly."

He shook his head and looked at Tis, his expression sad and serious. "So, ancient one? Tell me about Heaven. Tell me where I'm supposed to find my wife."

Kera looked at Tis, curious as to how she'd answer. She hadn't given much thought to the issues of Heaven and Hell as real, but if the gods existed... "Wow. So those places exist too?"

Tis stared at her feet, and Kera could tell she was thinking.

"Yes. Heaven exists. As does Hell. And Nirvana, Gan Eden, Vaikuntha, Hades, and Samsara. Whatever religion it is, the afterlife does actually exist. So, your wife will go to the version of Heaven believed in by the Vodun."

"Oh?" He pushed away from the tree and came to stand in front of Tis. His grief was almost palpable. "And what does that mean for me? I'm not a follower of any religion. Does that mean I never see my wife again?"

Tis took his hand, and Kera was surprised to see he didn't pull it away.

"Before the gods came out, what did you think would happen?" Tis asked.

Tears slipped down his cheeks. "I thought that was it. We'd get buried next to one another, and our bodies would feed the earth. Cycle of life and all that."

"And now?"

He began to cry in earnest, and Kera wrapped her arms around him, her own heart breaking.

"And now I know she's accessible, that we could, maybe, have some kind of eternity together. Except that even though I know her gods are real now, I just can't..." He choked on a sob. "I can't bring myself to go in there and pretend like I'm praying to the bastards. What does that say about me?"

Tis shook her head slightly. "It means you have your beliefs, just like she had hers. Yes, admittedly, it would be easier for you to see her again if you could believe what she did. But you don't, and faking it won't work very well. I suppose the new question is this:

now that you know the place itself exists, can you believe in it? Perhaps that's the best place to start."

He cried on Kera's shoulder until the drumming and chanting slowly eased, and when people began wandering outside, he pulled away and wiped his face with his sleeve. "Guess we have to play host, huh?" He wrapped his arm around Kera and gave Tis a small smile. "Thank you, Tisera, for your honesty. You've given me something to think about." He walked away, his shoulders slumped and his hands in his pockets.

Kera looked at Tis, trying to see her for the immortal she was, rather than the extremely hot and very pale woman she wanted sleeping in her arms tonight, but it didn't work. Right now, she just wanted comfort from the real, kind woman standing beside her. But comfort would have to wait. "I'm sorry. I should go talk to people…"

Tis leaned down and gave her a quick kiss. "It's okay, of course. Do what you need to do. I'll meet you back at the house later, okay? I'll talk to the others and see if I can get you access to your mom."

Kera nodded and watched as Tis walked into the grove of trees. Her dad wandered back over and put his arm around Kera's shoulders. When the heat shimmer surrounded Tis, Kera knew no one else could see the moment when she spread her glorious white wings and leapt into the air. Her dad stiffened, and she realized to him it would look like Tis simply disappeared.

"Believe me, you want to be ready for it when she shows you what she really looks like. Women worry about someone seeing them with no makeup on the morning after? Imagine them with fangs and feathers."

Her dad shook his head and plastered on a smile. "We'll talk more about that later. For now, let's say hello to your aunties."

Kera let him lead her away, though she looked over her shoulder a few times to see if she could spot Tis in the air anywhere. No such luck. As she started the round of pleasantries with her dad, she felt Tis's absence in a part of her she hadn't known existed. And it was very close to her heart.

Chapter Nineteen

Tis felt her phone ring in her pocket and answered it mid flight. She'd meant to call the office when she landed, but with everything going on, it had slipped her mind.

"Seriously. I was about to send out a search party. Where have you been?" Meg sounded utterly out of sorts.

"I linked with you and saw you and Alec in some weird situation, and I didn't want to distract you. Then, well, I got distracted. What's going on?"

Alec's voice came on a second line. "Things are getting a little crazy. We were called to Mount Sinai. The Big C and Yahweh both went there to preach. They wanted to show a united front, and maybe get some of that clarification stuff done in a big way. People came to listen by the thousands, but things went haywire. Rich people who wanted to be at the front, closest to their gods, got in their Humvees and literally drove over people to get there. Who does that right in front of their gods? It was like they're not connecting religion with right or wrong."

Meg took over, sounding a little less harried. "And then, when the gods were talking, people started shouting questions, not listening. Someone threw a punch at another follower, and all of a sudden, it's a holy mosh pit. People beating the crap out of one another, saying they're right and the other guys are wrong...even though the big guys themselves were *right there*."

As insane as it all sounded, Tis could believe it. Things hadn't always gone well when the Christian God, or the Big C, as they called him, came around. "So what happened?"

Alec laughed. "Well, we got involved with the jackasses who drove over people, and that got plenty of attention, slowed things down a little. Then Big C started in with the thunder and lightning, and Yahweh started smiting a couple of the particularly nasty instigators. When fried bodies started flying through the air, folks settled down considerably."

Tis landed on the cliffside waterfall and sat down, letting her feet swing in the rushing water. "And do you think people actually listened then?"

"They seemed to, yeah. But there wasn't any more soft speaking. It was all thunderous voices and threats of damnation, you know?" Meg sighed. "It was pretty awesome to see in action again, to be honest. But the people…the way they just ignored their gods and turned on one another…it was creepy. It's like people needed to see their vengeful sides to remember what they are."

"The thing is, Tis, there's talk that the coalition has made them weak. That they've gone soft because they aren't allowed to…well, to be gods."

Tis could tell Alec was treading carefully, not wanting to offend her. "Who said they couldn't be gods? Certainly not me. As a group they agreed to no killing off the believers of other groups and to directing their own believers not to kill. I find it hard to believe they can't be gods without those things."

There was silence, and Tis knew her sisters didn't have answers, just as she didn't.

Meg finally said, "Are you coming home soon? I have a feeling they could use your logic and reasoning in their meetings."

Tis thought of Kera and her promise to stay with her during this difficult week. She thought of Kera's dad's tears, of the loa lounging in the caves below her. *I promised.* "Not until the end of the week. I made a commitment I have to see through here. And you know, maybe it's good for the gods to see that it's not going to be easy being gods. Maybe it will be good for them to have to work at it and actually try to make the world better. Let's see if they can step up."

"They're calling Jesus the hippie god, and he's taken to it like a mushroom to the dark. But I have a feeling, if you need an ally, he's going to be the one to go to. Buddha is always good for a chat, too."

Tis ran through her mental list of gods and their attributes. "As much as I love our peaceful colleagues, I think I may have to appeal to our more moody ones to make real impact. I'll see when I get back. How are you two doing?"

"Alec and Selene are too busy trying to make little demi-fury babies to hang out with me." Meg sounded like she was pouting. "Hey! Stop that."

Tis laughed, knowing that Alec had probably pinched her wing. "Babies?"

"That's just our sister's way of letting you know she's not getting any, and she's jealous."

"I blame Selene. I was getting plenty when the gods had nothing better to do. Now everyone's rushing from this place to that temple. Hardly anyone came to my party last weekend."

Tis shook her head. Trust Meg to be put out that people actually had to go to work now and weren't looking for ways to fritter away their time. "I'm sure things will settle out eventually, and you'll get your harem back."

"I don't need a harem. They're too much work. I'd settle for a hard body with a—"

A touch on her shoulder made Tis jump so much that she nearly tumbled off the edge of the cliff and into the waterfall. A strong hand pulled her back, and she looked up to see Erzulie smiling down at her.

"We're having dinner and wanted to know if you'd like to join us?"

"Who is that? Who are you with? That's not your girlfriend, is it?" Meg's curiosity blared through the phone.

"Please give your sisters my love, and come down when you're ready." Erzulie gave her a mischievous smile and walked away, her multicolored silk skirt swaying sensually.

"It's Erzulie. I'm at her place with Papa Ghede."

Alec whistled. "Nice. I haven't been to Vodun country in ages. Have a good time, and keep in touch, okay? At least that way we can keep you up to date so you know what's breaking loose here, and you don't come back blind."

Tis loved Alec's ever present concern for her. "I will, thanks. And shout whenever. If I can't answer, I'll get back to you as soon as I can."

"Ooh, find out if Erzulie can still do that thing with her thumb and forefinger—"

Laughing, Tis hung up and headed down into the caves. Although the situation with believers and the gods was worrying, for the moment, here among those who didn't need to get involved in the politics of it all, she could relax. Stress would be her bread and butter once she returned. For now, she'd take all the time with Kera she possibly could. Their time together once they left Haiti was uncertain at best. If she wanted passion and something resembling romance, even for a moment, this was her chance. Once she left, it was absolutely possible both of their lives would become too chaotic to sustain anything more than an occasional phone call or text. The thought made her incredibly sad. For the first time in so long, she'd found someone she really wanted to spend time with. But Kera wasn't a fan of the immortal set, and when she returned and saw the chaos, she'd probably be even more inclined that way. What could that mean for them? *And what if I agree with her?*

Kera rested her chin on her knees, her arms wrapped tightly around them. The heavy night air buzzed with cicadas and a distant Latin beat. Her father gave a deep sigh next to her, and she flicked a bit of condensation from her beer at him. "Thoughts?"

He gave her a tired smile. "It's nice to see how many people loved your *mamacita*. But I wish I could be alone with my thoughts of her, you know? Instead of listening to everyone else's memory of her."

"I get that. I think some people need to tell you about their time with her, though. Not for you, necessarily, but because they need the person closest to her to validate their experience of her."

He sipped his beer and looked at her contemplatively. "When did you become so jaded, mija?"

Kera shook her head. "Not jaded. Just practical."

He reached over and touched her hand. "Was it that bad? What happened?"

She gently moved his hand and sat back, just out of reach. She couldn't have him touching her, not with that topic at hand. "I don't want to talk about it."

A shadow fell over them, blocking the night sky briefly before Tis landed lightly in front of them, her beautiful white wings and hair nearly glowing against the black night. She took Kera's breath away, and her heart felt like it could burst.

Her father grunted and raised an eyebrow. "That's something I won't get used to." His smile was softer, more open. He looked at Kera. "Back to the subject. It might be good for you to talk about it."

"And since he asked," Tis said, "I'd also like to hear the story. I enjoy our well-built entourage, and I'd chalk it up to you being absurdly wealthy, but that doesn't fit. Not to mention, they weren't with you in France, which suggests there's some new issue you're facing."

Kera frowned slightly. She didn't want Tis thinking about how well-built her bodyguards were. She'd have to get Petra to send her some weakling guys instead. Eunuchs, maybe. Or trolls. "Really? We need to do this tonight?"

Her father stretched and settled more fully into his chair. "I don't have anything better to do. You, Tis?"

"Nope. I'm all ears." Tis leaned down and gave Kera a soft, lingering kiss, before moving behind her. She straddled the lounge chair Kera was sitting on and pulled Kera back between her legs. She nuzzled her neck slightly and said, "Please."

Kera sighed and closed her eyes. She liked the soft, warm embrace of Tis's arms, the way she felt safe and grounded. She pictured her mother, how kind and generous she'd been. Maybe her father was right. Maybe now was exactly the right time. She pushed back against Tis, who seemed to understand and hugged her tighter.

"Mom was so brilliant. Really incredible. The discoveries she made moved science forward decades. After I graduated from college, we started working together on a joint project. She was really interested in researching airborne diseases and in trying to figure out ways to stop them." Kera felt the weight descend on her chest as she started reliving the story. "We hit some roadblocks with funding, and Mom decided it was time to retire. She loved the research but not the politics."

Her dad laughed. "I can't think of anything she hated more."

Kera smiled at him, and the knot in her stomach eased slightly. "Right? So, she retired, but I kept going, trying to play the game while still getting the work done. And it turned out, I was damn good at politics. But then all our funding was cut, right when we were really getting somewhere, and we had to shut the lab down. And then…these guys showed up. They said they were researchers out of Moscow, and they'd read the little bit we'd published about our work. They said they were opening a new lab in Siberia and were willing to fund our continued research."

Kera could still smell the leader's cologne, could still see the scar beside his left eye. She breathed deeply and kept going. "I gathered a small team, and we went to Siberia. There's a reason they send criminals there as the harshest penalty, let me tell you. It really is godforsaken." She gave a dry laugh and tapped Tis's leg. "Is it?"

"In a way. Since most of the people there are criminals, their prayers aren't usually answered."

Kera loved that Tis gave a serious answer to a sarcastic question. It made her grateful all the more for her presence. "Yeah, that makes sense, I guess. Anyway, the lab was state-of-the-art. High quality everything, and anything I asked for, I got. Suddenly, I made a breakthrough, and my research took off. There was a problem, though."

"You didn't like what you found?" Tis said.

"Because I was looking for a cure, I had to create versions of diseases within the lab, so I could then create antidotes on test matter. But there was a crazy mutation, and one of the diseases turned out to be so virulent it caused death within minutes. And then it started to happen with another virus, too. It was like some kind of horrifying contagion that attacked other viruses and couldn't be contained properly. I decided I had no option but to shut down the entire program."

Her dad stared at her, clearly horrified. "That kind of weapon…"

"Yeah." Kera took a long drink of her beer. "The guys who were paying my way showed up just as I started burning everything. They stopped me, gathered my team. Then…then they started asking questions."

She'd never been so glad for comfort as she was when Tis wrapped her wings around her. The soft feathers, along with the strength of her arms and her steady heartbeat against Kera's back, allowed her to breathe again. She paused to steady herself. No one but Ajan knew this story, and she hadn't had to say the words out loud to anyone else, ever. Now she was saying them to two of the most important people in her world. "They demanded all the notes. They wanted me to tell them everything. I'd encrypted the notes in my own little code and kept a lot of it in my head. I refused to tell them."

Her dad stood and held up a hand. "Wait. Let me get us another beer. You want one, Tis?"

"Please." When he'd gone inside, Tis rested her head against Kera's. "I've seen enough to have an idea what happened next. Are you sure you want to go on?"

Kera considered the question seriously before she answered. "You know, I think I do. Dad's right. I need to say it out loud to someone other than law enforcement."

"You never told anyone?"

"And risk putting them in danger? The only person I talked to about it is Ajan. He came to stay with me after I got back to the States, and I asked him to work for GRADE. He said he'd only do it if I told him why I kept waking up screaming. He brought me through the worst of it. Anyway, at least here, with just you and my dad, I know no one else is listening."

Her dad came back and handed them both frosty cold beers. "Okay, mija. Go on."

She wondered if her dad had needed the break or if he'd known she needed one. Either way, she was grateful. "They locked me in a cell below ground with no windows. Each night they brought me upstairs and sat one of my staff in front of me. They demanded answers and beat the hell out of my staff member, until eventually they shot them." Kera choked on the words and felt bile rise in the back of her throat as the smell of blood and gunpowder flooded her senses. The defeat and sadness in her staff's eyes as they watched her, knowing full well she wouldn't trade any of their lives, including her own, for the kind of information that could kill millions. "When there was no one left, they started on me. No food or water. The kinds of thing I imagine our own CIA do to people. But I wouldn't give in."

He wiped tears away, his shoulders hunched forward as though to ward off blows. "Oh, mija. Damn those men. If I'd known—"

"That's why I never told you. Or anyone else."

"How did you get away?" Tis's voice was soft, but Kera heard the anger in it.

"I thought I was about to die. I was lying there, watching the rats moving in the shadows, and I knew it was my last night. I regretted a lot of things, but not being able to say good-bye to you and Mama was the worst." Kera wiped away her tears, but they kept falling. "And then the cell door opened, and some guy I'd never seen came in. He said, 'Time to go,' and carried me out of the cell. I passed out, and when I came to, I was in an American chopper with an IV in my arm and an oxygen mask on my face."

"How did they know where to find you? Or that they needed to?"

Kera shook her head and relaxed into Tis's embrace. The worst of it was out. "Apparently, one of my staff members had managed to get out an incomplete SOS call right after we were captured. He sent it to a friend in a lab he'd worked at in Geneva. It took the guy a while to decode it, but once he did, he got in touch with the American embassy. My staff member had told him just enough about what we were doing that he knew we were in serious trouble, and had a damn good idea of why. When he told the embassy, they put together a rescue crew. Of course, by the time they got there, I was the only one left."

"Did they catch the bastards?" Her dad's grip was so tight on his bottle his knuckles were white.

"No. The place was empty when they arrived. Someone must have tipped them off. The FBI wanted to put me in witness protection, but I refused. I'd been under guard and constantly watched in that hellhole, and I wasn't about to go into that shit again consensually. But Petra found a lead on the head guy that suggests he's still watching me." She gestured toward her bodyguards, who were sitting under palm trees just far enough away to be out of range of conversation, as usual. "And so, I've got the Burly Twins."

They stayed silent, and Kera wondered what was going through Tis's and her father's minds. Finally, he stood and opened his arms. Kera left Tis's warm embrace and stood. Her father enfolded her so tightly she could barely breathe, and she hugged him back just as fiercely. He pulled back and held her chin in his hand.

"You did right, mija. Your mama would have been proud, no matter what."

Kera sobbed in her father's arms. When the tears were gone, she realized Tis had enveloped both of them in her wings.

"I think that's enough for tonight." Her dad kissed Kera's forehead and, to her surprise, planted a light kiss on Tis's cheek as well. "You know where I am if you need me."

He walked to the house, looking deep in thought, his shoulders hunched forward. Kera wondered if she'd done the right thing in telling him.

"He deserved to know, baby. It's a parent's right."

Kera turned into Tis's embrace and rested her head on her shoulder. "It doesn't feel right. He's already mourning my mom."

"And now he can be happy that he didn't lose you too. Coming that close to death can make someone realize just how much they cherish a person. I'm sorry those bastards weren't on my list. There are so many bad people in so many places, we can't get to them all.

And Siberia has always been outside our general parameters. But if they ever do come near you again…" Tis pulled on her hand. "Let's walk down to the beach."

They headed toward the sound of the ocean. Kera thought about what she'd told them, about their unwavering support. The terrible guilt had eased, if only a bit. She'd been accused of having a savior complex when she'd been researching medicine, and she knew it was probably still true. Not only did she feel the need to make up for the death of her team, but she wanted to do good, to compensate for the nearly disastrous mistake she'd made, and for the blood splattered on the cold white lab walls. She'd almost been responsible for killing untold numbers of people.

"Almost only counts in horseshoes and hand grenades."

Startled from her thoughts, she looked at Tis. "What?"

"The worst didn't happen. Some terrible things did, it's true. But the absolute worst thing that could have happened, didn't. You can't beat yourself up for something that didn't happen. Almost only counts when it's horseshoes or hand grenades."

"Did you read my mind? That's totally not fair." The possibility made her uncomfortable. She wanted to share what she wanted to share, not the stuff she kept inside.

"It doesn't take a mind reader to know what you were thinking. I'm connected to you, but I won't invade your privacy that way." She grinned. "Though I will check to make sure you like what I'm doing when you're incapable of speech because of what I'm doing to your body."

Kera started to laugh, and soon Tis joined her. When they sat on the beach and Tis pulled her close, she felt something she'd never felt before.

Home.

Chapter Twenty

The rest of the week slipped past. The days were often spent at Ben's restaurant, surrounded by people telling stories about Kera's mother, and they loved telling Tis plenty of stories about Kera's exploits, too. More than one of the people there had needed to forgive Kera for introducing their daughters to the carnal pleasures of life.

On Wednesday, Ajan showed up with his new charge. The beautiful little girl looked nothing like the frightened, desperate child they'd rescued from the rubble. She was all smiles and was brought into the fold as Ajan was welcomed home by family and friends. Tis loved watching it all; the genuine love and friendship this community shared was something she'd experienced only rarely in her entire existence. And although, as always, she was an outsider here, she still relished the beauty of it going on around her.

One night, while the ceremony was going on inside, Tis relaxed on a lounger under the stars, contemplating the simplicity of where she was. The believers here accepted the limitations of their lives, even with the gods among them. She wondered why that was and realized she actually rarely saw the Vodun gods among the people. *Familiarity breeds contempt.* The old adage made her soul weary. Perhaps that was part of the issue. When people came face-to-face with their gods, they saw the human side, and deep down, humans had little respect for humanity.

A small touch startled her from her thoughts. She looked down and saw Ajan's new daughter standing beside her. She raised her arms, and Tis willingly picked her up and cradled her. She thought about Meg teasing Alec about Alec and Selene having little demi-fury babies. Tis had held plenty of children over the centuries and had even been in the lives of several for a prolonged period of time. Though she enjoyed them, she'd never wanted one of her own. Now though, holding on to Ajan's daughter, she was able to take comfort in the small child asleep in her arms.

Ajan and Kera walked up beside them, and Ajan laughed.

"That child always finds the best places to curl up, I swear. Last week I found her sleeping in a pile of pillows beside the couch." He gathered his little girl up and hummed her a lullaby as he headed toward the house to put her to bed.

"You ever want one of those?" Kera nodded toward Ajan.

"You know how life is. Far too busy for lifeforms that need lots of attention." Tis gave her a wry smile to take any sting out of her words. "How is the ceremony going?"

Kera lightly traced Tis's fingers with her own. "Good. I can't believe tomorrow is the last day." She glanced at Tis and then quickly looked away. "I don't suppose you've had a chance to ask the oldies if I can say good-bye?"

Tis raised Kera's hand to her lips and kissed her knuckles. "I wouldn't call them that, if you want something from them. But yes, you can."

Kera's head snapped up and she searched Tis's face, as though expecting a joke. "Really? I don't have to die myself, right? It's not some kind of twisted setup, like where you ask for eternal life but forget to ask for eternal youth."

"It's absurd how often that happened when the gods were among humans last time. But no, that's not the case. They're making an exception because I've asked and because you're a daughter of a special priestess." Tis could see the warring emotions in Kera's expression. Glad to be able to say good-bye but heavily heartbroken to have to.

"Thank you—"

A cacophony of voices slammed into Tis's mind, and she held her head to try to make sense of what she was hearing, cutting off whatever Kera was about to say. At the same time, her phone began to ring.

"Baby? What is it? What's going on? Do I need to kill something? Are *you* killing something?" Kera's tone was slightly panicked, and Tis sensed her bodyguards move closer.

"Hold on…give me a second." Tis focused and saw chaos. Humanity First placards were burning, people were fighting and pushing, there was screaming and crying. She grabbed her phone. "What the hell is going on?"

Alec came on, her voice tight. "Humanity First has been on a media blitz, pointing out all the flaws in the gods. People are listening, especially the ones who are most in need and not getting anywhere. But the true believers are fighting back, sometimes literally. The gods are trying to do more, pressing their powers to make things better for people…but you know how that goes. Skirmishes are breaking out all over the damn place. And there have been a few more incidents involving that weird black spaghetti stuff in people's heads, along with missing souls when the death crew come in."

"Anger builds and resentment becomes the norm. I don't know what the hell to say about the black stuff. Are there any plans?"

"Right now, it's all about putting out fires, and there's no time to come up with something to stem the bleeding." Alec hesitated. "We need you, Tisera. No one can do what you can."

Tis closed her eyes, torn. She needed to go home, to do what she did best, and try to figure out how to keep the world from tearing itself apart. She felt Kera's hand on her back, rubbing gentle circles between her wing blades. And she also needed to be here, for the woman she'd grown to…yes, to love. For centuries, she'd given herself freely to her work. Just this once… "I need one more day, Alec. If you can send me a company plane, I'll get on it first thing day after tomorrow. But please, buy me two more nights."

Alec was silent for a moment. "She must be pretty damn special, Sis. Okay, I'll get you another day, and I'll get the plane sent over."

Tis breathed a sigh of relief. If she could count on anyone, it was Alec. "Thank you. Do me a favor. Tell Zed I want a major council gathering of the gods. Both the high council and the underworld council. I want them all in one room so we can figure out a strategy. If the world burns, there won't be anyone left to play god to. And we need to figure out who's behind the black string."

"You got it. See you then."

Alec hung up, and Tis closed the images out of her mind. She turned to Kera and was surprised to see unshed tears in her eyes. "What is it, baby?"

"You'd let the world go to hell, just to stay with me?"

Tis grinned. "Well, technically, the world can't go to hell, just the people in it. And even then, they've got so many versions of it, that isn't technically right either."

Kera laughed and swiped at her eyes. "Good to know. Thanks for correcting my idioms."

Tis ran her fingertips over Kera's cheek. "I promised, and I keep my promises. I'll have to leave before sunrise after the final ceremony, but I'll be here with you for it."

Kera stood and held out her hand. "I can think of a million ways to thank you, but doing it with my fantastic body and equally amazing tongue seem like the best way."

Tis laughed and took her hand. "I've been thanked plenty of times, but never quite the way you do it. Lead on, gorgeous."

❖

It's not creepy unless she knows. Kera grinned inwardly, glad for a moment to watch Tis sleep. Unguarded and relaxed, her beauty was truly breathtaking. Her pearlescent wings shone against the blue sheets, and her porcelain skin looked so incredibly soft it was all Kera could do not to stroke it. But she didn't want to risk waking her when she had some busy times ahead.

"I'm not sure if I should be insulted that you'd rather leave me sleeping than awake and talking to you." Tis opened one eye and gave her a sleepy smile.

"You said enough with your body last night. I could use the quiet and the rest."

Tis stretched, and Kera batted away a loose feather. "Insulted, then."

Kera tweaked her nipple. "I don't think I could ever get enough of looking at you."

Tis leaned over and kissed her. "Let's hope not. So, what's on the schedule for today?"

Kera stood and felt the soreness from their marathon sex session in her thighs and back. *Nice.* "Today, Dad will cook a shit ton of food, and everyone who's been attending the ceremonies all week, as well as some freeloaders, will show up and eat and talk all day. Things will get added to the altar throughout the day, and then tonight, we call on Papa Ghede to take my mom over." She turned to Tis. "I'm not sure when your friends come into it."

Tis got out of bed and moved so she could wrap Kera in her wings. "To be honest, I'm not sure either. We'll have to wait and see, although I have a feeling it will be when the crossing is due to happen. Are you ready?"

Kera thought about it. Was she? How could anyone ever be truly ready to say good-bye? Even if she'd been there when her mom had passed, would she have been ready? "I don't know. How about we grab breakfast, and I'll talk about it over huevos rancheros?"

Tis kissed her quickly before spinning around to get dressed. "Perfect. I'm starving. Who knew sex with a human could be so exhausting?"

"Yeah? Well, who knew it would be so easy to keep up with a goddess?"

Tis threw a pillow at her. "I'm not a goddess."

"You are to me. In fact, if I ever plan on praying, I'll gladly get on my knees for you." Kera gave her a lascivious grin, and Tis shook her head, laughing.

They got ready and headed to her father's restaurant. Big pots of food were already making their way out of the kitchen and onto long trestle tables against the far wall.

In the kitchen, Kera's dad directed them to a small side oven, where their breakfasts were already plated and being kept warm. Kera blew him a kiss as they went to a shaded corner outside to eat.

Once they'd started, Kera began thinking. "Tis, can I ask you something and get a straight answer?"

Tis looked wary. "I think so. I'll try."

"I guess that'll have to do. I need to understand why the gods didn't answer the prayers for my mother's health." She felt the tears well up and tried to push them back down. "It wasn't just her praying. It was lots of other people too. Why?"

Tis set her fork down and sighed. She stared off into the distance, and Kera knew that meant she was seriously considering her words. She waited, hoping Tis could give her some concrete reason.

Tis looked around as though to make sure they were alone. "What I'm about to tell you, I tell you because I trust you, and because you're not a believer anyway, so it won't affect your faith in any way." She paused and took a sip of tea. "Religion, and the relationships between men and their gods, is incredibly complex. But when it comes to certain things, there's an order, things that can't be changed. Biology and sickness, for example. The gods aren't in charge of science—of germs and illness. Those are biological processes, things that happen no matter what god someone believes in. Cancer, immunological diseases, even biological weapons…the gods have no part to play in those things, because science isn't pliable to prayer."

Kera took that in. "The gods are limited by science? But isn't the entire planet science based?"

"There are aspects that are inevitable, yes. Birth, death, climate change, the seasons. The gods have no control over those things. That's why they can't do anything when things like severe droughts or terrible flooding happen. They can create small changes in the weather, briefly, but the natural order of things eventually takes over again."

"So, all those prayers were wasted?" Kera's anger began to simmer. "If people knew the gods couldn't do shit, they wouldn't waste their time. Are the gods so narcissistic they want prayers for doing nothing?"

"That's the thing, though. If all those prayers had been for your mom to, say, make a breakthrough in a certain process, the gods might have been able to grant that by helping her make the necessary connections. Or if they prayed for your dad's restaurant to be successful, they could influence people to eat there. If someone prayed for a bomb not to hit their house, and that prayer was received in time, they could do something about that."

"What do you mean, received in time? Isn't someone always praying their house doesn't get hit?"

Tis sighed and closed her eyes. "I shouldn't be telling you all this. You see, prayers are sent constantly. Millions per second and must be dealt with that quickly. The gods answer them as they come in, but sometimes, that means one prayer gets answered, so the opposing one can't."

"Like when two sports teams pray for a win before the same game."

"Simplified, but yes. Whichever prayer comes in first, gets answered. *If* it's something the gods can interfere with. Although sometimes there's a reason not to grant a prayer. For instance, if someone prays they can manage to kill someone else, the god won't grant that prayer. That's something that happens without divine interference."

"So they can do something about who wins the fucking Super Bowl, but nothing about someone dying of leukemia. Ain't that grand." Kera pushed her plate away and stood. "I need to go for a walk."

Tis nodded, looking incredibly sad. "I understand. I'll see you in a while."

Kera left and headed toward the water. Her trusty brick shithouse bodyguards fell in behind her, but today she wasn't bothered by them. Recounting what she'd been through years ago had reminded her that jackass was still out there. She'd even thought she'd seen him on the plane on the way to Haiti, so she was prepared to admit Petra was right, that there wasn't any harm in having them nearby. Not that she'd tell Petra she was right about anything, ever. Right now, she wanted to think about what Tis had said. Tis was about to go back to a shit storm of biblical proportions. *And for what? For gods people think actually make a difference, but really don't? So they can win the fucking lotto but not keep them safe in a war zone?*

She took her shoes off when she got to the sand and made her way to the water's edge. The warm water lapped gently over her feet, and she let the tears fall. *All that prayer. All that begging, to be allowed to live, to get better. For nothing. Because no one knows the gods are nothing but half-full bags of wind. I miss you, Mom. I wish you could explain all this shit to me.*

She stayed there, staring out at the horizon, until sweat began to roll down her back from the rising heat. Determined, she headed back, ignoring the twisting in her gut.

Tis was sitting at a table in the shade, reading a book. She looked so lovely, so sweet, Kera nearly lost her nerve. But that was the thing with the gods. They weren't what they seemed. She dropped into the chair opposite Tis and forced the words out.

"I want you. I think you're the most amazing woman I've ever known. But you're also one of them, and not only that, you defend them and what they are. And they're liars. People think they need them, that they'll help if they only pray hard enough, act good enough. They even go to Heaven or Hell based on those lies and inadequacies. And you help perpetuate that lie." She finally looked up at Tis, but her work mask was on, and Kera couldn't tell what she was thinking. "I can't be a part of that. I wanted to make the world better, and I nearly fucked it up instead. Now, I'm trying really hard to make things right. I don't think I can do that and sleep with someone who isn't on my team."

Tis stayed silent for so long Kera didn't think she was going to respond. Finally, so quietly Kera could barely hear her, she said, "I can respect that. To some extent, I can even understand it. There are parts you don't know, things you haven't seen. They do a lot of good, too." She leaned forward so Kera could see the red of her eyes. "Tell me something, high and mighty one. If I looked closely at your business dealings, would you be as white as my wings? Or would you be walking a fine line between being in my bed or on my blacklist?"

Kera swallowed the tiny ball of fear rising in her throat. It was one thing to see Tis in action in the field. It was another to have that intensity focused on her. Especially when there was some truth to it. "I never said I was spotless. I'm doing good things, helping people. And if I have to get my hands a little dirty to do it, so be it. That's apparently more than your colleagues are willing to do. And you? What do you do to make the world better? Sure, you deal with a lot of scumbags. But you don't kill them, do you? You fuck up their minds, and then leave them here among us schmucks, for us to deal with. Does that make things better? Okay, maybe they don't rape again, or abuse kids, but what other shit do they do you never know about because you've 'dealt' with them?" Tis's eyes were getting redder, and she could see the tips of her fangs. Maybe calling a fury out wasn't a great idea, but her mouth was way ahead of her reasoning skills.

Tis stood and looked down at Kera. "I think we're done here. I'll see you at the ceremony tonight." She leapt into the air, and the downdraft of her wings blew sand into Kera's face.

"Nice. Thanks for that." Kera shouted at her retreating figure.

She flopped against the chair, feeling utterly, horribly alone.

Chapter Twenty-one

Tis sat on the buoy, the gentle rocking of the ocean beneath her calming. She'd needed space and had flown twenty miles into the Atlantic to make sure she was away from everyone. Normally so logical, she was drowning in emotions she didn't know what to do with. She was furious with Kera, though she couldn't pin down exactly why. For giving up on them, on what they could have, because of who she was and who she worked for. That was why. It wasn't like she hadn't known. *But she didn't know what I told her about their limitations.* Perhaps not. And if she knew the rest, she'd probably be even more pissed off. It wasn't like Tis hadn't been trying to figure out the point of it all herself.

But now, as she watched a pod of humpback whales surface and dive again, she knew what the point was. It was the very issue she'd be up against the moment she got back. The gods weren't useless. They *did* answer prayers, they did tell people how to behave, what stupid things not to do. Yes, people twisted their teachings, but now that the gods were back among them, they were trying to put things right. Prior to the recent upsets, wars had dropped dramatically, people were getting along, even murders and general crime had decreased. That made the world better. If they could just get a handle on how to keep that momentum going, then faith, religion, would actually do what it was meant to; it could be what Kera thought it should be. Just without the meddling in science and biology.

Kera doesn't even believe, and she's pissed off the gods have limitations. No wonder believers are going crazy. But deep down, she felt like it was more than that. There was something else at play, something she hadn't figured out yet. The strange black spaghetti filling people's minds, who then lost their souls; that hadn't happened as far as she could remember, and that was truly frightening. There was a piece missing, and she needed it for this puzzle.

She thought again of Kera's words, and although she was heartbroken in a way she hadn't been in centuries, she also wasn't about to apologize for who, for what, she was. She and her sisters stopped the monsters, and she wouldn't apologize for not taking lives. Maybe Kera was right. Maybe, as amazing as it felt to be with her, they couldn't find middle ground.

She'd promised, and she'd stay for the final ceremony tonight. She'd help Kera see her mom off, and then Tis would head home. *Where I belong.*

Furious rhythmic drumming and frantic chanting filled the night. Kera looked at the massive crowd swaying around her. *If they only knew.* Her stomach was in knots, and her heart ached like someone had used it for a punching bag. Tis stood next to Kera's father against the back wall, her expression impassive. Kera and her father had done rock-paper-scissors to determine which of them had to host tonight, and she'd lost rock to his paper. That meant she had to stand by the altar and accept all the offerings left to the gods as well as people's condolences. Although she appreciated the concept, she wondered how well any of them actually knew her mother. Among the mass of mourners, she felt totally isolated, as though she was watching everything from inside a bubble. She wanted to take back everything she'd said to Tis, but knew it would just come up again later. Tonight, though, of all nights, she wished Tis was at her side rather than across the room, looking for all the world like something far removed from it.

She smiled at Ajan, who slid an expensive cigar into her shirt pocket and then placed an apple on the altar. His little girl hugged Kera's leg before taking Ajan's hand and moving to the back to stand near Tis. It was nearing midnight, and the oppressive heat from the crowd and summer night was giving Kera a headache. Suddenly, the priest leading the show raised his hands, and the crowd fell silent.

"Papa Ghede! Mama Erzulie! We call on you to take our beloved sister, our mother, your priestess, home to you. She served you well, and now it's time for you to give her the peace she deserves."

The doors blew open, and the scent of apples filled the air. A soft murmur went through the crowd as Papa Ghede and Erzulie entered side-by-side. They didn't appear to be walking, but rather, floating. Erzulie kept her eyes locked on Kera as they made their way toward her. *Well, that's not unsettling.* Papa Ghede looked solemn, far more intense than he had when he was playing taxi driver. When Erzulie stopped in front of Kera, she stayed there for a long moment, staring at her.

Kera leaned forward slightly. "You're kind of freaking me out," she whispered.

Erzulie's lips twitched in a tiny smile. "Tisera made a request for you. I needed to see if you were strong enough."

"And?" Kera couldn't believe how desperately she wanted a particular answer.

"You are." Erzulie looked at Papa Ghede and inclined her head slightly. He turned around to address the crowd.

"Your prayers are heard and answered. Tonight, we take our sister to the lands beyond time, where all mortal souls must eventually make their way." He raised his arms. "Continue to drink, to fuck, to celebrate, to love. Light your sister's way across the river with your passion, the same passion she had while she walked with you."

There were shouts of amen and lots of other things Kera wasn't interested in. Tis had come up behind Erzulie, and Kera thought she saw a hint of sympathy in her eyes.

"It's time, girlie. You sure you want to do this?"

Kera looked from Tis to Papa Ghede. "Yeah. As long as I don't have to go kill a hydra or skin a golden goat or something."

He smiled at her and shook his head. "Only if you want to do it for fun." He looked at Tis. "You mind carrying her? It will go faster if we don't have to walk."

Tis raised an eyebrow and looked at Kera, but she didn't say anything.

"Please." Kera couldn't think of anything else to say and certainly not in front of other people.

Tis nodded and turned. Kera followed Papa Ghede and Erzulie from the building, wanting to scoff as they both touched followers' hands and heads as they passed by. But the desire to weep was stronger. They made it outside, and Kera took a deep breath of fresh air. Papa Ghede turned to her.

"We're only doing this because Tisera asked, and you don't turn down a fury when she asks for something. But, girlie, you listen to me." He lit a cigar and took a puff. "Living people don't go where we're going. That means you stick with us, you hear? You get to say good-bye to your mama, and then you're gone. No wandering around on your own, or you won't be coming back. Hear?"

Kera saluted him. "Got it, boss. You want to put a leash on me, just in case?"

He grinned and blew an O-ring of smoke at her. "I'll leave that to the women you bed down with."

Erzulie cleared her throat lightly. "It's time. Tisera?"

Tis moved to Kera's side. "It will be easier for both of us if you get on my back and wrap your arms around my neck."

Any other time, Kera would have made a wisecrack about gladly riding Tis's back. But this didn't seem like the right time. "Sure. Whatever works for you."

Tis turned around, spread her glorious wings, and Kera pressed her body against Tis's back, careful not to press too hard on her wings, although they felt more like rock than muscle. *Or bone. Or feathers. What the hell are her wings made of?*

She gasped as Tis leapt into the air, and held on tight, managing to wrap her arms around Tis's torso rather than her neck, which seemed like a bad idea. She felt the strength of her, the heavy pumping of her wings, and was reminded just how not-human Tis was. *Not that I need a big ass reminder, since I'm riding her like she's a fucking dragon.* She tried to see over Tis's shoulder but saw only water. She wondered where Papa Ghede and Erzulie had gone, since they didn't have wings. *Maybe they fly like Superman or some shit.* She shouted when Tis suddenly dove toward the water and wind rushed past them. She squeezed her eyes shut as they were about to slam into the ocean, realizing just how stupid she'd been to piss off a fury and then get on her back for a ride to death-land.

Cool air made her skin goose pimple, and she opened her eyes. The ocean was gone, and now they flew above cracked, dry land under an inky black sky with no stars or moon. Ahead, the sky lightened.

"Tis? Do you know where we're going?"

"Of course I do. I spent a good portion of my early life in the underworld."

Of course she did. It wasn't like a normal conversation, where you asked where someone went to high school or what their first job was. Tis lived in the underworld and fucked goddesses. She'd been around for an amount of time Kera couldn't really even fathom.

Tis slowed and started to descend. She touched down, and Kera quickly let go, feeling the loss instantly. Tis lowered her wings, and Kera could see what was ahead.

"What the fuck?"

Tis laughed. "It's changed since the last time I was here."

"It looks like…like…a really bad version of Vegas." A massive river was bordered on both sides by gaudy buildings with neon lights. Many of the lights were broken and missing letters, and there was a sense of gloom about the place even though it was brightly lit. There were saloons straight out of an old Western, brothels, casinos, and even a few churches. Papa Ghede and Erzulie materialized out of the darkness. Between them walked her mother.

"Mama," Kera whispered.

Her mother held out her arms, and Kera rushed into them. "Baby girl. If anyone could make it right down to the river, it would be you."

Kera let her tears fall. All the years of isolation, work, fear, and guilt welled up inside her and flowed away with her tears. "I'm so sorry I wasn't there at the end. I'm so, so sorry. I made so many mistakes—"

"Hush, mija."

Her mother held her at arm's length, and Kera realized Tis and the others had moved away a bit to give them some privacy.

"Life is about mistakes, baby. Some are worse than others, but at some point," she looked around them, "we all end up here anyway. So stop beating yourself up, baby." She held Kera's face in her hands. "I love you, and I'm so damn proud of you. Never forget that, no matter what happens." She let go of Kera's face and motioned toward Tis. "And remember that not everything is black-and-white."

Kera started to protest, but her mother cut her off with a look.

"No, mija. At some point you have to accept that there's always more to the story, and you're not always right. If there's one last piece of advice I can give you, it's to open up, and be prepared to be wrong. Learn to say you're sorry, and learn to forgive."

Kera laughed humorlessly. "Now I know I'm not among the living. As if."

"You'll learn, baby."

Erzulie moved closer to them. "I'm sorry, but it's time. Kera can't be here longer than necessary."

Kera looked at her mother, a million things she wanted to say jumbled in her head, and none of them coming out. Finally, she whispered, "I love you so much. Thank you for being the most amazing mom in the world."

Her mom took Papa Ghede's outstretched hand and stepped back. "Oh, baby, I know you loved me, never doubt that. And you were my greatest gift. I love you. Tell your papa..." She looked up at the onyx sky. "Tell him I'll be waiting for him."

Kera felt like she was choking on the desperation to keep her mother with her. She looked at Erzulie. "Could I go with her?" She heard Tis's sharp intake of breath.

Erzulie shook her head. "No, child. No one crosses the river without having finished what they were meant to do while alive. And you're not done yet."

Kera hugged herself, and when she felt she warmth of Tis's wing curl around her, she leaned into it gratefully. She watched as

Papa Ghede led her mother to a long dock, where a riverboat waited for them. An impossibly thin, tall man took her mother's hand and helped her into the boat. She sat next to Papa Ghede, who put an arm around her. She looked over her shoulder and waved.

Kera waved back and let go of the sob she'd been trying to hold back. Tis pulled her close, and they watched as the boat floated away, under a bridge, and out of sight.

Kera sobbed in Tis's arms, unaware of time passing, and feeling the loss of her mother as keenly as a bullet wound to her soul. At some point, Erzulie touched her shoulder.

"It's time for you to return, child."

Kera lifted her head from Tis's shoulder, embarrassed by the massive wet patch on her shirt. "Sorry about that. I'll get it dry-cleaned for you."

Tis gave her a small, sad smile. "Don't worry about it."

Kera stepped back and pulled herself together. She looked at the two of them. "Thank you. For allowing this." She looked directly at Tis. "For coming." She motioned around them, trying to ground herself a little bit. "What is this place?"

"It's Hypnos, and that's the River Lethe. There are five different rivers that are used for the crossing. This is the river of forgetfulness. Your mother will drink some of the river water when she gets to the other side, and she'll be content with where she goes. Those who don't drink sometimes end up haunting the living, unable to let go of the lives they once had."

Kera knew there was some kind of folk tale lesson in that information, but she didn't have the energy to analyze it now. "And it looks like a beat-up version of old people's Sin City because?"

Tis laughed. "There's not a lot of point in making it really glitzy, since most people who come here aren't happy about it. Basically, these are places they can spend their time until they're finally ready to cross over."

"Like I said, this is only one of five rivers. The one on Phlegethon, the river of fire, is really something to see. Fireworks all the time, animal shows…quite exciting. Still, people tire of it and eventually cross."

"What do they cross to?" Kera asked, staring down the river where she'd last seen her mother.

Erzulie started walking into the darkness, and Tis turned her back to Kera, indicating she should get on.

"It's different for every religion. Your mother will go where all Vodun go, and she'll be happy."

Erzulie faded into the dark, and Kera hung on as Tis leapt into the sky. Instead of looking around, she rested her cheek against Tis's strong back. It wasn't an answer, but she could live with it. As they emerged into daylight beside a stunning waterfall, she blinked at the bloom of dawn and the beauty of it, and of living in general. She laughed and pointed below them at an enormous pod of dolphins playing in the waves, and Tis joined her. As always, her laughter lifted Kera's heart.

Too soon, Tis landed on the beach in Haiti. The sun was just beginning to peek over the horizon, and Kera felt like she'd been reborn, somehow. Like life was a gift she'd never truly appreciated, as cheesy as that was.

Tis kissed her softly and stepped back toward the water.

"Tis…wait. Can we talk? I don't want to leave things this way."

Tis shook her head, her shoulders slumped. She pointed to the dock down the beach, where a large, sleek black SUV was parked. "They're waiting for me. I'm sorry. Have a safe flight home." She looked like she was going to say something else, but shrugged and spread her wings instead.

Kera watched her fly away and knew she'd made a terrible, terrible mistake.

CHAPTER TWENTY-TWO

Tis barely noticed the clouds speeding past and hardly spoke to the captain, Aeolus. He was the god of the winds in ancient Greece, and had come to work for Afterlife once he'd become more fable than worshipped god. He seemed to sense Tis's state of mind, and after giving her a quick hug, he left her to her thoughts. The only other person onboard was an Aurai, one of the nymphs of breezes, and like the water sprites, she was more elemental than person, making a conversation with her more work than Tis felt like doing.

They'd be back in LA by mid-afternoon thanks to the capabilities of the Afterlife ability to mess with time, and Tis was so beaten down emotionally, part of her was looking forward to being able to shout at the gods. The other part of her, though, desperately wanted to turn around and work things out with Kera. *What's to work out, though?* Kera made her feelings clear, and if Tis told her anything else about the gods, it would likely just drive her further away. *How do Selene and Alec do it?* Maybe it helped that Selene was a demigod. Maybe Selene was more open-minded. *Less pig headed stubborn.* Maybe, though…maybe they were meant to be together, whereas Tis and Kera weren't. She blinked back hot tears and tried to think about anything else. Finally, she put the seat into bed position and went to sleep, hoping she wouldn't dream about Kera instead.

"Get up, get up, get up, get up."

Tis opened one eye and watched Meg bounce on the bed beside her. Thankfully, she hadn't had any dreams at all, and had, apparently, slept through the entire journey.

Meg put her face up to Tis's and squished her cheeks with her hands. "How can you sleep when life is so exciting?"

"Because she's not a nutcase who feeds on drama the way you do?" Alec said from the doorway.

Meg jumped off the bed and pulled at Tis's arm. "Come on. They're all waiting for you, and I so want to see you get all bossy sexy-pants on them."

Tis laughed, her sisters buoying her as they always did. She followed them down the metal stairs and into the sunshine, and as Meg skipped ahead of them like a child, singing some nonsense about lightning bolts and burning bushes, Alec put her arm around Tis's shoulder.

"That bad, huh?"

Tis sighed. "You know, no matter how many times it happens throughout the centuries, you forget how much it hurts."

"That's the truth. Any chance of fixing it?"

"I've asked myself that, but I think we're just too different." She got into the Hummer's passenger seat. Meg was already in the back, lying down with her feet on the ceiling. Alec reached back and knocked them down.

"Hey!"

"I don't know where your feet have been. You'll give my car cooties."

"I haven't done anything with my feet in ages, I'll have you know."

"Excuse me, but can you let me know what I'm walking into?" Tis always enjoyed her sisters' banter, but she needed to be somewhat prepared before they got to the office.

Alec held up her hand when Meg sat up and started to speak. "Let me. If Meg does it you won't get facts." Meg huffed and put her feet back on the ceiling. "Nearly all the gods, upper and lower, are waiting for you in the main hall. I thought they'd be pissed off at being called in, but it turns out, being a god is hard work, and pretty much all of them were ready for a break. Who knew?" She grinned and ticked points off on her fingers. "Seriously, there are a few different issues. Issue one is Humanity First. They're doing what Frey Falconi started to do, but because there are so many, they're really building a batch of followers. Issue two, it's not just them. The followers of a lot of the religions are getting pissed off at a lack of answers, and they're standing right next to the Humanity people at protests. Issue three, we've had more murders committed by people who just have that black ooze in their heads, and when Dani's team gets there, the soul is already gone. We've had reports from our sisters in other countries saying the same thing. The research team can't figure it out, and we're not sure what step to take next."

Tis picked up a rubber band and started twisting it around her fingers. She often thought better with something in her hands. "Anything else?"

"Anubis is having sex with Freya. I'm hoping they're going to have little dog-headed Viking babies." Meg prodded Tis's shoulder with her toes. "And at my party last week, Ganesh blew bubbles from his trunk. He's allergic to the incense in his temples."

Tis swatted Meg's foot away. "Alec was right. I think her information is a little more useful right now."

They drove past Afterlife, and Tis gasped at the amount of protesters outside. Like Alec said, believers stood next to Humanity First people. Placards read things like, *Give us answers, not wine* and *Go back to where you came from.*

"I'd rather have wine than answers any day. Answers are boring. Wine is fun." Meg sat up and looked out the window.

Tis noticed that although Meg's words were blasé, her body was tense.

They pulled around to the back gate and went inside through the back door. They stepped into the elevator, and Alec touched Tis's arm.

"We're with you, all the way. Whatever you need, okay? If it gets crazy in there, we can leave."

Tis hugged her tightly. "Thank you. But I can't just leave. In fact, it's good to have something to concentrate on right now. I'll throw myself into work and everything will be fine."

Meg rested her head on Tis's shoulder. "I'm really glad I'm not you right now."

Tis laughed and kissed the top of Meg's head. "Thanks for that."

The door opened, and Tis readied herself. *This is what I'm good at. This is where I belong.* An image of Kera, naked and tangled in the white sheets, came to mind. And then, how crushed she'd looked standing on the beach as Tis had flown away. Her stomach turned, and she took her sisters' hands.

"Let's go play with the gods, shall we?"

Zed was pacing outside the hall doors when they stepped out. He opened his arms and crushed Tis in a hug. "Can't tell you how glad we are you're back." He turned to Meg and Alec. "Would you mind making sure no one is getting out of hand?"

Meg saluted him, and Alec grinned. "Anything for you, big guy." Alec winked at Tis, and Meg flung open the doors dramatically.

"I know you missed us, but don't crowd around." Meg blew a kiss at a nymph, who giggled and tossed her hair.

Tis shook her head and turned back to Zed as the doors closed on the cacophony. "How are you holding up?"

He leaned against the wall and tugged on his beard. "It's insanity. When we all worked here, I could keep an eye on everyone, make sure no one was stepping out of line. Sure, sometimes it happened, but that kept things interesting, right? But now…"

He looked so forlorn, so tired, Tis knew it was bad. "Now they're out doing what gods do, but you're still supposed to be in charge over the lot. And they're only okay with that when they run into trouble out there and don't know what to do about it."

"See? This is why we picked you for the job." He gave her a small smile. "The thing is, when it was all mystery and all that 'everything for a reason' stuff, people believed without issue. But now, when they're asking us questions we can't answer without stepping in it, belief is wavering. Not in us as beings, but in us as deities. And not one of us, including me, knows what the hell to do about it."

Tis considered. "So we need to develop a line of rhetoric around answering the questions no god can answer without jeopardizing us all, and it needs to be a party line everyone sticks to. Got it."

He gripped Tis's shoulder with his massive hand. "I'm so glad you're back."

She nodded. "Let's get started." *This is where I belong. These are my people.* She'd doubted it for a while, felt apart and disillusioned. But now, with Zed beside her and her sisters at the front of the room looking like beautiful sentries, she knew she'd never doubt again. *No matter who I'm in love with.*

Kera sipped her beer and let the sun dry her tears. One of her bodyguards had made an attempt to talk to her, but she couldn't stand the pity in the brick wall's voice, and she'd waved her away. They sat in the shade, as usual never far away. At some point she'd grown accustomed to their presence and wondered what that said about her. She'd opened her laptop and thrown herself into work for several hours after changing her flight plans. Building permits had finally come through for her downtown LA plans, and she'd sent out the emails to contractors to get renovations started. Focusing on doing something worthwhile made her feel a little better. Still, she needed another day before she faced real life without Tis in it.

"You look like shit."

She gave a humorless laugh but didn't open her eyes. "You shouldn't talk to your employer that way. And what's so important you couldn't wait another day to tell me?" She finally opened her eyes and squinted at Petra, who looked just as cold and imposing as she always did. "And aren't you boiling? Jesus, woman, take off some clothes."

Petra rolled her eyes. "I can't even imagine the number of times you've said that to someone." She took off her long-sleeve jacket to reveal a form fitting black T-shirt with Kera's company logo on the chest. She sat beside her and took a long drink of Kera's beer. "There's nothing like cold beer in hot climates."

Kera took it back. "Get your own." She glanced up when someone set two more bottles on the table. "Hell, that's service."

Ajan sat beside Petra at the table. "I don't know why we put up with you. I bet that three-headed dog the gods use to guard their office would be nicer."

Kera winced internally at the reminder of the gods. "Yeah, well, I'm sure they're hiring bodyguards these days. Go for it, with my blessing." She looked at Petra. "What's up? Or did you miss me so much you couldn't stand to be away from me for another day?"

"I could go lifetimes without seeing you and not remember your face." Ajan laughed and toasted her. Petra leaned forward. "I've got information, and I don't like it. I wanted to make sure you get home."

"That's chivalrous of you. I'm touched. But isn't that what they're for?" She waved at her bodyguards, who looked far more relaxed now that Ajan and Petra were sitting with her. In fact, one of them appeared to be ogling the waitress.

"Shut up and listen." Ajan tapped Kera's bottle with his own. "Has anything weird happened since you've been here?"

Kera laughed. "What would you consider weird? The week-long ceremony to send my mother to her final resting place, complete with beheaded chickens and offerings of cigars? Or maybe that I spent most of it with the most beautiful woman I've ever seen, who also happens to have wings and fangs, and looks mighty terrifying when she's pissed off? Ooh, I know, how about that trip I took to the underworld, where people were gambling and whoring?"

"Humans don't go to the underworld."

Petra glared at her, and Kera realized she was glowing slightly. "I did. Why do you look like you've got a lightbulb under your skin? That's weird too, by the way."

She sighed and looked at Ajan, who answered for her. "People have started going back to Petra's ancient temple and offering sacrifices to her. Although she retired, it's reigniting some of her goddess status."

Kera sat back and stared at her. "So, you're one of them again, is that it?" Unreasonable rage started to build.

Petra shook her head. "No. I was, and it's nice to have it happening. But I gave it up far too long ago, and I've seen too much to go back."

Kera shoved her chair back and pointed at her. "You're still one of them. If someone can leave some flowers and a dead animal for you somewhere and make you light up like you've ingested something nuclear, you're one of them. And I don't want you on my staff." She knew it was irrational, but she didn't care.

"Kera, don't be crazy—" Ajan said.

"No. I'm done with all of them, Ajan. Okay, I get that they help people to the other side, whatever the fuck that means. I still don't know, and I watched my mother float down some smelly river. But that doesn't make up for all the damage they're doing every day."

Petra stood and her light intensified. "Sit down."

Kera crossed her arms and stomped away a few feet. "No. What are you going to do? Turn me into a tree? Cut off body parts? Hey! Stop that!" Kera's feet left the ground and she floated back to her chair. The air slammed out of her as she was set down hard. "That was totally unnecessary."

Petra faded slightly and sat back down, looking pleased with herself. "I can see how this could be a benefit in working with you. Look, if you don't want me around after this, fine. But listen to what I have to say."

"First of all, can you do that any time you want? Because if you can I want you to do it to my bodyguards. Just for fun."

Petra sighed. "Sadly, no. Even that little bit will take me weeks to replenish. But it was worth it to see the panic on your face. Will you shut up and listen now?"

Kera motioned for another beer. "Fine. Go."

"I asked about anything weird because I've got a line on Degrovesnik. Word is that he's been building a new lab somewhere in the States. I haven't got an exact location yet. Nothing on why he's building it, but I think we can guess. My biggest concern is that he hasn't been seen for a few weeks. And thanks to this," she shoved a newspaper article across the table at Kera, "everyone in the world knows where you are."

Kera read the article, a short piece about the "wealthy playgirl" going home to her roots to take part in a voodoo death ceremony. "That's the best picture they could find? It's like, ten years old."

"Yeah, well, like I said, you look like shit. Anything weird?"

Kera sighed. "On the plane, on the way here. I thought I saw him, but when I looked again, he was gone. I figured it was my imagination. But nothing weird since I've been here, although I have had an ancient Greek fury at my side most of the time. That might put the bad guys off."

"But now Tisera is back at Afterlife."

Kera looked at Petra sharply. "How do you know that?"

"I'm privy to the gods' information once more. They're in the middle of a massive meeting, and Tisera is the main speaker."

They fell silent for a moment, and Kera wondered if they were expecting her to say something about what had happened between them. "Okay, well, I've still got my burly bodyguards."

Ajan took Kera's hand. "Right now, you need as many of us around you as possible. If he gets to you...we can't let anything happen to you."

The genuine worry in his eyes melted her stoic demeanor slightly. "It's only one more day. Hang out if you want to, whatever. We leave first thing in the morning."

"Wait." Petra looked like she was figuring out what to say. "I know you're angry with the gods. I know you're pissed off at their limitations, and you have a definite view on the world without them."

Kera shrugged. "So?"

"So, don't be a stubborn asshat."

"Sorry, I'm not sure what you mean by that. My ass is perfect and doesn't need a hat."

Petra looked at Ajan. "Can you give us a minute?"

He nodded and leaned over to kiss the top of Kera's head. "I'll come over for dinner with you tonight."

She waved him off, wanting to hear the rest of what Petra had to say.

When he was out of range, Petra continued. "Listen to me. Take off your blinders, Kera. You're being just as judgmental and intolerant as the people you fight against."

"What the fuck, Petra? How can you say that? No one prays to the bastards we deal with in other countries."

"You think their families don't believe in them? You think their siblings don't think they're absolutely in the right, no matter who they hurt?"

"This is an asinine argument. The gods tell people they can help them, and then they don't. People pray their asses off, and it doesn't do any good."

Petra shook her head. "That's not true. It doesn't do any good in some instances, maybe. But what about the prayers that *do* get answered, Kera? What about those? What about the people whose lives are better off because a god *was* able to answer their prayers? What about the hope it gives them, when life doesn't seem like it could get any worse?"

Kera stared at her blankly. She hadn't considered the positive side. "But those people are probably fewer than the others—"

"How would you know? You don't." Petra's tone softened. "This world is hard. You and I both know there are areas where just being alive is an act of bravery. Would you really take from people the bit of hope and relief they get from being believers?"

Kera thought about it. "And what about all the other shit that comes with it? The holy wars and killings in the name of god?"

"Do you really care what they call it? They can call it a holy war, or they can call it a land conflict. They can call it monkey shit butterfly wars. They'll always find a way to fight, Kera. That's the human way. If there are beings that can help, even in small ways, why would you deny them that?" She stood and looked down at Kera. "Believe what you want. Do what you want. You always do. But if you ruin what you've got with Tisera because you're being a stubborn cow, you'll have no one to blame but yourself."

Kera squeezed her eyes shut against the sudden tears forming. "Thanks for the pep talk. I don't think I've ever been called so many names when someone is trying to cheer me up."

Petra scoffed, and her smile was gentle. "I'm not trying to cheer you up. I'm trying to keep you from being a douche. You'll be impossible to work with if you screw this up." She nodded at the bodyguards, who straightened back into pay attention mode. "I'll come with Ajan to dinner tonight, after I meet up with some old friends."

Kera knew without asking Petra would be going to see the gods. "Tell them I said hey, and thanks again. It really did mean a lot."

"Tis must owe someone a massive favor, if they really took you to the underworld. Like I said, don't be stupid."

Kera watched her walk away, appreciating as she always did the sculpted body and perfect ass. It wasn't that ass she wanted to touch, though. It wasn't that body she desperately needed to feel against her. She picked up her beer and headed to the beach. Nothing cleared her head like the ocean, and she couldn't wait to get home and back onto her boat. She needed to process what Petra said. Was it true? Was she letting her bias against the gods blind her to anything good about them?

She sighed, missing Tis and thinking about her directing a room full of gods. *That's my girl. How do I fix this?* She thought about Petra's information about Degrovesnik. If he came after her, it might give her the chance she needed to deal with the bastard the way she needed to. *If it's self-defense, does that mean I won't end up on the naughty list?* The thought of facing Tis in her pissed off avenger form made her shudder. She had enough nightmares without having them fed to her by a fury. But even more, she couldn't stand the thought of losing Tis completely. *If I haven't already.*

CHAPTER TWENTY-THREE

Kera threw the last of her luggage into the SUV and wiped the sweat from her forehead. She looked at her bodyguard, who leaned against the car with her eyes closed, her face tilted toward the sun. "No, I've got it, thanks."

"Figured as much." The bodyguard didn't bother to open her eyes, but she smiled slightly.

Kera grunted and walked away to join Ajan and Petra. After dinner with her father, they'd drank themselves into the kind of stupor where everything sounds illuminating and brilliant, but Kera appeared to be the only one suffering from mild alcohol poisoning the following morning. It was beyond irritating.

Petra handed her a bottle of green juice. "This will help."

"Help what? Help me puke out the poison?" Kera tried to wave it away, but Petra captured her hand and pressed the bottle into it.

"It'll help us not want to kill you before we even make it to the airport."

Ajan laughed and slapped Kera on the back. "I can't imagine anyone more perfect to replace me." At Kera's glare, he held up his hands. "One day."

The ingredients included spinach, garlic, and spirulina, among a zillion other things people shouldn't mix together and ingest. But given the throbbing in her head and the way her stomach was threatening to revolt, she'd try it. She held her breath as she started to drink, but realized it tasted like apple juice and relaxed. She drained the bottle and nodded her thanks to Petra.

"That's enough vitamins and protein to replace some of what you killed off last night." Petra pointed at the line of SUVs. "I'm riding in the front car, Ajan is riding in the rear car with his daughter. Your bodyguards will be in your car."

"What, no Vodun god taxi driver this time?" It had only been a week, but the day they'd arrived in Haiti seemed forever ago. *Not exactly the way I'd planned on leaving.* She swallowed the sense of loss she'd had from the moment Tis had flown off.

"They don't tend to do you favors when you insult them." Petra stared at her as though she knew what Kera was thinking.

"Is this little convoy really necessary? What are we going to do when we're back at the office? Will I have someone attached to my ass all the time there, too?"

Petra shook her head and looked at Ajan. "You talk to her. I'm not officially in the position where I have to deal with it yet." She went to the first vehicle and opened the driver's side door. "Let's go."

Ajan gave Kera a quick hug. "We'll figure out what to do when we're back in the States when we actually get there. For now, one issue at a time, okay?"

He went to the rear car, where Kera could see his little girl already buckled into the passenger seat and playing on some device. Seeing the way his face lit up when he leaned over to kiss his daughter on the head made Kera well up again. She'd thought, for just a moment, she might have found that kind of...of...what? Caring? Love? Whatever it was, she'd had it with Tis, if only for a heartbeat. She sighed and got in the car.

One bodyguard was at the wheel, the other in the passenger seat. Kera slumped in the backseat, glad they weren't a talkative pair. Saying good-bye to her father had been difficult, but he'd promised to come see her for Christmas, maybe even for an extended stay. She'd make it a point to get back from whatever country they'd be working in. That he was her only family had really hit home after he'd gone to bed, and she didn't want to have to traipse through the underworld again in order to say good-bye next time.

She was dozing, enjoying images of Tis in the throes of an orgasm, when she heard one of her bodyguards swear. An accident ahead of them blocked the road, and two men appeared to be shoving and yelling at one another.

Petra slowed to a stop, well away from the accident. They'd taken Route Nationale 1 instead of going straight through the city, which should have meant they'd get there faster. But they'd passed the city and were near Fort Dimanche. That meant they'd have to backtrack to the nearest city road. *Good thing Petra is so anal about getting to the airport early.* Kera started to lean back, more interested in her previous thoughts about Tis's body than getting to the airport, when she saw Petra jump from her SUV and run at Kera's car, waving her arms. Kera heard "back up" but couldn't make out the rest.

It was too late. An explosion rocked the vehicle, sending it flipping onto its side and skidding along the dirt and rocks beside the road. Kera was flung against the shattered window, since she hadn't bothered with her seatbelt. Screeching metal and exploding glass filled the air. In the distance she heard gunfire and raised voices.

Shit shit shit. The SUV stopped moving, and she groaned as she tried to maneuver to her bodyguards. Neither looked conscious, and the driver's neck looked wrong. *Fuck. I never even knew their names. I'm such an asshole.* She'd just managed to get her feet under her and was reaching toward the passenger seat bodyguard to check for a pulse, when the rear door above her was wrenched open. The person, backlit by the sun, reached in and grabbed her shoulders. She couldn't help but cry out as she became aware of the pain in her left wrist and side. The man dragged her over the edge of the door and into the sun.

The world had become surreal. All three SUVs were mangled masses of metal, smoke and flames rising from the one Petra had been in. Masked gunmen trained rifles at Petra and Ajan's daughter, who were on their knees. When Kera saw Ajan sprawled face down, unmoving on the pavement, her knees buckled and she fell to the ground, only to be lifted roughly back to her feet and shoved toward a black van with no windows. Only then did their attackers' voices filter through her disorientation, and she shuddered. Degrovesnik. She took one last look over her shoulder at the trio on the ground before she was pushed into the van and the door was slammed shut behind her.

"Kera Espinosa. So nice to see you again."

Fear threatened to overwhelm her, but she kept it together. "Degrovesnik. Couldn't you think of a better way to get to me? This is rather messy, don't you think?"

He grinned. "I like messy better. And this way, you got to see your friends the moment before they died. Just like before, yes?"

She closed her eyes and swallowed the bile rising in her throat. *Petra's a goddess, kind of. She'll get them out of this.*

"Now, I need you nice and quiet for the rest of our big trip."

One of his crew grabbed her from behind and pulled her arms up painfully behind her back. She screamed as he put pressure on her wrist, and she knew it was broken.

Degrovesnik held up a fat needle so she could see it. "To help you sleep. I want you rested when we begin chatting."

He stabbed it into her neck and depressed the plunger. Within seconds, she began to feel woozy, and the bastard holding her let her drop to the floor of the van.

Tis. Baby, I'm so sorry. If there's any chance on this earth you can hear me, I'm in trouble. Ajan and Petra are in trouble, too. And those damn bodyguards. Please, please hear me. It was the closest she'd ever come to real prayer, and she had no idea if it would work. After all, Tis wasn't a goddess, as she'd often explained. As the world began to grow dark, she felt Degrovesnik's boot connect with her side and flip her onto her back. Her head slammed into the metal wall, and she had no more time to hope.

Tis grew to her full height and extended her wings. She let her fangs show and her eyes turn, making it so everything and everyone was tinged red. "Stop." She said it calmly, but the weight of it calmed the crowd instantly. Once they'd settled, she lowered her wings and looked around the room, making eye contact with the loudest of them. The moment she'd taken the stage they'd started yelling questions, and it had quickly erupted into a shouting match. Meg and Alec had moved onto the stage beside her, and she knew they were ready to defend her at any cost. Throughout the night, the variety of gods had raised question after question, several times arguing among themselves. They'd even had to break up a fight between a new, upstart god and an older one, when the young one had suggested the old one simply didn't have what it took anymore. Tis was tired, and she'd had enough.

"Now. If we're going to work things through, you need to listen. I'll hear you out, and we'll come to a decision." The underworld gods were mostly clustered together at the right, although a few of them whose position in their pantheon was more fluid sat with the rest of their groups. "I understand you're scared. I understand you're frustrated, and you want answers. I understand you're worried about fading and that things feel like they're out of control. And you're not sure if anyone is listening or going to help." She watched as many of them nodded. She knew suggesting the gods were frightened could piss them off, but she also knew it was true and needed to be said. "Now you have some sense of what it is to be human."

An uncomfortable silence filled the room. She waited for that to filter in before she continued. She flicked on the overhead projector. Ama had been taking notes all night, and during a break they'd worked together to come up with some primary questions, along with possible answers.

"The decision for the gods to move among the humans once again was not one made lightly. It was made because entire floors were fading, because followers had lost faith. The only way to show them that their gods existed was for you to show them yourselves. I, and the high council, still believe that to be true."

Tis paused, not because she didn't know what to say next, but because she had a sudden, emphatic feeling of danger, so intense it was like someone had thrown a blanket of cold moss on her. She tried to move past it, as the audience waited for her to continue. "Did you think it would be easy? Did you think there wouldn't be any issues to deal with, or questions? Have you forgotten what it means to be not just a god, but one truly attached to their people?"

The feeling of unease and danger grew to the point she could barely focus. Her pulse raced and she grew dizzy. She held onto the podium. "Yes, there are difficulties. One of the main questions is what to say to people when they ask why you didn't save their loved ones from cancer, or why you aren't helping with the drought. You can't answer without admitting to things humans can't know." She watched them nod and knew from experience the very fact they'd been heard would help calm them down. "I believe this is where we need to learn from those who are experts at deflecting questions with questions." She stepped back and motioned the woman waiting to the side forward. "And so, I've asked Atropos to speak to you today. Many of you won't have met her or her sisters. She's one of the three Fates, the woman who decides how someone will die. They are, of course, also the creators of oracles and omens. Who better to tell you how to be vague?"

There were titters of laughter along with a general sense of awe and wariness. The Fates not only measured out the humans' lives, they held an immense amount of power over the gods as well.

Atropos stepped up to the podium and began to speak. Tis moved aside and Alec put an arm around her and drew her off stage. "What's wrong?"

Tis hugged herself and gasped for air. "I don't know. Kera, I think. Something bad."

Meg stood on the other side of Tis, and she and Alec wrapped their wings around her. "Concentrate on her," Meg said.

Tis focused on Kera's essence, the unique quality each human held from the moment they were born. She saw smoke, flames. Petra, kneeling over Ajan, her hands on his chest. Then, almost as though Kera was right beside her, she heard her plea. *"Tis. Baby, I'm so sorry. If there's any chance on this earth you can hear me, I'm in trouble. Ajan and Petra are in trouble, too. And those damn bodyguards. Please, please hear me."*

Tis opened her mind so her sisters could see and hear the same things. She focused on Kera and felt her moving, saw the walls of a vehicle. More than anything, she felt Kera's terror and anguish like firebrands along her nerve endings. And she was in pain, so much pain. And then, nothing.

Tis jolted from the vision and stared at her sisters. "Where did she go?"

Alec frowned, clearly thinking. "I think they knocked her out. It's too complete for her to simply be asleep."

Meg's eyes were unfocused. "Hold on. I'm talking to Petra."

They waited, and Tis looked at Atropos, who held the audience captive with her lesson on rhetoric.

"You are *gods*. Don't forget that when you're scared and uncertain. You're goddamn gods. You don't have to explain yourselves to anyone, and you can damn well remind them of that. Simply say there are things humans aren't meant to understand, and it isn't their place to question the ways of the gods. There are reasons, and they must have faith. Faith is the foundation of the love and support they get from you, and you need to remind the snotty little primates of that whenever you can. Sure, be humble if that's what your followers want, and phrase it with goopy flowers and kindness. But for the rest of you? Take charge, and tell them they'll know what they need to know when you want to share it with them and not before. Some things are only knowable after death."

Panicked as she was, the lecture made Tis smile slightly. That was exactly what the gods needed to hear. Getting an audience with Atropos hadn't been easy, but once she'd convinced the secretary, Mnemosyne, how dire the situation was, the three Fates had met with her in a glass walled conference room overlooking the sea. They'd known she was coming, and they knew why. In fact, they already knew the outcome of the whole damn thing, but they'd let it take its course. Tis wanted to shake each one of them and demand answers. An ancient Greek had once taken their all-seeing eyeball and only given it back once they'd given him the answers he needed. Tis wished she could do the same, but an all-seeing eyeball was beyond archaic now. Today each of them sat at a massive desk with several computer screens on each and the constant hum of computer servers beneath their classical music station on the radio. No one, not the gods, not the furies, not even Zed, pushed the Fates.

"Okay. Petra says the bastard who took Kera before, ambushed them. Because she's still mostly human, she couldn't stop them, but she protected the other two people who were hurt. She says they took Kera in a black van with no windows, and they took the road that leads to the military base."

They stood there silently. "What do I do?" Tis finally whispered. "I can't leave in the middle of this, but I can't just let them take her, either."

"I can go," Alec said. "Let me see if she's at the military base."

Tis shook her head. "Meg, can you ask Petra to do it, please? It doesn't make sense for us to go when we've got someone there. See if any of the Vodun gods can go too. We have to know where she is before we can do anything to help her."

Meg hugged her tightly. "That's my wonderfully logical ice queen of a sister. I'd already be halfway across the ocean ready to rip people's heads off." Meg closed her eyes to concentrate on her mental conversation with Petra. "She says she'll head there now, and question whoever is around. She'll also get hold of the loa to help. The four other survivors of the attack have been taken to the hospital, so she can do what she needs to do."

Atropos held up a book to show the audience. "If you want more information and guidance, our new book, *Answers for Gods*, is available at reception and through our website."

Alec began to laugh. "The Fates have a website? Did you know that?"

Meg and Tis shook their heads, and Atropos left the stage to thunderous applause. She joined them, and her wide smile disappeared the moment the crowd could no longer see her. Her eyes reverted to the misty night sky, and her serious, ancient self was back in place.

"My dears," she said with a mysterious smile. "Don't look so stressed. Everything will work out in the end. It always does."

"But who will it work out for?" Meg asked.

"And isn't that always the question?" Atropos tilted her head and stared at Tis. "We never know what's just around life's corner or what choices we'll have to make."

The sentiment echoed the same words of the Vodun goddess. *At some point, you'll have to make a choice.* "But whatever we do, it's what we're meant to do, because we can't do anything other than what you've already decided. Isn't that right?" Tis tried to stay calm, though she wanted to let a snake loose on the old woman.

"Perhaps. Or maybe there's more free will in the world than you think."

"You drive me insane, you know that?" Alec shook her head. "You've driven me crazy since we were kids."

"Yes, Alectho, I'm aware. You told us often, when you'd come eat cherries with us in the summer."

"Good times," Meg murmured.

"Now, I must get back to work. People being born and dying every moment, you know."

They watched Atropos leave, and Meg blew out a windy breath. "I've never been as nervous around anyone as I am around them."

"I can't imagine what it must be like, to be born of Necessity and Night. Not really very warm parents," Alec said.

Tis nodded, but she was barely listening. She kept trying to make contact with Kera, to feel her or get a sense of her surroundings. Alec startled her back to the moment.

"I think it's probably a good time for a break, don't you?"

Tis nodded, grateful for the respite. She went back to the podium and motioned for silence. "I think you'll have found what Atropos had to say is extremely helpful. I know I did. On that note, since we worked through the night and you all have things to attend to, I suggest we take a break until tomorrow afternoon. Get back to work, and put some of what Atropos said into practice. We'll meet back here after lunch tomorrow and tackle some of the other questions and issues."

The atmosphere was lighter and more hopeful than it had been when Tis had arrived, and she was thankful she'd bought more than twenty-four hours to try to find Kera without walking away from her duty.

Meg came up beside her. "Petra says she found two guys at the dock who watched a group of five guys unload a van into a seaplane. They didn't see a woman with them, but there was a rolled up carpet that looked unusually heavy. The guys offered to help and had guns pulled on them as thanks. But neither she nor the loa can find any trace of them now."

"Tell Petra thank you, and to let us know how everyone else is doing." Tis thought furiously. *A seaplane. If Kera stays unconscious, I won't have any idea where they're taking her.* But seaplanes, for the most part, couldn't land in any kind of rough water. That ruled out large coastlines. *But it leaves a zillion lakes.* She'd never felt so helpless. Logic and strategy couldn't help her until she knew where to start.

Come on, baby. Wake up. Just for a minute, so I can get to you. Whatever else happened between them, Kera was special, and Tis wasn't about to let some evil bastard hurt her again. *And when I find you, asshole, you're going to wish for death.*

Chapter Twenty-four

K era's throat was on fire, and her head pounded. Each time she'd managed to swim back to consciousness, a needle was jabbed into her neck, and she'd blacked out again. This time she stayed completely still and made certain her breathing didn't change. She slowly took stock of her body, starting with her feet and making her way up. Her ankle hurt and her boot felt too tight around it. *Swollen, but not broken.* She kept going, and when she concentrated on her ribs, she knew they were badly bruised, but again, they weren't broken. A quick survey of her arms let her know her wrist was probably broken. Her neck hurt where they kept jamming that goddamned needle into her, and her head was pounding like someone with a jackhammer was trying to get out via her eye sockets. *But not dead. That's something, right?*

She had no idea how long she'd been unconscious, or where they were. She could hear an engine but couldn't figure out what kind it was. Given that she wasn't on a bed of feathers drinking ambrosia, she guessed her mental phone call to Tis hadn't worked. *Not a big surprise, really.*

"Wake up, sleepyhead. We're almost home."

The voice sent a chill down her spine and made her want to vomit.

"Come on. We can tell by the monitors that you're awake, Dr. Espinosa. No need to play opossum."

She opened her eyes and closed them again, the light making the pounding in her head worse.

"Ah, of course. Dmitri, turn down the lights. You see, the little concoction we've been using to keep you asleep has some side effects, and I'm afraid a truly noxious headache is one of them."

Even with her eyes closed she knew the lights had dimmed, and she slowly cracked her eyes open again. Degrovesnik held a plastic cup with a straw in it.

"I imagine you're quite thirsty, too."

She wanted the water more than she'd ever wanted anything but couldn't bear the thought of taking it from him.

"It makes no sense to deny yourself. As you know, true dehydration is very uncomfortable. And unnecessary."

She struggled to sit up in what she realized was a hospital bed, and Degrovesnik moved around to raise the back of it for her. She took the cup from him and drank deeply, never taking her eyes from him. "What do you want?" she asked, her voice hoarse.

"What all men want, I suppose. Love, sex, money. All the base things. But then, I also want revenge. And death. There are those things, too."

"Where am I? And where are you taking me?"

He sighed dramatically. "Such mundane questions. I expected better. But okay. For now. You're currently on a train headed for an airport. Once we've reached that airport, we'll take a flight to a high security, extremely remote location where I've got a truly exceptional lab setup. There, you'll have all you need to continue the experiments and research that were so rudely interrupted when your American friends removed you from my care."

He used almost the same words he'd used so many years ago to entice her to his lab in Siberia. "Russia, again? Do you miss it that much?"

He gently pressed on her injured wrist, which was wrapped and clean. She jerked it away. "No, Kera. After you left, I did some soul searching, and I came to understand I was too narrowly focused. No, this time we'll go where I can reach many, many more people with little effort. And with your help, I'll let the Western world know how impoverished and fragile they can be."

"You know I won't help you. I watched good men and women die because I wouldn't help you."

His smile was pure evil. "But will you allow children to die?" He nodded at the guard at the door. "I don't think you will."

"What the fuck does that mean, you overzealous cologned prick?" She sat up and immediately fell back as the room spun.

"Soon enough, Dr. Espinosa. Soon enough." His voice grew faint as the door shut behind him.

The guard moved forward with that fucking long needle in his hand again. She raised her hands to ward him off, but he just shoved them aside and jammed it into her incredibly sore neck.

He turned away, and Kera let the tears fall. She thought of Petra and Ajan's daughter watching as she was taken away, as they knelt over his inert body. *Please, please don't let him die.* She wasn't praying, because she didn't know how, or who she'd even pray to. The only one she'd ever known that listened… *"Tis, I know you can't hear me. But if there's a snowball's chance in hell that you can… I'm so sorry."*

❖

Tis gasped and shook Alec awake. "I heard her."

Alec nodded and struggled out of her cramped position on the sofa. "Give me your hand." She nudged Meg's leg with her own. "Meg. Get up. Give us your hands."

Meg groaned and stretched her arms out, still face down on the lounge chair. Tis and Alec took her hands in theirs.

Tis concentrated on the energy flowing between them, using it to spread her awareness of Kera's energy as far as she could. The words were brief, but they lingered. "She's moving…a train? She's far away, I can't quite get her…" Tis opened her eyes and dropped her sisters' hands. "I lost her. They must be keeping her sedated. Did you get anything?"

Alec shook her head, her expression sympathetic. "I'm sorry, Sis. Like you said, she felt far away. I wouldn't say she's in this country, but I couldn't get a read on where she is. It felt like she was in less pain, though. That's something, right?"

Meg said something, but it was muffled because she was still face down.

"Flip over, fang face." Alec nudged her again as she went to make coffee.

"You're a fang face." Meg rolled onto her back and looked at Tis upside down. "She was definitely in less pain, but she's scared. She knows the guy who took her."

Tis jumped to her feet. "The research team. I can get them to see where the guy is, right? They can run him through the system. And Petra. She was doing something to do with him too. That's why Kera had bodyguards."

Meg stretched. "I'll call Petra. You call the research team. I'm taking a shower."

"I thought you were calling Petra?" Alec said.

"Where better to talk to her than while I'm naked in hot water? Have you seen that woman's body?" Meg grinned and headed into the bathroom.

"I feel stupid for not thinking of this before," Tis said, taking a mug of coffee from Alec.

"To be honest, Petra's probably a better bet than the research team. Granted, he might be a religious bad guy, but if he's not a believer, he won't be in the system anywhere." She sipped her coffee contemplatively. "He's letting her wake up long enough to call out. Hopefully, when they get to where they're going, she'll be awake long enough for us to get a flag on her location."

"I hate that we have to wait. I hate every second she's with him."

Alec gave Tis a tight hug. "We'll find her. And you know we'll take care of the bastard when we do." She looked at her watch. "Until then, I need to run home and see Selene before we go back to the meeting this afternoon. But if you hear anything more and need me, just shout and I'll come right away."

Tis hugged her back, not wanting to let her go. "Okay. See you soon. Tell Selene I said hi."

"It *will* be okay. I promise." Alec kissed her cheek and left.

Tis drank the rest of her coffee while staring out over the ocean. They'd gone back to her place when they'd left the meeting and ordered pizza. Meg had put in some absurd movie that made a mess of the fall of Troy, and they'd distracted themselves by tearing it apart and talking about what had really happened. They'd all fallen asleep where they were, and Tis's wings ached from sitting in the egg-shaped chair all night.

Meg came into the room looking refreshed and vibrant, as she always did. She wore Tis's jeans and one of her tighter T-shirts, and Tis wondered if she looked as good in them as her sister did. Tis envied Meg's all-out approach to life, something she'd had even when they were children. Nothing ever fazed her. But then, she didn't seem to actually let anyone genuinely close, either.

"Okay, I've had a chat with Petra." She took a piece of paper from the drawer and started writing. "Here's all the information she found on the guy they think took her. She was worried about something like this happening, which is why she was there in the first place. Bummer she couldn't stop it, but at least she's there with Ajan. And he's going to be okay, by the way. Concussion, but no big deal. Humans have such soft heads, don't they? It's amazing they manage to live past their first year."

Tis called the research team and spoke with the head of research, Lu, a former Chinese god of knowledge. She gave him every detail she could recall from her conversation with Kera, as well as everything Meg had learned from Petra. He promised to work fast and get back to her as quickly as possible.

She put the phone down and looked at Meg blankly. She had no idea what to do next, and the weight of it all felt utterly overwhelming. In an instant, Meg had her in her arms.

"You know, it's strange." Meg's tone was measured, as it sometimes was when she was being serious. "We were born without human belief. Death, the Fates, and us. None of us need belief to stick around. And yet, not one of us has ever left the job the way some of the gods have been able to. We serve, and keep serving, even though we don't have a boss and can't get fired. We do it because we were born to do it, and I think you're the only one who's ever questioned why." Meg leaned back to look at Tis. "Did you come up with an answer before everything went to shit?"

Tis laughed slightly. "I think I did, actually. And you're right. We were born to it. It's who we are. We can't just change jobs like other people can. I'm proud of what we've done for the world, and even if we can't fix all of it, at least we do something. So, yeah, I think I'm okay."

"But Kera didn't see it that way?"

Tis sighed. Trust Meg to get right to the point. "No, she didn't. We tried to get past it, but she's angry about the limitations and that the gods don't live up to people's expectations."

"And of course you couldn't explain the whole shebang, because you'd be in violation of every Afterlife code going." Meg shook her head. "That's why I've tried to keep my distance from humans all these years. It's too messy. Alec lucked out that Selene has that demigod thing going on."

It was true, Alec had lucked out. But Tis hadn't, and there didn't seem to be any way to fix it. "Well, regardless, I have to get her back and make sure she's safe. After that…" She shrugged.

"The first thing you need to do is shower. You smell like an overripe goat. And you look like a plastic shopping bag, you know, the ones that float around in the air on a windy day? How will the gods have confidence in you if you look like a homeless fury?"

Tis winced and laughed. "Thank you for that lovely description. Good thing you're my sister."

Meg poured herself a cup of coffee and flipped on the TV. "That's what sisters are for. Go, stinky hoofs."

Tis took off her clothes and saw how wrinkled they were. She looked in the mirror on her way to the bathroom and grimaced. *A plastic bag for sure.* Her hair was tangled, and her feathers were matted. She turned on the overhead rainwater faucet as well as the wall jet and let the hot water stream over her. She scrubbed herself raw until her hair and feathers squeaked when she ran her hands over them. She thought of the hot showers she'd taken with Kera, of the way their soapy bodies had slid over one another, and how

Kera's fingers had felt inside her. She rested against the wall and remembered as she tugged at her nipple with one hand and circled her clit with the other. Kera's mouth, her tongue, her fingers, her moans…

The bathroom door flew open, and Meg stood there with a towel in her hands. Tis was about to tell her off when she saw the look on her face. "What is it?"

"Come see." Meg threw the towel to her. "And before you ask, it's not about Kera." She turned and left.

Tis quickly toweled off, feeling far better than she had when she'd woken. But something had rattled Meg, which meant it had to be really bad. She threw on some clothes and went into the living room. Meg sat staring at the TV, her hands pressed to her cheeks and tears in her eyes. Tis focused on the news anchor.

"It's an unprecedented wave of destruction. That these attacks could be carried out almost simultaneously in so many countries is unbelievable, and yet, it's true. There's no word yet on the number of casualties, as most of the fires are still burning too intensely for firefighters to get anywhere near the buildings."

Smoke filled the background behind the reporter, but as a plume thinned, Tis recognized the blackened walls. She looked at Meg, horrified. "Meg?"

"Churches. Temples. Mosques. All over the world at the same time." She looked at Tis and tears streamed down her cheeks. "They're destroying Zed's temple."

Chapter Twenty-five

Peaceful. Thank fuck. Kera slowly climbed back to consciousness, aware only of the absolute silence. She'd woken briefly when they'd wheeled her onto the plane, but they'd quickly knocked her out again. Now, there was nothing moving, no engines chugging, or people talking. Her eyes felt like they had weights on them, but she forced them open and rubbed the grit out of them. Her wrist was wrapped in clean bandages and throbbed like a son of a bitch. She was dressed in a kimono type thing with a lot of ugly flowers on it. *They're already torturing me.* She sat up slowly, stayed still until the wave of dizziness and nausea passed, then looked around. *At least it's not a dirt cell this time.*

It was a large bedroom, and it had the feel of a cabin. There was lots of wood everywhere, including the big four-poster bed she was sitting on. There was a large window across from the bed, and she wondered if she could be so lucky, or her captors so stupid. She slid off the bed and stumbled toward it, but dropped to her knees when her legs wouldn't support her. She had no idea what day it was or how long the assholes had kept her drugged, but her legs felt like they were made of water. She crawled to the window and hefted herself up using the window ledge. She couldn't see any locks on it, but no matter how much she pushed at it, it didn't budge. But whether that was because it wouldn't open, or because she was too weak, she didn't know.

The door to her room opened, and Degrovesnik walked in, followed by an extremely tall Amazonesque woman with long blond hair in two thick braids. A guard closed the door behind them.

"Good morning, Doctor. I'm very glad to see you awake and already out of bed. How are you feeling?"

"Yeah, this is nice. Reminds me of a place I stayed in Vermont. Three weeks with a trio of friends who couldn't get enough of… well, anything really. But right now, I'd feel a whole lot better if I was on a plane home with a cute flight attendant waiting for me in the staff area."

"Yes, I imagine you would. Your appetite for women is well known. And along those lines, let me introduce you to Sasha. She's a good friend of mine, but she's willing to be a good friend of yours as well."

The Amazon gave Kera a small smile and brazenly looked her over. Her eyes were cold, and her smile could have been carved from ice. Kera gave her a fake smile in return. "That's quite thoughtful. But she looks like she could break me. No offense, sweetheart."

The woman's eyebrow quirked, but she didn't say anything.

"Oh, she could, Doctor. I wouldn't leave you with just any woman. You see, I'd like you to be as comfortable here as possible, and I'll try to provide for your needs. That includes women like Sasha. You're going to be here for as long as it takes for me to get the result I need, and I've always been a firm believer that happy employees are better employees." He moved to the window next to Kera and looked outside. "If you were wondering, this window is sealed shut. It's also alarmed, as are all the windows in the house, should it be broken. We're ninety miles from the nearest town, most of which is abandoned. There is no main road for nearly two hundred miles. The area is heavy with bears and mountain lions, both of which are very hungry this time of year."

He turned to look at her, and she shuddered at the lifeless evil in his eyes. He saw her reaction, and it seemed to please him.

"If you do as I ask, this will be like working in a luxury resort. Beautiful surroundings, good food, lovely women, and high-end equipment."

"And if I don't?"

He sighed. "That would be a shame. I'm aware from our previous encounter how little you value the lives of those who work for you. That's why I didn't bother with your sidekick back in Haiti."

The little bit of strength Kera had was failing, but she didn't want to fall in front of the bastard who had made her life hell. Just when she knew she'd have no choice, Amazon Sasha came over and draped an arm around her waist. She led her back to the bed, and although Kera tried to keep her back straight, she knew she'd failed miserably. She crawled back into bed and pulled the comforter up over her. "I cared deeply for the innocent people you killed. I just wasn't about to let you kill even more."

"If you had truly cared, you would have done as I'd asked, and we wouldn't be here today." He pointed at her, and his face flushed. "And I wouldn't have had to put my plans on hold until I found a way to get to you, until this place was ready to go. You've made me wait far too long, and now you *will* do as I say. If you don't, I will kill every employee you've got, and I'll go back and have a long talk with your father that will end with him going to see your mother." He closed his eyes, clearly calming himself down. "However, I have a much more interesting incentive for you on site. Someone will bring you dinner shortly, and then I'll give you a little tour." He turned to leave and ushered Sasha out ahead of him. "Oh, and if you think your pretty pale girlfriend can help you, you should know this house was built by atheists and was later turned into an astronomy academy. Thanks to their studies, the cabin is densely insulated and has a surprising amount of metal built into it. Something to do with their telescopes or aliens or something. I know you're not religious, but after seeing that beauty you've been spending time with, I wouldn't be surprised if you'd changed your mind. I just wouldn't want you to get your hopes up, you see. Prayer won't work here."

She could hear him laughing even after the door shut and locked behind him. Kera slumped against the pillows and tried to think, but she was exhausted and defeated. She had no idea what he meant about the atheist or metal thing. She and Tis hadn't talked about the way prayer worked. *Is that all it takes? A bit of tin foil and someone who doesn't believe? Fucking hell.* She closed her eyes, and though she fought it, she drifted to sleep once more.

When she woke up, the room was dim, with just the final rays of sunlight pushing into the evening sky outside. A tray of food sat on a cart beside the bed, and it looked like it had long gone cold. She quickly drank the large glass of water and then the milk, even though it was warm. She tore into the bread roll, not bothering with the butter. She wasn't sure when she'd last eaten, and the hard roll tasted like a delicacy.

The door opened, and Amazon Sasha came in with a fresh tray of food. She turned on the light and swapped the trays, all without saying anything.

Kera finished chewing, though the smell of the pasta dish was making her salivate. "Do you speak? Or did our Russian Romeo out there cut out your tongue?"

She pushed the tray toward Kera. "I speak. If I want to. My tongue is very useful." She turned away and went to the closet. "I can assume you would like to change clothes before we go out, yes?"

"No, thanks. I love flower dresses. I've always wanted one but could never give myself permission. Now that I'm in one, I don't ever want to let it go." The food was excellent. That, or she was so hungry bear scat would have tasted gourmet.

"There's no need for sarcasm."

"I disagree. Sarcasm is the most honest language I know."

Amazon Sasha brought over a pair of jeans and a white T-shirt. "I'll be back in thirty minutes. You don't want to keep him waiting."

"Actually, that's not true. I'd very much like to keep him waiting. Until he's dead, in fact."

Amazon Sasha left, and Kera was irritated she didn't rise to the bait at all. She felt like a good fight. More sleep and no more drugs meant she had some energy, and the food was doing wonders for her too. She finished, all but licking the plate, and got dressed. There were socks but no shoes. She opened all the drawers, and there wasn't so much as a pencil in them. Amazon Sasha came in again, but this time she had a wheelchair with her.

"Is that for you? Is it too exhausting, walking around with all that height?"

"It's for you, Doctor. The area is very big, and you are not healthy yet." She stared at Kera for a moment. "Please do not make this difficult. There will be plenty of time for you to be difficult later."

"Choose my battles, huh? Okay, Amazon Sasha. Let's go for a ride."

Kera sat in the chair, unwilling to let the woman see that she was already tired from the exertion of getting dressed and eating. Her wrist throbbed, and the rest of her body felt like she'd been hit by a bomb. *Oh, right...*

Amazon Sasha pushed her down a number of long hallways and down several ramps in place of staircases, and Kera was surprised at how massive the place was. It wasn't just a cabin, it was more like a hotel, but the doors they passed had signs that read things like "white dwarves," "black hole assignments," and "corona conjunctions." Names she assumed were meant to be funny to those in the know, but which just reinforced what her personal psychopath had said about the building. They stopped at an elevator and took it to the basement. When they got out, Kera's old nightmares hit her full force.

It was a lab. Pristine, shiny, new. A few people in white coats tapped away at computers, but for the most part, it was empty. Degrovesnik entered from another door across the lab.

"Doctor, I'm glad to see you look better. Welcome to your new work station. I've taken the liberty of having all your old workbooks and notes left on that desk there. Anything else you need, you have but to ask."

"I told you, I'm not—"

He held up a hand. "Yes, I know." He motioned to Sasha, who pushed Kera's chair across the room. "If you wouldn't mind, please have a look here."

Kera stared at the long glass wall, the dinner she'd eaten threatening to come back up. "You're a fucking monster." There were children, at least thirty of them, ranging in age from about six to ten. Some huddled together, some sat alone. Many were crying, a sound she could hear faintly through the vent at the top.

"Without question, Doctor. But I'm a monster with a mission, and if you don't help me complete that mission, I will kill one of those children every time you oppose me. If I think you're stalling, or trying to deceive me, I will kill one. I'll leave their bodies outside for the animals directly outside your bedroom window, so you can see what your integrity has cost. And of course, they'll always be right here to remind you of that." He turned to Sasha. "I think our doctor would like to rest now. Doctor, I'll give you some time to get your strength back and to understand the rules of this game. I'll come see you tomorrow."

Back in her room, Kera crawled into bed and pounded on the pillows. "Fuck. Fucking murdering psycho bastard fuck!"

Sasha turned at the door. "You should conserve your strength."

Kera threw a pillow at the door as it shut and then curled up on her side, the images of all those children like a horror movie in her mind. She had to think of a way out. For all of them. *"Jesus, Tis. If I ever needed someone in my life, I need you now. If you can hear me, now is the time."* She thought about the crap Degrovesnik had said about the building and hoped like hell it wasn't true.

Chapter Twenty-six

They flew as fast their wings would carry them, the ocean a blur of turbulent white-tipped glass. Tis's thoughts were flying even faster than she was, but without any direction, they were far less useful. When she heard Kera's voice, she nearly lost her balance and fell into the ocean.

"Kera. Baby, where are you?"

"YES! I promise to believe in every god you want me to. Just get me the fuck out of here, fast."

"But where are you? I can't feel you the way I should be able to."

"That's creepy, but we'll talk about it later. I'm pretty sure I'm in the States, but I'm in the wilderness. All I can see are trees, but he said there are bears and mountain lions. And he said something about it being an old astronomy building. Does that help at all?"

Tis motioned to Meg, and they landed on the shore. She grabbed Meg's hand and brought her into the conversation.

"Trees and animals don't help much, baby, but the astronomy thing does. And thank the gods I can hear you. Are you hurt? Papa Ghede said he could hear you too, but he couldn't figure out where you are."

"Well, at least the telepathy thing works, right? I'm not great, but okay. But things are going to go to hell if you can't find me."

"Can you stall? If you can keep talking, I'll try to zero in on you. But it may take some time."

"I'm okay, and I can fake sick with the best of them. Someone's coming..."

She faded away and Tis looked at Meg, who shook her head.

"That's weird. If she was somewhere like they took Alec last year, we wouldn't hear her at all. But I can't get a read on her location. It's like she's just in the air somewhere."

Tis nodded and tried to focus on Kera, but she'd stopped talking, and her energy had faded away. *Astronomy means science. If there hasn't been faith in it, it's like the place they took Alec.* Meg touched her arm.

"Now that we know she's safe, and she's not hurt, we need to get to the office. We'll go get her, but, well. You know. Zapping and burning and angry gods and stuff."

"And stuff." Tis sighed. "Yeah, I know. Let's go."

They flew the rest of the way to Afterlife, and Meg back-winged when they were in sight of the building. The walls were shaking, several windows were broken, and the air crackled with furious energy.

Without looking at her, Meg said, "Have I mentioned lately how glad I am I'm not you?"

"Not within the last few minutes. Thanks for the reminder. Let's go in the back door."

The inner courtyard was a flurry of agitated gods, some sitting by themselves, others in clusters. When they saw Tis and Meg fly over, they began heading toward the main building.

"So much for a stealthy entrance."

"I want to see Zed first, but I'm not sure how to get to the fourth floor—"

Just then, a door opened above the fire escape to the fifth floor. Clotho, one of the Fates, opened the door and waved her and Meg over. They landed on the metal steps in front of her, and she motioned them inside.

"You'll never make it through the crowd down there." She closed and locked the door behind them, then led the way through the dimly lit back hallways. She opened a cleverly hidden side door that looked like the rest of the wall. "This leads to Zed's office. Good luck." She walked away, humming what sounded like a carousel tune.

Meg rolled her eyes. "Some people are so dramatic." They made their way quickly to the door leading to Zed's office. Before she turned the handle, she looked at Tis. "They don't play tricks anymore, do they? Like, we're actually at the gate to Hades and have to make it back in time to save Christmas or something?"

Tis gave her an incredulous look, and Meg shrugged. They entered Zed's office, and Tis ducked as a vase shattered against the wall beside her. The air smelled like…bacon.

Meg sidled around the table and grabbed a piece of pizza from the box.

"It was just ham, until Big Man here lost his temper and crispied it with one of his lightning bolts." Ama sat in Zed's desk chair, pieces of her hair standing on end like someone had rubbed her head with a balloon.

"MY TEMPLE. MINE. They're wrecking MY TEMPLE." Lightning cracked against the glass wall as Zed spoke with his hands. "I haven't done anything wrong."

Tis fluffed her wings to get out the electricity. She hated when they were full of static. "Zed, I need you to calm down. I need to understand what's going on, so I can get out there and help."

He turned to her, his face flushed, and his eyes alight with rage. "It's like they're saying on the news. Every major religion has had at least one sacred place set on fire. And each one was started at the same moment as the others."

"And was anyone caught setting the fires?" Tis was lost. As organized as Humanity First was, it didn't seem like something they'd do. They were against the death of innocents, and any one of those temple fires could have killed people.

Zed seemed to calm down slightly. "They've caught a few, but no one has gone to speak with them yet. Thanks to the laws we've put in place, none of us thinks we could question humans properly without killing them."

"That's remarkable self-restraint. I'm impressed." He tilted his head in acknowledgement, and Tis could see the flames in his eyes as he watched his most beloved temple fall. "Meg, can you go to the Hindu temple in Malibu and see if anyone there was caught? Let's start close to home."

Meg swallowed the last of her pizza, saluted with one hand, and licked the fingers of her other clean before she went to the secret door in Zed's office. "Will do. Listen for me and I'll shout if I've got anything. Alec says she and Selene will be here in a minute."

Tis waved as Meg left and was glad that she'd have Selene's cool, philosophical approach there soon. She turned to Ama. "The temples on fire—are all those gods here?"

"They are. Some of their underlings are out in the world trying to deal with things, but like Zed says, there isn't a single god who doesn't know he'll fry the person who has desecrated his temple the moment he sees them."

"Okay. Let's go to the main hall."

The three of them made their way past gods in various stages of distress. Unable to stop herself, though she knew she should be focused on the here and now, she called out to Kera and was weak with relief when she answered right away.

"I'm here. Can you hear me? Are you coming?"

Tis felt the question like a blow to her soul. *"I'm going to, baby. We just need a better handle on where you are. And I'm kind of in the middle of a crisis..."*

There was a long pause, and Tis thought she'd lost her again.

"Yeah, I understand. I'm sure I can figure my way out of it. Don't worry about it."

Kera faded, and Tis nearly doubled over from the sense of loss. *"Don't shut me out. I'm coming, baby. I promise."*

There was no answer, and Tis felt the tears well in her eyes. They entered the foyer, and her knees weakened at the sight of Alec and Selene talking to Cerberus. Alec opened her arms, and Tis let herself be wrapped in her sister's embrace.

"Tisera, we need to get to the assembly room." Zed's voice was sharp, his stress loud.

Alec looked at Tis, her expression searching. "Meg says you can hear her."

Tis nodded. "I can. But I can't leave."

Selene took Tis's hand. "If you don't, who will? So, the world is falling apart. It's always falling apart. Save it today, tomorrow some other part will burn." She pressed her palm to Tis's chest. "Sometimes, Tisera, you have to make a choice. One only you can make."

Tis flinched inwardly. It was the third time someone had told her she'd need to make a choice. *By the gods, I hate oracles.* She thought about the way Kera made her feel, about the way Kera's touch made her ache and soar, and about how disappointed and detached she'd sounded moments ago. She thought about how lonely she'd been before Kera came into her life. She looked at Selene and Alec and let her tears fall.

"Tell me what you would say. As a stopgap, what would you tell them to go do?" Selene asked.

Tis thought fast. "They need to overstep the line and take drastic measures. They need to use the weather to put the fires out in the temples and take care of the people in the affected areas. They need to go be among their humans, right now, at their sacred places, so they can see they haven't been abandoned and their gods do care, no matter what the physical space may look like. They need to calm their believers, grant as many prayers as they can, as fast as they can, while the rest of us figure out what happened and who caused it."

Selene took Alec's hand. "Go." She grabbed Zed's forearm and pulled him along. "Leave her alone. We've got this, and she'll hardly be gone for any time at all."

Zed stared at Tis, his eyes wide. She hadn't seen this kind of fear in him since they'd stopped worshipping at his temples centuries ago. "I'll be right back, I promise," she whispered, knowing he'd hear her.

Tis ran to the side entrance, flung open the emergency door, and leapt into the sky. *Kera, baby, talk to me. I'm coming for you.*

❖

Kera ate slowly, watching the people in lab coats move carefully through the lab. The door to her room had opened just as Tis had let her know she wasn't as important as her job, and she was glad for the interruption. At least she hadn't been able to say anything she'd regret later. *We discussed the fact that our jobs come first. For both of us. She never lied to me.* That fact didn't stop the needle of pain in her soul, and she wished she could change things between them, somehow. *Not that I'll have the chance. I won't make it out of this alive, not again.*

Her guard had escorted her to the basement lab, but hadn't said a word, no matter how she'd tried to provoke him. Sasha had met her in the lab and explained that they wanted her to start getting used to the operation and the people she'd be working with. What better time than over dinner? She bent the plastic knife in her hand. Clearly, they didn't trust her not to do anything stupid. *Good call.* She motioned Sasha over. "What am I supposed to be creating? Once I've healed from the injuries your boss gave me."

"He has the records you left behind. He was careful they were preserved. You'll continue working on the project you failed to complete previously."

She looked so impassive, so like a crazy big mannequin, Kera wanted to see her crack. "Have you ever been told you look like a really big Barbie doll? I mean, if Barbie came in Amazon flavor."

Sasha studied her for a moment before leaning close to her ear. "I don't believe killing the children will work on you. I believe only your own pain will drown out those pretentious morals of yours." She stroked Kera's hand with her own. "If I were in charge, I would take a little piece of you every day and place it in a glass box where you could see your body parts mounting, until you finally did as you were asked. But I'm not in charge, and I've been told I'm to see to your particular needs."

She stepped back and smiled sweetly, and Kera shivered at her cold, soulless eyes. "Then I guess I'm glad a woman isn't in charge, for once. And I have to say, you've taken a serious hit in the fuckability department. I wouldn't be able to get off for worrying you'd go all nutty on me in the act."

Sasha shrugged and turned away. "You're not as funny as you think. And if you anger Degrovesnik further, he may let me have my way after all." She motioned at the guard. "Put her in with the children for the night. Let her get to know their sweet little faces, the ones she'll be responsible for feeding to the animals."

The guard pulled Kera to her feet, and she winced at the pain in her ribs. Not one of the lab workers looked up as she was marched past them, and she wondered where they'd been taken from. Quiet, frozen fear emanated from all of them. A door in the glass wall slid open, and the guard roughly shoved her inside. Two of the older kids put themselves in front of several of the younger ones and eyed her warily.

She put her back to the wall and slid to the floor, already exhausted. Somehow, she knew Tis wouldn't be able to hear her from the basement, so she didn't try. *Not to mention she's busy.* Kera looked at the cluster of kids nearest her. "So, what are you in for?"

"Probably not the same thing you are," a tall boy answered.

Kera grinned. "No, probably not. What's your name?"

"Greg. I'm the oldest."

"Well, Greg, I'm going to say you aren't the oldest anymore."

He pointed and proceeded to tell her every child's name and age. She'd remember them all, whether she took their names to the grave or if she managed to get the hell out of this place.

"Any chance of breaking out, Greg?"

He shook his head. "There's always two guards when they bring our meals, and one always has a gun. They never open the door except to give us food."

"What about bathroom breaks? Any chance of a child-stampede then?"

He pointed at the back of the room. "There's a bathroom back there, off to the side. Everything is bolted down. I checked."

Kera nodded, exhaustion stealing over her. "Well, that's all rosy news. I think I'll take a little nap and dream about more pleasant things, like famine and plague." She opened her eyes again when she felt a nudge at her shoulder.

"Take this. Looks like you need it more than I do right now."

She accepted his balled up sweatshirt and used it as a pillow. When a little girl crawled over and snuggled against her, she put her arm around the child. "Thanks, Greg. I'll make it up to you sometime."

He nodded and sat beside her. Several of the children came to sit beside him. *What kind of world is it where a kid has to parent other kids in the madhouse of a psycho?*

She fell asleep with a child against her and far too many more around her. Degrovesnik had played his hand, and she was going to have to fold.

❖

Tis flew in loose circles somewhere over the Midwest. She'd followed Kera's trail as long as she could feel any hint of it, but it was gone and Kera wasn't answering her anymore. Her phone rang, and she ignored the disappointment of it not being Kera. "Hey, Aulis. How is everything going?"

"Aside from the world burning to the ground, great, thanks. I was calling to make sure you weren't in any of those flaming temples."

Tis watched a herd of deer bounce through the trees below her, unaware they were being stalked by a massive cat of some kind. "I'm in the air at the moment. Kera's been kidnapped, and I'm trying to find her. Meg and Alec are handling things at the office."

There was a moment of silence before Aulis began to laugh. "Well, that was a succinct plot rundown. Trust you to put the end of the world into such simple terminology. How can I help?"

In her desperation to find Kera, it hadn't occurred to her to use anyone else's help. "Maybe…Aulis, if someone has broken an oath of any kind, do they end up on your list?"

"It depends on the level of oath broken. If it's a little thing, a white lie, then we take note so we can keep an eye on them for bigger stuff later. If it's a medium thing, we pay a visit but don't leave lasting punishment. If it's a big thing, well, then we pop brains and fry cells."

"I've got a last name and a little bit of information. If I give you that, can you check your database for me? I'm trying to find a bad guy, and bad guys break their promises all the time, right?"

"That's been my experience, yes. Give me what you've got."

Tis told her what little information she had, and Aulis hung up after saying she'd get back to her right away. Tis saw a massive lake and headed to it. Since she couldn't go any farther, she might as well rest her wings. She landed beside an enormous oak and climbed into its sturdy branches. She curled up against the trunk and thought about Kera. She didn't know where their paths would end, but she wasn't going to give up on her, not until it was definite there was no way forward. With the temples falling, believers and non-believers both turning against the gods, and her own heart mixed up in it all, Tis wondered if her kind could have a breaking point. She called Alec, who said Selene had told the gods exactly what Tis had told her to, and they'd done as instructed.

"In fact, I think they were just glad someone was there to tell them what step to take next. I bet plenty were ready to let the temples burn and then move on to retribution." Alec chuckled. "Anyway, any luck with Kera?"

"I don't think it needs to get to retribution stage. And no, I can't get a read on her. Aulis is doing some checking for me, and I'll keep calling. Hopefully, she'll answer. Any luck on old astronomy labs?"

Alec's tone was gentle when she said, "She'll answer, honey. And then you can bring her back here while we go fix the world. And no luck so far, but we'll keep searching."

Alone in a massive tree, Tis thought about that phrase. *Fix the world.* That's what Kera had been trying to do with all her charity projects. That's what Tis was trying to do now. *If we're both trying to do it, why can't we do it together?*

She closed her eyes and listened to a pair of owls calling to one another. She needed to figure out so many answers to questions she couldn't even phrase yet. The only thing she knew for certain was that she had to get Kera back, no matter what.

Chapter Twenty-seven

Kera watched the kids eat breakfast, some kind of horrible instant oatmeal with pieces of dried fruit on top. They were also given individual cartons of orange juice. *Keeping them healthy until he kills them. Until I kill them. Goddamn him to whatever hell he believes in.* Unless she could figure a way out, she'd have no choice but to do what he wanted her to. Although, if she could get hold of Tis and get enough of her time to get out…then she could go to the authorities and get the kids released. But that idea meant getting back to her room long enough for Tis to zone in on her, or whatever it was she did. She thought about calling out to the loa, but Petra said they weren't big fans of hers after she'd insulted everything about them, which meant they probably wouldn't come for her even if they heard her. Although Tis had said Papa Ghede had tried to zone in on her, too, which was both comforting and weirdly discombobulating. And if she was going to talk telepathically to anyone in her final days on the planet, it was damn sure going to be Tis.

Greg sat down next to her. "You should eat. You don't always know when they're going to bring food."

She looked at the porridge. "Pretty sure I wouldn't keep it down, buddy. I've eaten a lot worse in countries where that would have been a luxury, but right now, it's not very appealing."

He shrugged and swallowed a big spoonful. "My foster mom always said we should be grateful for whatever we got." He eyed a piece of dried fruit. "Even if it came with a punch or two."

Little pissed Kera off more than child abuse. Her parents had loved her so much, she couldn't imagine coming from a home where parents were sons of bitches. The vision of Tis in her full power mode came to mind. *Yeah, okay, that makes sense. She's got the right of it there.* "Where are you from?" she asked, trying to banish Tis from her mind for the moment.

"Georgia. Oklahoma. Kentucky. Florida was the last one. A Southern kid, I guess."

"Any idea where we are now?" Kera felt a flicker of hope.

"Not really. It took a long time to get here, though. Like, three or four days, I think. A bunch of us were packed into a big rig, so it was hard to tell time. There were always guards in there with us, though, and when they got out I could tell it was different times of day."

"Smart kid. Did you see anything else on the way in? Any landmarks or weird buildings?"

He thought about it. "A lot of trees, mostly. But I did get a quick look at water. I mean, it looked like the ocean, but it didn't feel like it. Does that sound stupid?"

Kera shook her head. There were only a few bodies of water in the States that looked like the ocean. "The Great Lakes. We're somewhere in the far North." She punched his shoulder lightly. "Nice work."

"Thanks, for all the good it does us. Knowing where we are doesn't get us out of here." He set his bowl aside and looked at her seriously. "You're something to do with why we're here, aren't you?"

"What makes you say that?" Kera could tell plenty of other kids were listening, and she didn't want to frighten any of them.

"It's not like they throw any other adults in here with us. We're not stupid. What do they want from you?"

Fuck. This is why I don't have kids. So many questions. Her mother had once told her that if a kid was old enough to ask a question, they deserved a real answer. The problem was, Greg wasn't the only one waiting for an answer. "They want me to create something, a disease that could hurt a lot of people, all over the world."

He stared at her, and she could practically see the thoughts whirling around in his head. He looked away from her at the other children and gave a sharp nod. "I get it."

He didn't ask anything else, and she knew he was protecting the other children from the knowledge he now had, but probably didn't want. "I'm going to do everything I can to get us all out of this. I promise."

"Promises don't mean a whole lot to this group. Good luck." He got up and went to sit with a group of the youngest children, one of whom climbed into his lap.

The door slid open, and the guard motioned to her. "Let's go."

She looked back at Greg as she left, but his back was rigid and he didn't turn around. Kera sighed and stretched her aching muscles as she walked back through the lab. A brief glint caught her attention, so fast she almost missed it.

"Shit!" She stumbled and fell to the floor, knocking various empty glass beakers and cylinders to the floor. They shattered, and she cut her hands on them as she braced against her fall. One of the lab techs was instantly beside her, and Kera knew she saw her slip the silver scalpel up her sleeve. They made eye contact, and she saw the fear in the girl's eyes, though her expression remained impassive.

"Let me help you up." She helped Kera to her feet and led her over to a sink, where she carefully washed the glass fragments from Kera's hands and bandaged the cuts. The guard stayed too close for them to speak.

"Thanks. I owe you."

The girl tilted her head slightly and went back to work without another word. Kera pretended to limp forward. Buying time meant she needed to look like she couldn't work yet. "After you, big guy." She followed him down a long hall she didn't recognize to a beautiful, candlelit room. On the dining table was fresh fruit and bagels, and her stomach grumbled at the smell of bacon. The guard whispered in Sasha's ear before he left and closed the door behind him.

"I'm sorry to hear of your mishap. It's not surprising you aren't steady on your feet yet." She came over and lifted one of Kera's hands to inspect the various bandages. "And we can't have you working with open wounds, can we?"

She turned away, and Kera was again struck by the woman's icy demeanor. "Nope, can't have that. Can I have a bagel?" She moved slowly and carefully, desperately trying to keep the scalpel from showing up against her sleeve.

"That's why you're here. Help yourself."

Kera sat in an overstuffed chair and nearly groaned with relief. "You know, you should put a few of these in with the kids. I think they'd love them."

"There's no point in allowing those little gutter rats to have what they can't keep."

Kera wondered if she could throw the scalpel hard enough to do any serious damage but thought better of it. She'd have one chance, and she had to time it just right. "Are you his girlfriend? Confidant? Psycho escort service?"

Sasha smiled. "I'm his business partner. I had the money, and he had the dream. Together we're making it a reality."

"So what's your gripe? Bad childhood? Someone take your toy or piss in your cereal?"

She was silent for so long Kera didn't think she was going to answer.

Finally, she said softly, "It was a bomb. American made, American dropped. They said they were going after insurgents. But the bomb they dropped hit a hospital and a school. Everyone died. Including my grandmother and my youngest sister." She finally looked at Kera, her eyes like flint. "The entire village lost someone that day. I'm tired of watching people in countries die because of extremists on both sides of the missiles. It's time to put an end to it. We'll cure the world of its preoccupation with other cultures and give people something to think about other than tearing apart other countries for oil or weapons."

Kera knew there was no one more dangerous than someone who felt they had nothing to live for. "I'm sorry for your loss."

Sasha stood and wiped her palms on her jeans. "Yes, well, you're going to make up for what your country did. Enjoy your meal."

She closed the door behind her, and Kera was left with her thoughts.

Chapter Twenty-eight

Tis stirred as the buzz of her phone woke her. She opened her eyes to find two tawny owls on the branch next to her, also dozing.

"Hey."

"You didn't give me much to go on. That name you gave me is pretty common in Russia, and it comes up a lot." Aulis paused. "There's one that seems odd, though. He's a bad guy, but he doesn't seem to have actually broken any oaths. But because he's been in the outer nowhere of Russia, he hasn't been on any of our serious watch lists."

"Godforsaken places." Tis stretched and her owl companions fluttered slightly before settling back down.

"Right. He seems to have killed some people, but there weren't any oaths involved, so not one of our cases, and since there aren't any specific gods assigned to that region, there wasn't anyone around to serve any justice."

"Any current address?"

"Siberia is the last one I could find. I'm sorry, honey. Still no word?"

Tis watched as the sky turned from a bruised nightshade to a candy pink. *If only life worked that way too.* "Nothing yet. I know I'm close, but I don't know how close."

"Let me know if I can do anything else. I'm helping at some of the temples, but I'll come if you need me."

The thought of having such an amazing friend, one who would drop everything even when the world was going to pieces, gave Tis a modicum of comfort. "Thanks, Aulis. I'll let you know how it all turns out."

She hung up and headed back into the sky. She flew in lazy circles, scanning the earth below, hoping to see something, anything, that would lead her to Kera.

"Hey. You there?" Kera's mental tone was cautious.

Tis's pulse raced. *"I'm here. Keep talking. Are you safe?"* She flew north, feeling Kera's energy signature like a neon sign.

"For the moment. Some cuts and bruises, but things are pretty fucking bad here. Can you find me?"

"I can and I will. I don't think I'm too far away." Kera sounded tired, defeated, and Tis ached to hold her.

"One of the kids here told me there are a lot of trees, and a massive lake. I think I'm near one of the Great Lakes, but I don't know which one. A lot of this place is underground. Whenever they take me out of my room I can't reach you."

"That's great. It will narrow things down for me." Tis flew as fast as she could, holding on to Kera's energy as tightly as she could. *"What kids?"*

"They're holding a bunch of kids hostage to get me to do what they want me to do."

Tis understood the hopeless feeling in Kera's tone now. There was no way she'd allow children to die. *"Yeah, well, I'll deal with that when I get there."* Tis closed her eyes and focused on Kera's energy, which was stronger with every mile that passed. She pulled back slightly and concentrated on the location.

"Tis? I'm sorry. I've been an ass, and if I don't make it out of this, I hope you know you're the most amazing woman I've ever met, and by far the best lay I've ever had."

"Well, then I guess I'd better save your obstinate ass. She felt Kera's energy waver. *What's going on?"*

"They've come for me. Tis…I love you. I should have told you sooner."

Abruptly, Kera's energy shut off, like a switch being flipped. Tis's stomach lurched at the break in contact, as well as at her final words. *She loves me.*

❖

Kera followed her guard dutifully down the maze of corridors, memorizing them the way she had been from the first. She'd been left in that dining room after breakfast for hours, and eventually she'd moved to a couch and gone to sleep. When she woke, there was no guard, so she'd moved quickly back to her room, managing to guess correctly the few times she wasn't sure which way to go. Now, on her way back to her kidnappers, she hoped like hell it had given Tis enough time to track her. *At least I got to tell her.* She hadn't planned on it, but the seriousness of the situation was weighing heavy. She kept thinking about Greg and the way he'd protected the other kids, and had even given her his sweatshirt to use as a pillow. *The lives of the many or the lives of the few?* It was an impossible question, and she prayed she wouldn't have to answer it.

They entered the lab, and this time there were several techs waiting for them. Sasha motioned her to a seat.

"Good morning, Doctor. I trust you slept well? My apologies you weren't taken back to your room sooner. It seems the man guarding you fell asleep on duty."

Kera felt the guard next to her tense. Degrovesnik didn't take incompetence lightly, and she was willing to bet his batshit crazy counterpart didn't either.

"Fortunately, he's given us an excellent opportunity."

Kera barely registered the gun in Sasha's hand before it went off, the bullet punching a small, neat hole directly in the middle of the guard's forehead. The tech staff all jumped, and one of them turned away to vomit. The guard fell to the ground with barely a sound.

"We're going to place him outside your bedroom window, so you can watch firsthand what will happen to those sweet little children should you fail to do as we ask." She motioned with the gun, and two other guards stepped forward to take their comrade's body away.

"That's very kind of you, but unnecessary. I've seen what animals can do to people." Kera let the implication hang in the air, but as usual, Sasha failed to bite.

"The team has been assembled so you can begin discussing your previous work and how you're going to continue your research. Detail for them what you'll need, and if you need supplies, we'll get them in."

She walked out of the lab, almost daintily sidestepping the small pool of blood still on the floor, and Kera looked at the team in front of her. All young, all scared. "I think we should get drunk while we talk." She turned to the guard at the door. "She said we could have what we need. I think we need beer."

He stared at her and then looked at his colleague, who shrugged and nodded slightly. The guard turned to leave and she said, "That's right, bellboy, off you go." She turned back to the team. "I'm guessing you know who I am. Who are you?"

They gave her their names and seemed to relax slightly now that someone without a degree in *international psychopath* was in charge. She lowered her voice and whispered, "Okay. I say we discuss, at length, the best Marvel movie heroes. But use big, science sounding words to befuddle the masses. In fact, describe the movie and hero in science terms and see if we can guess who it is. Got it?"

There were a few smiles and nods. The guard brought back a box filled with bottles of beer, and she handed them out. If they were all going to die here, at least they'd have some fun first.

They spent most of the day playing their game, opening and closing notebooks as though they had something to do with the conversation and trying to keep a straight face any time Sasha walked through. Kera's hands hurt, her wrist ached, and she was utterly exhausted, but she tried hard not to show it.

The far door opened, and Degrovesnik strode across the lab. He looked every inch the bastard she needed to deal with. She looked at her team. "You know how there's always someone to help the guy in tights? People who step in give the hero the time he needs to do what needs to be done?" She made eye contact with each of them quickly. "I always hated the stormtroopers. I mean, who did they fight for? Whoever was strongest, right?" Degrovesnik was nearly with them. *So close.* "And is it one, two, three, go? Or go on three? Someone is always left scrambling. But that's okay, I guess. Someone to tie up loose ends."

When Degrovesnik was within striking distance, Kera tapped her fingers on a bottle, and made eye contact with each staff member. *One. Two. Go.* The guards were bored and inattentive, and totally unready for what happened next. Two staff members each jumped a guard and brought him down, managing to disarm them quickly. Kera's attention was on Degrovesnik, though. She kicked a stool and sent it flying at him, and she was right behind it. He batted it away, but that left him open, and when she crashed into him, she managed to spin him so he landed face down. She rammed her knee so hard into his crotch she wondered if he could taste his balls. He screamed, and she straddled him, yanking his arms behind him. She slid the scalpel she'd secreted away the day before from her sleeve and held it to his neck.

"This ends now. No more child hostages, no more dark cells. I've owed you this for a long time." She leaned back slightly to shove the blade into his neck.

The door crashed open, shattering the glass around it.

And there in the doorway stood the most beautiful woman Kera had ever set eyes on, in her truest, most terrifying form. The snakes on her head writhed and hissed, her eyes were the color of fresh blood, and her fangs were fully extended. Her wings glowed magnificently, spread out behind her.

She looked at Kera. "Don't. He's mine."

Kera trembled. If she let him live, Tis would fill his mind with agony and horror, but he'd still be walking the planet. If she did what she had to do, she'd lose Tis forever, and potentially end up being the one with a gray matter makeover.

"The children are watching." Tis didn't take her eyes away from Kera, but Kera knew it was true. They'd already seen the guard from this morning killed, most likely. They didn't need to see it happen again. *They can get therapy. This fucktard will keep killing people.* "Please."

Kera groaned and got off Degrovesnik, but not before giving him a quick punch in the kidneys. As much as she hated him, she wouldn't risk losing Tis, and maybe she could save the kids' innocence, if they had any left. She stumbled away, but heard a shout and turned.

Degrovesnik lunged at her with a hunting knife, his eyes wild with fear and rage. "I should have killed you years ago."

Kera raised her hand to deflect the knife at the same time as she jabbed with the other hand, her martial arts training kicking in automatically. She buried the knife in his neck, and he dropped his own weapon as he fell to the floor, gasping and holding the artery as blood pumped between his fingers.

Kera looked at Tis, panic engulfing her as the man who had tortured her dreams lay at her feet, very quickly dying.

"Self-defense. Doesn't count." Tis tilted her head and looked past Kera. "Down!"

Kera didn't need to be told twice. She dropped to the ground and looked behind her. Sasha, her expression feral, pointed her gun at Kera.

"You've ruined everything! I told him you would, but he wouldn't listen."

Suddenly, Sasha flew backward, as though someone had punched her in the chest. She hit the back wall but didn't let go of the gun. Even doubled over, she pointed it at Kera and pulled the trigger.

Kera had no idea what happened to the bullet. All she knew was that one minute Sasha was there, the next she was a disgusting puddle of human goo on the floor. She looked like an egg put in a microwave too long, and her dead eyes suggested it wasn't a pretty bright light she'd seen in her last moments.

Tis lowered her hands back to her sides, her eyes blazing, and her fangs glistening under the glow of the fluorescent lights. "Are you okay?"

Kera nodded and tried to ignore putrid smelling slush-human on the floor. "Thanks to you. We've got a lot of people here, though. Can we get them all out?"

Tis looked around the room. The tech staff were still on top of the guards, and all of them were looking at her in obvious terror. Several of the children were pressed up against the glass wall, staring in awed fascination. Greg stood with his arms around two younger children, his eyes wide, even as he tried to turn them so they couldn't see the carnage in the lab. "I can hear the other guards fleeing. Were these the only two in charge?"

Kera nodded.

"In that case, Petra and Ajan can come help. We'll let them know you're at a ranch house in the Wilderness State Park in Michigan, on the edge of Sturgeon Bay. They can help clear everyone out."

Kera hadn't been able to think about Ajan without seeing him lying on the road, his daughter beside him. "He's okay?"

"He'll be fine once he heals. But I'm fairly certain he's going to retire now."

Tis moved closer, and Kera looked up at her. When she looked at Tis, she didn't see a monster or an immortal. All she could see was the woman she loved. "You came for me."

"You knew I was coming. All I needed was a good connection. Like you said, a lot of this place is not only underground, but it's also got metal walls. It was built years ago by people hoping for extraterrestrial visitation, and then turned into a place for actual astronomical study, but it wasn't on any register because of its history with the alien adherents. That's why I could hear you so clearly sometimes and not others. I'm sorry it took me so long to get to you."

Kera touched Tis's face and winced slightly at the pain in her wrist. "But you had something going on, and you still came. You must have pissed someone off."

Tis laughed, a strange but not unwelcome sound in her true form. "I'm sure I have. But I realized something important." She pulled Kera close and wrapped her wings around her. "When it comes down to it, I'll always choose you."

Kera closed her eyes, the simple statement unraveling her emotions and making her weak-kneed.

"How badly are you hurt?"

Tis leaned back to look down at her, and Kera realized she'd never again be able to fib to someone whose hair stared at her as well. She decided to ignore the cloud of hissing snakes and focused on the crimson fire in Tis's eyes. "Not too bad. My wrist, mostly. I'll be fine. Especially if you sleep in my bed as soon as possible. For observational purposes, obviously."

Tis looked behind Kera and smiled.

Kera turned around and pressed against Tis. "Okay. Now I need fresh underwear."

The extremely tall figure in a black cloak, who also held an enormous scythe, moved gracefully toward them, almost delicately stepping over Sasha's remains. "Geez, Tisera. Did you really need to make such a mess?"

The figure lowered its hood, and Kera felt like she could breathe again. "You're way more attractive without the terrifying getup, you know."

Tis hugged Kera to her. "Kera, Dani. Dani, Kera."

"Nice to meet you, Kera. I've heard a lot about you. Forgive the uniform, but it's part of the job." Dani smiled and motioned at the bodies on the floor. "If you'll excuse me, I have work to do."

Dani moved away to kneel over Degrovesnik's body, and Tis gently turned her around to face her again. "Baby, I'm sorry, but I need to get back to the office. Things are pretty crazy. Are you sure there's no one else here I need to worry about?"

"I'm pretty sure. I mean, there were guards, but we can deal with these two, and you said you heard the rest taking off. So, it's just like taking care of business in the other countries we go to, right?" Kera hated the thought of Tis needing to leave so soon.

"In a way. I'd take you with me, but I have a feeling you'll be needed here. Someone needs to take care of the children, as well as the staff. You should call the police, so they can confiscate whatever weapons are on the premises."

"Hey, now. This isn't my first bad guy rodeo, you know. I mean, I've never had to explain an over-easy body, but I'll work with it." Tis's smile didn't reach her eyes. "That serious, huh?"

"Pretty bad. As long as I know you're safe, I can concentrate on what I need to do. When you're done here, will you come to the Afterlife office? I have a feeling I could use your viewpoint on a few things."

The thought that Tis, a fury who could pop people like a pimple, would need her help made Kera feel like she could conquer the world. "Of course. Do I just ring the bell?"

"I can take her," Dani said as she moved away from Sasha, tucking a black sack into her backpack. "We're busy, but my crew has things in hand at the moment, and the gods are doing what you told them to, so things are level at the moment. I can spare some time."

Kera looked at Tis, unsure how to respond without offending the one being in the world she really didn't want to piss off, ever. But the thought of traveling with Death made her distinctly uncomfortable.

"That would be incredible, Dani. Thank you so much." Tis pulled Kera in for a hug and whispered, "She's a good friend, and you'll never be safer than you will be with her." She looked into Kera's eyes, and Kera saw the love in them.

"Yeah, okay. I'm sure I can keep from peeing myself long enough to come back with her. I'll get done here as fast as I can."

Tis closed her eyes and was silent for a moment before she reopened them. "Don't bother calling Ajan and Petra. I've already had Meg let Petra know our plane is on its way to get them. They'll be here as soon as they can." She leaned down and gave Kera a lingering kiss. "I'm sorry, but I really have to go. I'll see you back at the office soon." She looked at Dani. "Take care of her, okay?"

Dani waved her off. "Go. Save the world. I'll bring her back safe and sound, I promise."

Tis sighed and stepped away. She looked back at Kera and smiled. "I love you, too."

She disappeared down the hallway, and Kera felt bereft at Tis's absence.

"I hope someone looks at me that way, one day," Dani said from beside her.

She jumped and gave Dani a quick smile. *Death is lonely. Who knew?* "You never know. Maybe you just have to be ready to take the leap, you know?" Kera turned and surveyed the room, unable to cope with an existential conversation with Death about love. "Let's get started, shall we?"

Chapter Twenty-nine

Tis flew through the night, so high up ice crystals formed on her wings. The beauty of the cold, clear night matched the clarity in her soul. With Kera not only safe, but coming to her soon, she could truly focus on the job at hand. She let her gaze soften, and the stars blurred together. *Think. It's all related somehow. The kids and others with that black sludge and their souls already gone. The outbreaks of violence and the burning of religious centers…*It was there, a niggle in the back of her mind, but she couldn't quite grasp it. It felt familiar, but ancient, so long ago it was a memory buried in dust.

She flew lower, into warmer air, and smelled the faint acrid scent of fire. Below, a massive church was still smoking. Instinct told her to land, and she circled the glowing embers, searching for something, a hint of what was going on. She landed, making sure no one could see her, and walked the perimeter of the building. At the edge of the trees, she caught a sense of the thing, the something they'd been searching for, and her feathers trembled in the darkness.

She knelt and spread her hand in the dirt before she stood and pressed her hands to the tree next to her. But it wasn't there, not really. It wasn't a physical thing. Whatever it was had been inside someone, a person carrying something they didn't understand. She looked at the ruined building, at the one wall still standing. There, framed by the empty window, stood a person in the shadows across the clearing. Tis leapt into the air and dashed across the space, but when she got to where the person had been, they were gone, leaving only the terrible empty feeling behind. She waited, watching, but the person didn't reappear, and the strange feeling faded, leaving behind only a sense of confusion.

She spread her wings and headed for the office. She forced herself to put words to the feelings before they faded completely, and repeated them constantly, fighting off the strange disorientation she felt when she tried to picture the being. While she didn't know *what* they were, or who the person was, at least she knew for certain someone was behind it all. *No one can hide from every god on the planet. And if my sisters and I catch you...*

She landed at Afterlife just as the sun was coming up. Unlike the days before, the grounds were nearly empty and the building was, thankfully, still in one piece. Alec and Meg were outside waiting for her. The moment she was in reach, Alec handed her a huge mug of coffee.

She sipped it gratefully before asking, "So?"

They entered the building together, all of them taking a moment to scratch one of Cerberus's heads before getting in the elevator.

"Selene managed to calm everyone down and get them focused, the way you wanted them to. It's taking a lot out of some of the lesser gods, but they're managing to put things back in order. Consequently, because they're actually helping people on the ground level, the people are responding in kind. No more religious spaces are being attacked at the moment." Alec held the elevator door open for them as they headed for Zed's office.

"That's good news. I've got some of my own, but I want to tell Zed and Ama about it at the same time."

Meg was uncharacteristically quiet, and Tis gave her a questioning look.

"Just feeling a little rundown, you know? I haven't had a spa day or manicure in ages. I want some quiet time."

Tis put her arm around her and gave her a squeeze. Meg was always so up, she forgot how deep she ran. "Hopefully, we can work things out soon and get back to normal, whatever that is."

Zed saw them coming and waved them in. "I take it your personal issues are dealt with now?" He frowned at her, thunder rumbling around him.

"You're one to talk. How many times did we have to go after someone because you were fooling around with humans? Especially when you went through that shape-shifting phase." Tis sat down and finished off her coffee, wishing there were more. "And yes, thank you, I managed to resolve everything. But I saw something on the way back that I need your perspective on."

They sat down and looked at her expectantly. She concentrated and pulled the scene back to her. "There was a smoking church, and I felt the need to see it. When I got there, there was some kind of emanation everywhere—sticking to the ground, to the trees, and especially around the burned bits."

"What kind of emanation?" Meg leaned forward, looking like a child listening to a campfire story.

"Confusion. Despair. This subtle feeling of disorganized mayhem simmering, waiting. At first I couldn't figure out where it was coming from, but then I saw someone, something, in the distance, and I knew they were behind it. But by the time I got there, they were gone."

Everyone was silent until Meg said, "By the time you got there? How could anything move that fast?"

Tis hadn't even considered that aspect of it. "So, not human then. That's a start."

Zed drummed his fingertips on the table. "You couldn't see them? Anything at all? You've got the best eyesight I've ever known."

Again, that hadn't occurred to Tis either, and the cloudiness of her thinking made her incredibly uncomfortable. "Nothing. It was like…like…" She struggled to find the words, and then it was as though a wall crashed to the ground and she could think clearly again. She almost gasped at the sudden clarity. "It was like a living shadow. Darkness formed into a person. I haven't been able to think clearly since the moment I landed there. And I got the feeling I knew them, but I have no idea from where."

Ama's sudden intake of breath drew their attention. "I know." She took Zed's hand in her own. "So do you."

He shook his head. "It can't be. She's been gone for centuries."

"Um, excuse me? Who are we talking about? Confused fury here." Meg waved her hand to get their attention.

Zed stood and motioned them to follow. "Come with me."

They followed him to the disguised staircase and up to Level Five. The receptionist wasn't there, and they walked straight back to the Fates' offices. All three of them were standing in front of a massive door at the end of the hall, waiting.

"Is it true? Is she back?" Zed's deep voice bounced off the walls.

As one, they said, "It's true." Clotho stepped forward and looked at them impassively. "She can not be defeated until passion merges with destruction to create a new world."

Tis really, really hated oracles, and this wasn't the time for vague warnings. "What in Hades are you talking about?"

The Fates moved away from the huge door. As it slowly swung open, the tension in the small group was palpable. Tis wanted to spread her wings to protect them from whatever was about to walk into the room.

"Awesome. You've got a door into outer space. That puts my parties to shame." Meg leaned forward, and Alec put a gently restraining hand on her shoulder.

"It's so beautiful," Ama whispered.

Beyond the open door was a view of the cosmos, in all its brilliant colors, swirling masses of stars passing by in jet streams of superheated gasses. And then that sight was blocked by the person coming in. Tis felt the same pull and strangeness she'd felt at the fire and fought against it.

"Knock that off," Clotho snapped at the person.

The strange sensation vanished, and Tis focused on the figure. Or she tried to. One second she would swear it was female, with long flowing hair. The next instant, it appeared male, with shining black eyes. It was all of them and none of them, and even their clothes seemed to reflect the cosmos behind them.

Again, Clotho sighed and slapped the figure on the arm. "That's enough. Behave, or I'll shut you out there again."

The figure solidified and became an utterly stunning woman with jet-black hair down to her waist and eyes that looked like snowflake obsidian. She gave Clotho a mischievous smile before turning back to the group.

"Lovely to see you again. Please, call me Dis."

Tis stared at a being she hadn't seen in more than a thousand years, and understood why the world was imploding. *Chaos is back.*

Chapter Thirty

K era had been at her fair share of meetings with powerful people. She'd eaten with presidents in various countries, had slept with royalty, and shaken hands over billion-dollar deals.

None of that prepared her for sitting at a conference table with a bunch of gods. Nor did it help that her girlfriend's sisters were there, looking far more terrifying than the one she'd gotten used to. It was a hell of a way to meet someone's family. "So, let me get this straight. You're the reason all those pretty buildings out there are smoking piles of rubble now?" She spoke to the extremely sexy but extremely dangerous looking woman across from her.

As soon as she'd been able to, she'd given control of the situation to Ajan and Petra and hopped into Dani's car, which had entered a long underground tunnel and emerged shortly thereafter in LA. When she'd asked if she could buy one for herself, Dani had laughed heartily. "Only if you want my job, too," she'd said. The thought of being Death made Kera cringe, though she made sure not to show it. She'd choose life any day, even if it did mean she wouldn't get the cool travel toys. When Kera had arrived after a pleasant journey with Ms. Death herself, she'd been ushered straight past the enormous three-headed guard dog receptionist, and up to where Tis was waiting for her outside the elevator. It was like a really twisted urban version of Wonderland.

After a quick hug and kiss, Tis had explained she needed to stay in her meeting, but Kera was welcome to join it, as was Dani, since it also involved her.

Kera focused on the conversation going on around her, trying to keep up.

"I'm only partially responsible. I admit, it's very nice to be back."

"What do you mean, partially?" Tis swatted at Meg, who looked bored now that her initial curiosity had been satisfied.

"For centuries, humans have been content. Whether they believe in religion or not, they've had a sense of their place in the universe. They think they know about the origin of their species, whether that's from a place of faith or a place of science." She looked at Selene and smiled. "Occasionally, when a new epoch was ushered in, I was able to come out and play for a while, but eventually, creatures on this planet find a way to either placate or ignore their fears, and I'm relegated back to the infinite. The humans were settled for a ridiculously long time, until the gods decided to make their presence known. When that happened, it began another stage of evolution, in a manner of speaking. There are too many people who can't handle the truth, who see their gods and are unable to cope with it."

"Like the old days," Zed said thoughtfully.

"Like the old days," Dis agreed. "To look upon your god was to risk death or insanity, as the human mind couldn't handle it. Today, there are many people who can process it without issue. But there are also many who can't. Thanks to those people, I've been called back. They are the embodiment of me, and as they disintegrate mentally, it's me they understand, not their gods or their science. Only me."

Kera sat back and studied Dis. "Well, don't you sound like the happy little cosmic sadist. I don't suppose you feel any sympathy for the people you're ruining?"

Dis looked at Kera with a wry smile. "I was first, you know. Before all of the people around you, before everyone in this building. Even before the crones on the floor above us. I was the beginning, and everything came from me. And, eventually, to me everything returns."

"So, you've got a mother complex, too. What difference does that make to the people you're messing with?" Kera felt Tis squeeze her hand in warning, but she didn't care. As far as she was concerned, the woman was a bully with nothing better to do than hurt people.

"I am the origin and the cosmos. I am galaxies and universes you can't fathom. No, I don't care for insignificant human lives that last less than a flash of a second in the expanse of space."

"I have to admit, that does sound pretty selfish," Dani said in that quiet way she had.

"Doesn't it though?" Kera leaned around Tis to give Dani a high five. "So, how do we make you go away again, so you can go play with your neon gasses and balls of rock?"

Dis looked at Zed and Ama, obviously unfazed by Kera's sharp tongue.

"Until the world calms down again and people understand their places, Dis will be among us." Ama looked at the rest of the team. "That means we have to come up with a way to exist in this new world, quickly. But in the meantime, people's fear and confusion will call to Dis, and she'll answer."

Tis raised her hand. "Why did those kids blame Satan for the shooting?"

Dis shrugged elegantly. "When their brains are disintegrating, and they can no longer be rational, they find a way to explain what they're feeling and why. They use concepts they know to put a name to what they're experiencing. What or who they choose isn't my doing."

"But that one kid choked like he was murdered," Alec said.

"A biological reaction. His brain couldn't complete the process he was trying to rationalize, and it turned his own body against him. He quite literally choked on his words. Again, not my doing."

She seemed like she was enjoying the attention and was totally unbothered by the accusations. It was pissing Kera off. She turned to Tis and was calmed by the serious beauty beside her. "So, gorgeous? I think we need to figure out a plan. It sounds like your spacey friend here is going to be around no matter what, so let's work on getting the world back in order." Tis's smile held so much love and tenderness, Kera could have wept if it weren't for the badasses surrounding her. There was no way she'd show that kind of emotion around a bunch of immortals.

"I agree. Why don't we go to Meg's place since it's closest? We'll get takeout and discuss potential solutions."

Meg jumped up from the table and took Dani's hand. "We'll go get Thai food. I've been craving it for ages."

Alec shook her head as they left the room. Dani looked somewhat bemused as she trailed behind Meg. Alec clapped a hand on Kera's shoulder. "Glad you got out of that mess safely. It's nice to see my sister so happy." She sauntered out, whistling a tune from Snow White.

"I've been asked to have dinner with the Sisters," Dis said as she rose. "I'm sure I'll be seeing you often."

"Not to be rude, lady, but there's enough death and destruction without you here helping things along. I kind of hope I'll never see you again." Kera winced at how hard Tis squeezed her hand this time, and she noticed the one called Zed move slightly in front of her.

To her surprise, Dis laughed, an eerie sound that echoed like rocks falling into a canyon. "I like you, little human. I hope we can speak again."

She left, and Tis stood and pulled Kera up with her. "You're welcome to join us," she said to Zed and Ama.

Zed shook his head and put his arm around Ama. "This is your field and the whole reason we gave you the position. You'll know what's best, you always do. Just let me know what you need from me when you're ready. In the meantime, I need to go back out to my temple and help with the nearby crops. Ama is going to do the same. And it keeps my ex out of my hair for a while."

Kera had a hard time imagining the giant guy with the long beard wielding a hoe or dodging an angry spouse, but if it worked, she wasn't going to knock it. She'd promised herself she'd be more open-minded, and sitting among them, it helped to see them as less useless.

Tis turned to her. "Well, shall we go have a few minutes to ourselves?"

"That's an offer I'll never turn down. Let's do it."

❖

After a teenage-like make-out session behind the caretaker's shed, Kera and Tis walked to Meg's place, and Kera heard the TV newscast before they entered the room. She wondered what it meant for the world she'd dropped into.

"Tonight at the DNC, for the first time in American history, a Democratic nominee has come out in support of a religion other than Christianity. Gavin Jackson has stated his unequivocal support of the Buddhist belief system and has suggested that it's time America takes a new direction in both policy and faith."

Kera could think of a million things she'd rather be doing than sitting around talking about religion, and all of them included Tis naked. Instead, she smiled politely as Tis leaned down and gave Selene a hug before she made the introductions.

Selene got up and shook Kera's hand. "It's so nice to meet you. You gave us quite a scare."

Kera wasn't sure if Selene had a sense of humor, and it didn't seem wise to insult her with her enormous, black-winged girlfriend behind her, so she kept herself in check. Apparently, sometimes sarcasm wasn't the answer. "Definitely wasn't my intention, and I sure as hell hope never to do it again." She narrowed her eyes as she took a good look at Selene. "I really hope this isn't offensive, but you don't look like you belong here any more than I do."

Selene laughed. "I didn't when I first got here. I can imagine all the things going through your head. Most of them probably went through mine, too. If you ever feel the need to call someone who will experience gray hair and wrinkles while your partner remains ageless, just shout."

Kera ran her hand through her hair self-consciously. "I hadn't given that much thought. Thanks a lot."

Meg came in carrying two massive bags full of Thai takeout. "Don't let her fool you, Kera. She's a demigod. She just likes to pretend she's not one of us. It makes her feel unique."

Alec rolled her eyes and sat on the floor beside Selene. She handed out plates and served Selene's before she got her own.

"Not true. She's unique in every way. She doesn't have to pretend anything."

Meg made a gagging noise and flopped upside down on the couch beside Dani. Kera laughed with the others, the surrealness of the situation not lost on her.

Tis wrapped a wing around Kera and winked at her. "So, let's start. Any ideas?"

"First, let's lay out the exact problem so we're all clear what premise we're working under," Selene said. "And I'd like to discuss the political element we've just witnessed as well."

Tis ticked the points off on her fingers. "One. Chaos is behind the black spaghetti in people's heads, as well as the violent destruction going off like bombs all over the world. Some humans lack the capacity to withstand gods in their midst, and consequently, Chaos takes over. Two. There's general unrest among believers. Humanity First has people questioning their gods and what they get from them like never before in history. As people question, they fail to get answers, and they revolt."

When she stopped, Kera continued. "Three. The gods are useless asshats who answer prayer by email and can't help people with the most difficult parts of life. That pisses people off."

There was an uncomfortable silence before Meg burst out laughing. "I'd love to see you call Osiris an asshat."

Kera smiled at her. "Give me the chance."

"I'm fairly certain name-calling wouldn't get us anywhere," Selene said with a grin. "But I think Kera has raised a valid point, and one we need to add to the mix."

Kera raised her beer in salute. She'd expected more resistance and was relieved to see they were looking at the problem openly.

They ate contemplatively for a while, and when Kera moved to get another helping of pad thai, Alec pushed it toward her. In that instant, Kera started to formulate a plan. "Okay. So, let's set aside the Chaos thing. The woman gives me the creeps, and it sounds like all we can do is deal with her messes after they've happened. Right?"

"Entropy is the natural state of things, so she'll always be closer than we'd like her to be. While we may dislike her place among us, her existence is as constant as our own. Fortunately, she only comes to the fore when there's extreme change." Selene opened a soda and shared it with Alec.

"Like the plague," Kera said.

"I wonder what she'd be like in bed?" said Meg from her upside down position on the couch. "Would she be all airy fairy, or hot and electric?"

"Or gassy." Kera ducked the fortune cookie Meg threw at her. "So, we set gassy hot creepy woman aside for now. As I see it, the other two problems are inextricably linked. People are questioning because they have someone they can ask directly now, and they're not getting answers they like. But at this moment, while the asshats they pray to are out there actually helping people, things are better, right?"

"What are you thinking?" Tis leaned against her, looking tired. Kera wrapped an arm around her protectively.

"I say, put them under new management." Kera looked around, and she could see Selene knew where she was going. She nodded, and Kera continued. "When you run a business, you don't make it successful by putting the front line staff in charge of everything. You don't give them a few baseline rules and then let them loose."

Tis sat up and stared at Kera. "You manage them."

"Exactly."

Selene jumped up and ran to Meg's coat closet, where she pulled out a flipchart Meg used for game nights. At the top of the page she put a question mark, then drew vertical lines from the question mark down.

Kera got up and pointed at the question mark. "You need to have someone up here who understands business. Someone who understands management and can make decisions. Someone who can help managers delegate and someone to help with decisions."

Dani shook her head. "You want to make someone the boss of the gods? Zed's been trying since we moved to Afterlife. Have you ever tried to tell a god what to do?"

Kera crossed her arms. "I've sure as hell told them where to go."

Meg snorted and coughed on her drink.

Tis traced the lines on the chart with her fingertips. "In the past it wouldn't have worked. But the uprisings have rattled them. They always turned to Zed when things became difficult, but now that Zed's temple has burned as easily as theirs have, I think they'll respect and fear him less."

"He's a front-liner anyway. His people probably want him to do shit for them too, right?" Kera pointed at the question mark. "The gods wanted out of the closet, now they have to face up to what the world really is. Do you have someone other than the creepy as fuck old women who are having dinner with their creepy as fuck comrade tonight, who doesn't have folks dropping to their knees for them?"

"There are a few of us who don't have believers. The three of us," Tis motioned to herself and her sisters, "don't have followers. Nor does Dani, or Selene's mother."

Kera raised her eyebrow. "Who is your mom, anyway?"

Meg speared a wonton and stuffed it in her mouth. "The moon," she said around a mouthful of food.

"She's not the moon, but rather the personification of it. But yes, basically." Selene shrugged slightly.

"Of course. Silly me." The bizarreness of the situation rushed in on Kera once again. She turned her attention to Tis when she felt her next to her.

Tis took Kera's hand. "It's you."

"What is? Wait…what?"

Tis pointed at the question mark. "You know who we are. You know what we are. You understand some of the complications we face, and you know what people need and want from their gods."

"And you think I possess the subtlety and grace to tell gods what to do, do you? I'm still not sure how I feel about religion, and I'm not sure your colleagues would appreciate me telling them they're piss-poor at their jobs." Kera kissed Tis's hand. "I think you might regard me too highly, love."

"Oh, believe me, I see how rude and blunt you are. I know you're crude, childish, self-indulgent, and extremely stubborn." She smiled as Kera pretended to be wounded. "But don't you see?

Subtle and kid gloves won't work anymore. They need direction, guidelines. I've tried to draw those up, and I've got a baseline. But I don't manage people the way you do. Whether you like it or not, we're not going anywhere. So why don't we change the system that's tearing itself apart anyway? Even if we have to use someone like you to do it. Granted, they wouldn't listen to just you, especially with your mortality issue, so I'd have to work beside you to make sure you didn't screw up because of gaps in your knowledge or because you insulted someone one too many times and they removed your organs. I still think it's the best plan we've got. We manage them. Get them trained and working in the here and now. I don't know anyone better at getting people to do what she wants them to."

"I feel strangely insulted and complimented at the same time." Kera stared at the flipchart, seeing the sense of it. She'd always wanted to make a difference in the world, and she'd worked her ass off to do it as well as she could. If she had the gods working for her, how much more could she do? "I like it."

Chapter Thirty-one

A nd so, with the mega merger of Afterlife, Inc. and GRADE, with CEO Kera Espinosa in charge and vice president and white fury Tisera Graves acting as production manager, we usher in a new era of gods and man working in harmony to create a better world. What will this new way of life bring? Only time will tell."

Tis turned off the TV and lay on her side to face Kera. "It's really something, isn't it? I'm not sure how I feel about being referred to as the 'white fury' though."

Kera pressed her body against Tis's and nibbled at her neck, making Tis murmur appreciatively. "Uh-huh. We make a good team. And you are a white fury. Deal with it."

"Harsh." She gasped at the sensation of Kera's teeth nibbling along her collarbone. "We never did talk about the political thing Selene wanted to discuss." Tis closed her eyes and shivered as Kera ran her tongue over Tis's nipple.

"We'll be talking our fool heads off for years to come. Right now…" Kera pushed Tis onto her back and straddled her. "I want you to moan the way you did the first time we had sex."

Tis put her hand in the middle of Kera's chest and pushed her backward. "Then I suggest you stop talking and use your mouth more effectively."

Kera grinned and moved down between Tis's thighs. As her warm tongue slid over Tis's already aching clit, Tis moaned and lifted her hips. Kera applied pressure in just the right way, soft at first, then harder, until Tis was thrashing under her and she sucked hard, making Tis explode. As soon as she did, Kera thrust two fingers inside her and fucked her until she came a second, and third, time.

Kera crawled back up beside her, looking distinctly pleased with herself. Tis laughed, satisfied in a way she'd never felt in all her years on the planet. Her soul was quiet, her body sated, and most of all, her heart was full.

She stroked Kera's inner thigh, liking the way she pressed against her touch. "I thought I'd lost you." She looked down at Kera, not bothering to hide the tears in her eyes. "I've never felt pain like that. Like I'd lost a part of myself. I wouldn't have forgiven myself if anything had happened to you."

Kera wiped her tears away gently. "I was an ass, and if anything had happened to me, it wouldn't have been your fault. As it was, you saved me. From myself, and from a life without this." She pressed her hand over Tis's heart. "I thought I had everything. But when it came down to it, without you, it wouldn't have been enough." She stretched and smiled wickedly. "Now I've got the girl, the money, and I'm in charge of every god on the planet. I'd say I'm at the top of my game. Women like a woman with power. You'd better keep an eye out, you know."

Tis laughed and pinched her nipple, getting her attention. "Just don't get cocky." She spread Kera open and slipped her finger inside her. She made love to her slowly, building her need. "If there are other women, I'll choose them, and I'll make sure they leave when I tell them to."

Kera's eyes opened and she raised her eyebrow.

"You don't live for thousands of years and not enjoy all life has to offer. Somehow, I'd forgotten that." Tis pushed deeper, loving the way Kera's eyes fluttered shut and she thrust against Tis's hand. She watched every shift of her expression, the way every muscle tensed and released. When she came, Tis nearly came again just from the pleasure of watching her arch and cry out.

She moved back to Kera's side and spooned her. She brushed her hair away from her ear and whispered, "I love you. Thank you for believing in me."

Kera pulled Tis's arm tighter around her. "Thank you for choosing me. And for that amazing orgasm."

Tis laughed and listened as Kera fell into an exhausted sleep. They'd been insanely busy; from the moment they'd broached the merger and begun discussing it with the gods, things had been nonstop. Plus, Kera had her other operations that were still going ahead. Only now, she had the help of that region's gods. They'd have to wait and see how it worked out, but it looked promising. Ajan had retired and taken his daughter on an around-the-world cruise, paid for by Kera. He wanted his child to see the beauty of the world, since she'd already seen so much of its ugly side. Most of the children in the lab had been returned to their respective homes. A few, though, hadn't even been reported missing by their foster parents, and Kera had seen to it those kids went into one of the care centers run by GRADE. Greg, one of those kids, had asked if he could keep in touch with Kera, and she'd promised to pick him up for Christmas. Tis knew she meant it, and could tell she had a special soft spot for the boy. The lab itself had been pulled apart by the FBI, since they had jurisdiction because of the abductions crossing state lines. Though plenty of illegal things had been retrieved, there was no longer anyone to arrest for it. They'd complained bitterly about the mess Tis had made, and she'd tried to make amends by sending a cleanup squad from Afterlife.

Petra had taken over Ajan's position, and Tis found she really enjoyed spending time with her. Offerings were being left at Petra's ancient temple, though, and it was possible they'd have to make a decision at some point as to whether she could continue in her role with the company, or if she'd need to go be a front line goddess again.

All in all, it was a start, and one Tis thought might actually work. Plus, it meant she got to spend her days as well as her nights with the extraordinary, rash, cocky woman she'd fallen desperately in love with, and as far as she was concerned, that made it all so much the better.

She pulled Kera closer, knowing that whatever the future might bring, she had what she'd searched for her entire life, and she'd treasure every second.

EPILOGUE

Dis drew lazy circles in the stardust and then blew on it. It puffed into the air and formed a woman's body before dispersing back into the ether.

"She's not going to like it," the person lounging on the sofa behind her said.

Dis turned away from the window and unbuttoned her top as she made her way over to her lover. "I don't care if she likes it. I don't care anything about them. I'm having fun, and I'm going to make the most of it while I can."

Her lover sucked Dis's nipple into his mouth and bit on it, making Dis jerk and moan. He let go and said, "I've heard angering a fury can be bad for your lifespan."

Dis pushed her other breast at his mouth and sighed appreciatively at the warmth of his tongue. "I'm the only one of them that can't truly die. I'm not afraid of her. But I do want to see what those wings feel like before I rip them apart."

She closed her eyes and orgasmed as she thought of the beautiful darkness she'd soon unleash on them all.

About the Author

Brey Willows is a longtime editor and writer. Her passion is literature and the classics, and she has published a large handful of short stories and several articles and reviews. When she's not running a social enterprise working with marginalized communities on writing projects, she's editing other people's writing or doing her own. She lives in the middle of England with her partner and fellow author and spends entirely too much time exploring castles and ancient ruins while bemoaning the rain.

Books Available from Bold Strokes Books

Beauty and the Boss by Ali Vali. Ellis Renois is at the top of the fashion world, but she never expects her summer assistant Charlotte Hamner to tear her heart and her business apart like sharp scissors through cheap material. (978-1-62639-919-8)

Fury's Choice by Brey Willows. When gods walk amongst humans, can two women find a balance between love and faith? (978-1-62639-869-6)

Lessons in Desire by MJ Williamz. Can a summer love stand a four-month hiatus and still burn hot? (978-1-63555-019-1)

Lightning Chasers by Cass Sellars. For Sydney and Parker, being a couple was never what they had planned. Now they have to fight corruption, murder, and enemies hiding in plain sight just to hold on to each other. Lightning Series, Book Two (978-1-62639-965-5)

Summer Fling by Jean Copeland. Still jaded from a breakup years earlier, Kate struggles to trust falling in love again when a summer fling with sexy young singer Jordan rocks her off her feet. (978-1-62639-981-5)

Take Me There by Julie Cannon. Adrienne and Sloan know it would be career suicide to mix business with pleasure, however tempting it is. But what's the harm? They're both consenting adults. Who would know? (978-1-62639-917-4)

The Girl Who Wasn't Dead by Samantha Boyette. A year ago, someone tried to kill Jenny Lewis. Tonight she's ready to find out who it was. (978-1-62639-950-1)

Unchained Memories by Dena Blake. Can a woman give herself completely when she's left a piece of herself behind? (978-1-62639-993-8)

Walking Through Shadows by Sheri Lewis Wohl. All Molly wanted to do was go backpacking…in her own century. (978-1-62639-968-6)

A Lamentation of Swans by Valerie Bronwen. Ariel Montgomery returns to Sea Oats to try to save her broken marriage but soon finds herself also fighting to save her own life and catch a murderer. (978-1-62639-828-3)

Freedom to Love by Ronica Black. What happens when the woman who spent her lifetime worrying about caring for her family, finally finds the freedom to love without borders? (978-1-63555-001-6)

House of Fate by Barbara Ann Wright. Two women must throw off the lives they've known as a guardian and an assassin and save two rival houses before their secrets tear the galaxy apart. (978-1-62639-780-4)

Planning for Love by Erin Dutton. Could true love be the one thing that wedding coordinator Faith McKenna didn't plan for? (978-1-62639-954-9)

Sidebar by Carsen Taite. Judge Camille Avery and her clerk, attorney West Fallon, agree on little except their mutual attraction, but can their relationship and their careers survive a headline-grabbing case? (978-1-62639-752-1)

Sweet Boy and Wild One by T. L. Hayes. When Rachel Cole meets soulful singer Bobby Layton at an open mic, she is immediately in thrall. What she soon discovers will rock her world in ways she never imagined. (978-1-62639-963-1)

To Be Determined by Mardi Alexander and Laurie Eichler. Charlie Dickerson escapes her life in the US to rescue Australian wildlife with Pip Atkins, but can they save each other? (978-1-62639-946-4)

True Colors by Yolanda Wallace. Blogger Robby Rawlins plans to use First Daughter Taylor Crenshaw to get ahead, but she never planned on falling in love with her in the process. (978-1-62639-927-3)

Unexpected by Jenny Frame. When Dale McGuire falls for Rebecca Harper, the mother of the son she never knew she had, will Rebecca's troubled past stop them from making the family they both truly crave? (978-1-62639-942-6)

Canvas for Love by Charlotte Greene. When ghosts from Amelia's past threaten to undermine their relationship, Chloé must navigate the greatest romance of her life without losing sight of who she is. (978-1-62639-944-0)

Heart Stop by Radclyffe. Two women, one with a damaged body, the other a damaged spirit, challenge each other to dare to live again. (978-1-62639-899-3)

Repercussions by Jessica L. Webb. Someone planted information in Edie Black's brain and now they want it back, but with the protection of shy former soldier Skye Kenny, Edie has a chance at life and love. (978-1-62639-925-9)

Spark by Catherine Friend. Jamie's life is turned upside down when her consciousness travels back to 1560 and lands in the body of one of Queen Elizabeth I's ladies-in-waiting…or has she totally lost her grip on reality? (978-1-62639-930-3)

Taking Sides by Kathleen Knowles. When passion and politics collide, can love survive? (978-1-62639-876-4)

Thorns of the Past by Gun Brooke. Former cop Darcy Flynn's heart broke when her career on the force ended in disgrace, but perhaps saving Sabrina Hawk's life will mend it in more ways than one. (978-1-62639-857-3)

You Make Me Tremble by Karis Walsh. Seismologist Casey Radnor comes to the San Juan Islands to study an earthquake but finds her heart shaken by passion when she meets animal rescuer Iris Mallery. (978-1-62639-901-3)

Complications by MJ Williamz. Two women battle for the heart of one. (978-1-62639-769-9)

Crossing the Wide Forever by Missouri Vaun. As Cody Walsh and Lillie Ellis face the perils of the untamed West, they discover that love's uncharted frontier isn't for the weak in spirit or the faint of heart. (978-1-62639-851-1)

Fake It Till You Make It by M. Ullrich. Lies will lead to trouble, but can they lead to love? (978-1-62639-923-5)

Girls Next Door by Sandy Lowe and Stacia Seaman eds.. Best-selling romance authors tell it from the heart—sexy, romantic stories of falling for the girls next door. (978-1-62639-916-7)

Pursuit by Jackie D. The pursuit of the most dangerous terrorist in America will crack the lines of friendship and love, and not everyone will make it out under the weight of duty and service. (978-1-62639-903-7)

Shameless by Brit Ryder. Confident Emery Pearson knows exactly what she's looking for in a no-strings-attached hookup, but can a spontaneous interlude open her heart to more? (978-1-63555-006-1)

The Practitioner by Ronica Black. Sometimes love comes calling whether you're ready for it or not. (978-1-62639-948-8)

Unlikely Match by Fiona Riley. When an ambitious PR exec and her super-rich coding geek-girl client fall in love, they learn that giving something up may be the only way to have everything. (978-1-62639-891-7)

Where Love Leads by Erin McKenzie. A high school counselor and the mom of her new student bond in support of the troubled girl, never expecting deeper feelings to emerge, testing the boundaries of their relationship. (978-1-62639-991-4)

Forsaken Trust by Meredith Doench. When four women are murdered, Agent Luce Hansen must regain trust in her most valuable investigative tool—herself—to catch the killer. (978-1-62639-737-8)

Her Best Friend's Sister by Meghan O'Brien. For fifteen years, Claire Barker has nursed a massive crush on her best friend's older sister. What happens when all her wildest fantasies come true? (978-1-62639-861-0)

Letter of the Law by Carsen Taite. Will federal prosecutor Bianca Cruz take a chance at love with horse breeder Jade Vargas, whose dark family ties threaten everything Bianca has worked to protect—including her child? (978-1-62639-750-7)

New Life by Jan Gayle. Trigena and Karrie are having a baby, but the stress of becoming a mother and the impact on their relationship might be too much for Trigena. (978-1-62639-878-8)

Royal Rebel by Jenny Frame. Charity director Lennox King sees through the party girl image Princess Roza has cultivated, but will Lennox's past indiscretions and Roza's responsibilities make their love impossible? (978-1-62639-893-1)

Unbroken by Donna K. Ford. When Kayla and Jackie, two women with every reason to reject Happy Ever After, fall in love, will they have the courage to overcome their pasts and rewrite their stories? (978-1-62639-921-1)

Where the Light Glows by Dena Blake. Mel Thomas doesn't realize just how unhappy she is in her marriage until she meets Izzy Calabrese. Will she have the courage to overcome her insecurities and follow her heart? (978-1-62639-958-7)